All of Red Rock is still abuzz, speculating about "the gifts" Ryan Fortune gave at his recent Christmas party. Seems Ryan's near-fatal poisoning has made him appreciate life— and four special people who've helped in his hour of need. He gave each of these individuals a special gift. Considering the Fortunes' generous welcome to their newly discovered heirs, one can only imagine what *these* gift boxes contained.

Of course, all the inquiring minds in Red Rock also want to know—*who are these people?* It's no secret that Ryan owes his life to Dr. Maggie Taylor's expert, compassionate care.

But the others are a mystery. Visiting sheik Nico Tan-efi looked as if he'd just stepped out of the pages of the *Arabian Nights*. And not even the icy-cold champagne that freely flowed could douse the sparks between Sebastian Quentin and Jessamine Mitchell.

Well, only one thing's for sure—whenever those Fortunes hold a celebration, a wedding is bound to follow!

THE FORTUNES OF TEXAS

Barbara Boswell is a bestselling author who has written over twenty category romances. She is also the author of a single title about the Fortune family, *A Fortune's Children Wedding: The Hoodwinked Bride,* and contributed to the original FORTUNE'S CHILDREN continuity series with *Stand-In Bride.* Ms. Boswell loves writing about families. "I particularly enjoy writing about how my characters' family relationships affect them," she says. When this Pennsylvania author isn't writing for Silhouette and reading, she's spending time with her *own* family or writing popular single-title romances.

Jennifer Greene has written more than fifty category romances, for which she has won numerous awards, including two RITA Awards from the Romance Writers of America in the Best Short Contemporary category, and a Career Achievement award from *Romantic Times Magazine.* She lives near Lake Michigan with her husband and two children. Before writing full-time, she worked as a teacher and a personnel manager. Michigan State University honored her as an "outstanding woman graduate" for her work with women on campus.

Jackie Merritt is a bestselling author of over forty category romances, including her contributions to the twleve-book FORTUNES OF TEXAS continuity series, *A Wiling Wife* and *Hired Bride.* She and her husband live in southern Nevada, falling back on old habits of loving the long, slightly cool winters and trying almost desperately to head north for the months of July and August, when the fiery sun bakes people and cacti alike.

Gifts of
FORTUNE

Barbara Boswell
Jennifer Greene
Jackie Merritt

Silhouette Books

Published by Silhouette Books
America's Publisher of Contemporary Romance

Special thanks and acknowledgment are given to
Barbara Boswell, Jennifer Greene and Jackie Merritt
for their contributions to GIFTS OF FORTUNE

 SILHOUETTE BOOKS

GIFTS OF FORTUNE

Copyright © 2001 by Harlequin Books S.A.

ISBN 0-373-48438-0

The publisher acknowledges the copyright holders
of the individual works as follows:

THE HOLIDAY HEIR
Copyright © 2001 by Harlequin Books S.A.

THE CHRISTMAS HOUSE
Copyright © 2001 by Harlequin Books S.A.

MAGGIE'S MIRACLE
Copyright © 2001 by Harlequin Books S.A.

CONTENTS

*Meet the Fortunes of Texas—a family whose legacy
is greater than mere riches. As the family gathers
to thank four special people who stood by
Ryan Fortune in his hour of need, three special gifts
ignite passionate new romances that only a
true-bred Texas love can bring!*

CAST OF CHARACTERS

Nico Tan-efi: This darkly handsome sheik saved his country from a political takeover. But in doing so, he lost the one person dearest to him. Will Ryan's gift offer him a second chance at love?

Jessamine Mitchell: Love and family have eluded her grasp. Until one fateful night when she pulls Ryan Fortune from a burning car. Now the patriarch has his own scheme for rescuing Jessamine...from herself!

Sebastian O. Quentin: When this bad boy helped a beautiful stranger rescue the Fortune patriarch, he never imagined that one selfless act would completely change his life....

Dr. Maggie Taylor: She has devoted herself to finding a cure for her sister's rare disease, but now Ryan Fortune is determined to give this no-nonsense woman a life!

THE HOLIDAY HEIR
Barbara Boswell

Prologue

Oxford University, England
Eighteen months earlier

Esme couldn't move or speak. Breathing and swallowing were becoming equally impossible. Unfortunately, she could still hear and still see. And what she was hearing and seeing made her feel faint with pain and sick with sorrow.

Nico, her true love, the man she'd waited for her entire life—the man who had made her the happiest woman in the world two months ago by asking her to be his wife and share his life—was now taking it all away.

His proposal and pledge of love. Her dreams, her happiness. Esme stared at Nico, her dark eyes filled with tears, the delicate features of her face frozen into a mask of incredulity.

"I have to end it now, Esme," Nico repeated those terrible words. Each one slashed at her heart. "There is no other way." His voice was hard and unyielding.

She'd never heard him speak in such a tone. Whenever he spoke to her, his voice was filled with warmth or humor, sometimes both. And had always resonated with love.

Now she was hearing what must be the Official Voice of Nico Tan-efi, the king of Imarco, that oil-rich kingdom bordering her own country of Rayaz.

The two countries had been enemies for years, always in dispute over something. Currently, it was over the financing of an underground oil pipeline. Previous conflicts involved borders, water, camels, horses—none of which had ever been fully resolved and continued to simmer, waiting to erupt again at any given time.

But when she and Nico had been introduced here at Oxford, far away from the conflicts that obsessed their respective families, they had taken just one look at each other and fallen in love, right then and there. A classic case of love at first sight, and the following idyllic three months they'd spent together had reaffirmed what each had known the moment they met.

They were made for each other, soul mates, best friends and lovers, who were destined to spend the rest of their lives together.

Except a soul mate didn't avoid her gaze while he made his incomprehensible pronouncement. Best friends don't cause each other heartbreak. And lovers...

Esme gulped in a gasp of air, her lungs finally demanding oxygen. She and Nico had not yet become lovers. He had insisted on waiting until she was his wife to make love to her, properly following the traditional tenets of his family, his country, his religion.

She shared his beliefs, but deep in her heart she knew if Nico had simply asked her... If he'd wanted...

He hadn't wanted her enough. The sudden, harsh realization put his reluctance in an entirely different light. Esme winced.

Nico did not want her at all. He was telling her so, right now.

"It is important that you understand," she heard him say.

His voice might have held a note of desperation but Esme couldn't be sure. She wasn't sure of anything anymore, especially not this man whom she thought she'd known so well. Whom she loved so much.

"I've been given word that my uncle Amman is ready to make his move. Amman has always been hungry for power and after my father's assassination..." Nico's voice caught.

Esme knew that try as he might, Nico still couldn't speak of his late father's tragic death five years ago without a searing grief. But quickly, he composed his expression, his voice, back into that robotic imperial alien Esme did not recognize.

"You are aware that Amman has tried to wrest the throne from me before, but his attempts have always met with failure. Now, with my mother dead, and with me periodically spending time abroad—" Nico paused.

A pause filled with unspoken meaning.

Which Esme immediately, bleakly interpreted. "It's because you've been here with me. Spending time abroad to cement alliances and attract business for Imarco, would pose no problems. Everybody would approve and support you for that."

"Yes."

Reality was hitting her fast and hard, replacing her initial disbelief. This was really happening. Nico actually was going to end it between them.

"Being engaged to me was just the ammunition Amman needed to rally serious support for himself?" guessed Esme.

"Yes," Nico repeated, his voice was as distant as his eyes. "Amman has used our countries' enmity toward each other to whip a militant minority faction into a frenzy. They promise a civil war if a member of the Bakkar family from Rayaz becomes queen of Imarco. Our engagement was always somewhat controversial in Imarco, Esme," he added grimly.

"Somewhat? That is a master understatement, isn't it, Nico? Our engagement was extremely controversial and very unpopular. But I seem to remember you saying at the time that you could handle the fallout. That as king, your decision would be respected."

Esme tried to sound blithe, to inject a light touch

of sarcasm. Which was quite a challenge when all she wanted to do was to throw herself into his arms and beg him not to leave her. Her pride, however, would not permit that.

"Esme, I truly never expected Amman to escalate a minor issue into a conflict that could lead to bloodshed."

Minor. The word burned through Esme's brain. He considered their engagement to be *minor?*

"I hope you are aware that our engagement horrified my own family and country, as well," she retorted icily. "The difference being that we are a civilized people who won't start a war over something so *minor.*"

If it were possible to die of emotional pain, she ought to be on life support right now. She was nearly blind from the hot tears burning her eyes. But she just couldn't break down crying in the middle of a public park!

She suddenly realized Nico was counting on that; it was the reason he had chosen to break up with her here. He was counting on her not to make a scene! To make it easier for himself.

The flash of insight enraged her. And with her rage came a welcome force of energy. She didn't feel drained of her soul and her spirit anymore. She wouldn't collapse into a weeping heap—at least not right now.

"My family and my country are far more cultured, more tolerant, more supportive and kind and under-

standing than the small-minded, avaricious, hypocrit-
ical barbarians of Imarco!''

She watched Nico grimace as she insulted his coun-
trymen. Actually, she was being rather generous, from
a Rayaz standpoint. Her family members and fellow
citizens had far, far worse things to say about their
neighboring country of Imarco.

Nico squared his shoulders and took a deep breath.
''Amman and his rebels must be subdued for the good
of my country, Esme. I must put Imarco before
my—'' he paused and stumbled over the next words,
''my personal wants and needs. I can't marry you,
Esme.''

''You're right, you can't.'' Esme pulled off the exquisite emerald and diamond engagement ring he had
given her. He had chosen the stones and designed the
ring himself, displaying an artistry and sentiment that
had deeply touched her.

But it had meant nothing to him, after all. Just as
she meant nothing to him. ''I will never marry a—a
conniving camel thief from Imarco.''

Esme wished she could've come up with something
more cutting, more *original,* than one of those ancient
charges the citizens of Imarco and Rayaz had been
hurling at each other for years. But right now, she
seemed to have lost all creative power.

''Here, give this to your next fiancée.'' She thrust
the ring into his hand.

The brief contact electrified them both, and each
quickly, defensively stepped back, away from each

other. The ring hit the cement walk. They both stared at it for a moment.

Then Nico bent to pick it up.

"Esme, I want you to keep the ring," he said huskily, holding it out to her.

She recoiled, as if it were a piece of radioactive waste. "No."

Turning, she walked away from him, picking up her pace as the tears began to roll down her cheeks. She willed him to call her back, or even better, to come running to her. To grab her and pull her into his arms and tell her he loved her too much to let anything—even his duty to his country!—ever come between them.

But he didn't. A responsible, conscionable king did have a duty to his country, to his people. Even her romantic, broken heart knew that to be true.

She kept walking, leaving the park and Nico behind. She flagged down a taxi and gave the driver the address of her flat that she shared with Jackie Sloane, a British diplomat's daughter whom she'd met when the Sloanes were posted at the embassy in Rayaz. Thankfully, the taxi driver didn't comment on the fact that his passenger was weeping in the back of his cab. He weaved and bobbed through the traffic, listening to his radio.

Jackie was aghast as Esme trudged through the door into the flat. "You look terrible! Esme, what happened?"

Esme was crying too hard to speak. She held out her ringless hand to Jackie, who let out a scream.

"You've been mugged! Some bloody crook stole your ring right off your hand! Quick! We'll call Nico right away. And the police." She raced to the telephone.

Esme found her voice before Jackie picked up the receiver. "Jackie, there's been no robbery. I gave Nico his ring back." She gulped back a sob before explaining why Nico called off their engagement.

Jackie was indignant. "Why, he's a—a snake! A cobra!"

"He has to put his country's best interests first, Jackie." Esme felt ridiculously compelled to defend Nico against Jackie's condemnation. "And right now, that isn't me. Imarco is in crisis and Nico… He—he is the king, after all."

"Well, that's no excuse," spluttered Jackie. "Right here in England, we had that fellow—oh, I can't remember his name, but I know he gave up the throne for the woman he loved."

"It was Edward, the Duke of Windsor," Esme said wearily. "And the circumstances aren't even close, Jackie. Imarco could have a civil war if Nico marries me."

"So you forgive him for dumping you?" Jackie seemed incredulous. "You don't mind that he broke your heart?"

"I suppose I can understand why he did what he did." Esme's tears had stopped, and her dark eyes were glittering like icy jewels. "But no, I don't forgive him and yes, I do mind that he broke my heart." She lifted her chin. "From now on, Nico Tan-efi doesn't exist for me," she added, her tone regally Bakkar.

"Fine. Consider him obliterated," exclaimed Jackie. "Now wash your face and put on fresh makeup. You're coming to a party tonight with me."

Esme panicked. "Jackie, I can't, I—"

"You can and you will. Nico no longer exists and you are a beautiful, bright, single woman, Esme. There is plenty going on in this town, and you are going to enjoy yourself. I'll make sure of it!" She gave Esme a friendly shove in the direction of the bathroom.

Esme swallowed hard. She had a decision to make, one that stretched well beyond choosing to stay in and cry or to go out with Jackie tonight.

Though she couldn't have Nico, the true love of her life, she could not—*she would not*—waste her life pining away for what could never be. She would move on, both socially and professionally. She would have a meaningful career, teaching special-needs children, something she had planned to do before she'd ever met Nico Tan-efi.

After all, it wasn't as if she had grown up dreaming to be queen of Imarco. Even as a fanciful teenager, such a scenario would've struck her as impossibly far-fetched as becoming queen of England.

But her fateful meeting with Nico had occurred, and she had fallen deeply in love with him. Everything had changed then.

Just as everything had changed now.

She might as well get used to it.

"I'll be ready within a half hour, Jackie."

Chapter 1

Ryan Fortune's Double Crown Ranch
Red Rock, Texas
Two weeks before Christmas

The Christmas party was in full swing, with Fortune family members of all ages spilling out of the aptly titled great room, mixing and mingling throughout the other downstairs rooms. Patriarch Ryan Fortune's home, one of the big houses on the fabled Double Crown Ranch, resembled a Spanish hacienda on the outside. Inside the design was open and airy with one room flowing into another.

A mammoth Christmas tree twinkled with colored lights and traditional holiday songs played softly in the background. Hundreds of indoor luminaries provided glowing, old-fashioned candlelight and charm.

Nico Tan-efi stood alone, holding a crystal cup filled with eggnog, as he glanced around at the Southwestern decor of the place. There were the traditional leather couches and solid oak furniture, along with assorted prints, paintings and pottery by talented local artists. The stucco walls, high-beamed ceilings and large stone fireplace that dominated the room were nothing less than spectacular.

Nico mused that if a film director were to make a movie about a wealthy Texas family, Ryan Fortune's house on the Double Crown Ranch would make the ideal cinematic setting.

Nico's eyes returned to Ryan Fortune himself.

Ryan could star in that same movie as his ranch. In his mid-fifties, his rugged dark good looks still qualified as leading man material. And even though he had recently been critically ill, the tycoon projected a strong presence. He was everyone's focal point.

Nico watched him lean down to talk to a group of children at their eye level. Grandchildren, perhaps? Ryan was as attentive to the youngsters as he was to the adults at the party. He was a good listener, which Nico knew from his own experience with the man.

Nico thought of his after-hours hospital visits to Ryan Fortune's bedside as the older man gradually recovered.

Their conversations had centered on many subjects. One might not expect a middle-aged Texas billionaire and the thirty-two-year-old sheik of a Middle Eastern country to have anything in common except the oil business, but Ryan and Nico found it easy to talk about anything. Current events, books, sports, movies, food and wine. Women and life, in general and in specific.

Nico knew that Ryan was devoted to his wife, Lily, who was currently standing at his side and gazing affectionately at him as they listened to the children.

"Lily is the true love of my life," Ryan had confided, during one of Nico's late-night visits.

He had spoken fondly of his first wife, Janine, the mother of his grown children, whose death from cancer had sent him emotionally reeling. He'd loved Janine but in a wholly different way than he loved Lily.

Nico thought of his mother, Nadine, and had been tempted to ask Ryan if he remembered a passionate affair with a headstrong young woman from the Middle East, nearly thirty-three years ago. Had Ryan loved his mother at all, even a little?

Nadine hadn't gone into much detail when on her deathbed, she had finally confessed to Nico about her premarital affair with Ryan Fortune all those years ago. Only that she had used an alias to conceal her true identity. Even if Ryan Fortune had tried to contact her afterward, it would have been futile. Princess Nadine had passed herself off as an Egyptian girl named Jasmine during their monthlong European fling.

Worse, her true identity wasn't all that the future queen of Imarco had neglected to reveal to Ryan Fortune. There was also the tangible consequence of their liaison—their son.

Nico.

Nico, who had been raised by her unsuspecting husband, King Omar Tan-efi, as his own child. Nico, the only son, who had been groomed from childhood to take the throne upon Omar's death. Who had done so immediately following Omar's untimely assassination.

Nobody else knew that Imarco's young king was really half-Fortune. The shocking revelation still had the power to jar Nico. He was not who he'd thought he was; he was not what others believed him to be.

How did one successfully live a lie? His mother had done so, but she was no longer around to ask for advice.

Once again, Nico fought the urge to confide the truth to Ryan Fortune. *His father!* But strong as it was, he successfully suppressed that urge, yet again.

Now was not the time, just as the timing had been wrong during Ryan's hospitalization. Maybe the time would always be wrong for such a revelation.

"I have an announcement to make," Ryan Fortune's deep voice resonated throughout the great room.

Word spread quickly, and a respectful hush fell over the crowd.

"Although I've always been more of a man of action than a philosopher, since the last time we were all together like this, I've had lots of time on my hands to think," Ryan began.

"No doubt getting poisoned tends to make one philosophical, Dad," somebody interjected wryly.

Nico tried to see who it was. If Ryan Fortune was "Dad" to that person, then he, Nico, was a half brother. In fact, he was probably related to all the people at this party, a whole new tribe of brothers, sisters, nieces, nephews, uncles, aunts and cousins. Nico thought of his three younger sisters at home, all married with children of their own. Of all his aunts, uncles and cousins in Imarco. His family tree had been irrevocably altered and expanded, though only he was aware of that fact.

Wait until he told Esme he had a brother! Nico smiled.

Almost instantly, his smile disappeared. This eggnog must be strongly spiked, and as he rarely indulged in alcohol, its effect was hitting him hard and fast. Only that could explain his unexpected, forbidden thought of Esme.

His former fiancée was not permitted to slip through the impenetrable fortress guarding his heart and mind. At least not during his conscious, daylight hours. It was only late at night as he lay alone in bed and was drifting into sleep that images of Esme broke free.

And tortured him. He would be unable to sleep and would toss and turn, tormented by memories of their last terrible meeting, when he had to tell her he couldn't marry her. Her face, white with shock, her big dark eyes shimmering with tears would haunt him forever.

How he wanted to change all that, to see her smile at him again. To talk to her about everything and nothing, the way they used to. To hold her small, graceful hand and link his long fingers with her slender ones.

And to feel his body throb with anticipation and passion as he inhaled the alluring scent of her perfume, as he felt the warm smooth softness of her skin...

Hospitality rites notwithstanding, Nico set down the eggnog, as if it had also been doctored with poison.

The dangerously potent brew had knocked out his fierce self-imposed control and made him think of Esme in the middle of this crowded room. It was making him admit to himself how much he missed her, how desperately he wanted her back.

"I decided to have this party, not only to gather all my loved ones together again," Ryan's voice was a welcome interruption into Nico's torturous thoughts, "but also to give back to four special people who did something for me, out of the goodness of their hearts. With Christmas just two weeks away, tonight seems like an ideal time. Nico Tan-efi, Sebastian Quentin, Jessamine Mitchell and Dr. Maggie Taylor, will you please all come over here to me? I have something for each one of you."

Nico walked over to Ryan, feeling the curious glances of the crowd upon them all. He cast a few covert glances of his own at his fellow mystery gift recipients. They did likewise, each looking as surprised as he.

Ryan introduced all four, gave a brief summary of

what each one had done for him, "out of the goodness of their hearts."

Sebastian and Jessamine had been two complete strangers, to each other and to him, but they'd worked together to save Ryan's life a year ago, risking their own lives, to pull him out of a burning car. Maggie was the dedicated doctor who had worked night and day to come up with an accurate diagnosis and cure for the subtle poison he'd ingested.

"And last but certainly not least is Nico." Ryan fixed his penetrating dark eyes on the man he did not know was his own son. "King Nico Tan-efi saved my business reputation last year when some members of the Middle East oil cartel decided it would be good sport to make a fool out of the rancher from Texas. I would've lost big time, as the kids here say, losing both face and financially. But Nico tipped me off…though there was nothing in it for him to do that for me."

Nico cleared his throat. "Ah, but there was, Ryan."

If this were one of the Hollywood movies he so enjoyed, right now the music would swell to a crescendo, and he dramatically would announce their kinship. Instead Nico said quietly, "There was our honor as fellow businessmen at stake."

Ryan's eyes misted. "Business honor aside, you've been like a son to me, Nico, coming here all the way to Texas from Imarco to visit me in the hospital. I'll always treasure our late-night talks in my hospital room—and I have to confess, I admire how you slipped by those eagle-eyed nurses, getting yourself in and out completely undetected.''

The little joke broke the somber mood, and everybody laughed, remembering those strictly-by-the-rulebook nurses. Dr. Maggie defended them, but there was a twinkle in her eye as she did.

Ryan proceeded to hand out the special gifts to the chosen four.

Nico opened his own beautifully wrapped gift box a while later in Ryan's study, as the older man looked on, his expression eager with urgency and anticipation.

Nico snapped open a satin-lined box that held a heavy masculine gold ring with a distinctive double crown inlay. He stared at it, wide-eyed.

''The ring was given to me on my fifteenth birthday,'' Ryan explained. ''I know this is hard to believe but it was designed from a birthmark that I have, one that resembles two crowns. I've been told both the ring and the birthmark are absolutely unique.''

''Most unusual, I would have to agree,'' said Nico.

Although a ring designed from such a distinctive birthmark wasn't at all hard for Nico to fathom. Because he had that same birthmark himself!

"There has never been anything like this in our family. It is truly proof that you were born to be king, my son," his dear father, Omar Tan-efi, had often told young Nico, gazing lovingly at the boy, whom he believed to be of his own bloodline.

Nico swallowed hard. Thank God the father who had raised and loved him would now never know the truth about that birthmark. He gazed at Ryan—and decided that his biological father must never know either.

"Ryan, this ring should rightfully go to—one of your sons. Or grandsons. Or even to one of the girls. It is an heirloom and your heirs ought to—"

"My heirs have been very well-provided for, all of them," Ryan cut in. "No, this ring is not merely a sentimental piece of jewelry, Nico. It has power, a kind of mystical power that makes true love survive. And since you remind me of myself in many ways, you will need this ring, just as I needed it."

"A ring that has the power to make true love survive? Ryan, I mean no disrespect, but how much eggnog have you had tonight? I can attest that brew has a power all its own."

"I'm as sober as the proverbial judge, Nico. This ring has power, I swear. It worked its magic when Lily and I first fell in love, and our love lasted until we could finally be together thirty-five long years later."

Nico stared at him thoughtfully. "I am not certain if you are telling a tall tale derived from the old Aladdin's lamp story. After rubbing this ring, will a girl dressed in a belly dancer's costume fly in on a magic carpet, promising to grant me three wishes? Unless, in the Texas version, she'd ride in on a horse, wearing a ten-gallon hat?"

"How can I convince you that this is not a joke?" Ryan sighed heavily. "Nico, I want you to know the power of this ring. You need it, more than any of my own children who have all found their true loves.''

''True love.'' Nico grimaced. ''You Americans are certainly under the spell of that starry-eyed myth, thanks to all your Hollywood movies, I suppose. I enjoy them myself, but see them for what they are— enjoyable escapist fare. I also like the James Bond films, but I don't for one moment believe that in real life, a suave, infallible secret agent prowls in diplomatic circles and—''

''Nico, let's get back on topic,'' Ryan interrupted. ''I might as well admit this to you. I know all about what happened between you and Esme Bakkar.''

Nico froze. Just the sound of her name was enough to send a bolt of pain through him. He found it impossible to say a single word.

He didn't have to. Ryan was willing to do all the talking.

''Circumstances have changed since you last saw Esme, Nico. There is no longer danger of a revolt in Imarco. You've amassed the support of your people, your uncle Amman has been successfully neutralized and decided that he would be happier—and much safer—living abroad rather than in Imarco.''

''Yes, when word of Amman's private penchant for pornography was made public, his horrified supporters offered him the choice of permanently leaving the country, either with or without his head,'' Nico said wryly. ''I was able to remain rather loftily above the fray.''

Ryan grinned. ''Well, you've proven your mettle,

my boy. You've undermined your enemies and accrued global connections, your position as king of Imarco is unassailable. Now it's time to find a way to win Esme back. And you will with the power of this ring, because she is your true love.''

There was a long silence.

"Ryan, I appreciate what you would like to do for me,'' Nico said at last. "I thank you for your kind thoughts and good wishes. But this ring will need to possess the power of that mythical magic lamp that conjures up genies on flying carpets. Nothing less will bring Esme back to me.''

"How do you know that?''

"Because she loathes me.''

"That isn't a bad thing, you know.''

Nico was stunned. "It's not a bad thing when the woman you love hates you?''

"Don't worry, I haven't gone mad. I am older and wiser and see things more clearly than I used to. More clearly than a younger man, even one who is a very talented king.'' Ryan smiled. "Hate is the flip side of love, Nico. It's indifference that is the death knell of hope in repairing a relationship. Now just call Esme and—''

"Ask her out to dinner? Send her a box of chocolates and a bouquet of flowers with theater tickets attached?'' Nico was sarcastic. "Those tired old courtship tactics wouldn't even work in the movies these days.''

"How do you know for sure?'' pressed Ryan. "Did you try them? Have you even once tried to call her?''

Nico threw up his arms and began to pace. "Oh, what's the point in trying to save face? I have admitted this to no one, I have trouble admitting it to myself...but yes, I have tried to call her. Five times."

"Only five?"

"All right, dammit, nine times. At least."

Nico ran his fingers through his dark hair, remembering those phone calls, after the dangerous internal threat to Imarco had successfully ended. "She wouldn't take my calls. Each time, she told her friend Jackie to tell me that she didn't want to talk to me ever again. I heard her saying so in the background—as she no doubt intended."

"Hmm." Ryan pondered that. "Maybe you do need to try another tack."

"There is none. Esme's country Rayaz is an oligarchy," Nico said wearily. "You know, ruled by several powerful families instead of a monarchy like Imarco. Her family, the Bakkars, are one of those ruling clans. Another one, the Murads, have a son Bashir whom they all feel would be an ideal match for Esme, according to an unofficial source who is usually quite accurate in such matters."

Nico felt the bile rise in his throat, as it always did when he considered that odious possibility. "I don't know how Esme herself feels about it. We have been unable to gain any knowledge of her response, either pro or con."

"Well, I hear from my own unofficial sources that there's been plenty of talk about Esme's sister, Zara, who was widowed last year and left with those baby triplet daughters," Ryan said. "The Bakkars are frantic with distress, as I would be, as any parent would be, in that situation. And if I were Papa Bakkar, my total focus would be on my bereaved daughter with three small children."

"I am not understanding your point, Ryan. What does Esme's sister have to do with—"

"My point is that the Bakkars have to be thinking that the eligible Murad son would be a far better match for their unfortunate widowed daughter and her fatherless children than for Esme, whose current status is neither urgent nor tragic."

"Ryan, no. You can't possibly believe that the Bakkars could foist their daughter Zara, with *three* daughters of her own, on the Murads?"

"Of course they can. I've done my homework, Nico. I've learned that the Bakkars are richer and more powerful than the Murads, though the families are close friends. Still, I'm willing to bet that in Rayaz, as in the rest of the world, the richer and the more powerful inevitably get their own way."

"This is quite a different matter, Ryan. In Rayaz, females are not considered valuable commodities, but frankly, more like liabilities. That is why the Hassans didn't take Zara and the triplets in after their son's death. The Murads, with daughters of their own to marry off, will not welcome four more girls from the Bakkar family—and the Bakkars will understand because they would feel the same if the circumstances were reversed. In Imarco, we are far more enlightened about the value of women,'' Nico added with a touch of regal pride.

''With your sleazy uncle gone, you are on your way to becoming one of the most progressive rulers in the Middle East, Nico.'' Ryan gave him a warm paternal pat on the shoulder. ''And you need an educated progressive queen at your side—one who also happens to be your true love. That would be Esme, of course. She is currently living back in England, Nico.''

''I know,'' Nico said slowly. ''To my surprise, it seems that her family didn't object to her seeking an advanced degree there.''

''No surprise to me. That family is undoubtedly completely preoccupied with poor Zara and those triplets. For now, Esme is below the family's radar screen, as it were. An ideal time to catch the Bakkars unaware, Nico.''

''The hostility of the Bakkars is troublesome, but not an insurmountable obstacle, Ryan. I stood up to them before, and they grudgingly accepted my engagement to Esme.'' Nico shrugged. ''It is Esme herself who despises me far more than her family does. I wrote her a letter of sympathy when her sister's husband, Rez, died in the private plane crash. It was returned, unopened. My condolence letters to the older Bakkars and to the Hassans, the late husband's family, were politely acknowledged. Zara sent me a sweet handwritten letter.''

''I'm not surprised. The king of Imarco could be

seen as a possible prospect to raise those girl triplets."

Nico actually laughed. "You do have a cynical
streak, Ryan. Which makes your sentimental faith in
this ring amusing yet touching."

He slipped the ring on his finger and unconsciously
rubbed his thumb over it. "I confess that I do wish
it could be as simple as you make it sound. That true
love really can survive and overcome impossible ad-
versity."

"It can and it does, Nico. And with the power of
that ring, true love will prevail. Of course, you'll have
to do your part. Nothing comes to the hapless fool
who stands by passively waiting as life and opportunity pass him by. Fortunately, you are not of that
ilk, son."

Nico cleared his throat. It felt as if something were
lodged in it.

"This situation does call for more than the good
old traditional courtship methods," Ryan continued.
"Candlelight dinners, tickets to the theater, candy and
flowers can't achieve results if she won't take your
phone calls. And you most definitely can't wait thirty-
five years for true love to prevail. You must be as
aggressive in romance as you are in politics, Nico."

"And what aggressive tactics do you suggest I use,
Ryan?" Nico asked, clearly humoring the older man.
"Kidnap Esme and keep her with me until she agrees
to be my wife?"

Ryan Fortune was not one to be humored.

"Yes!" Ryan thrust his fist into the air in a gesture

of victory. "That's exactly what I was going to recommend! It's uncanny how mentally attuned we are, Nico. You really do remind me of me. The best parts of me," he added proudly.

Chapter 2

A week later, an obviously nonplussed Jackie Sloane
stood in the doorway of the Oxford flat she shared
with Esme, and stared at Nico Tan-efi.

"The security in this building is deplorable." Nico
frowned. "I simply walked in the front entrance and
up the stairs to your door. And when I rang, you
opened it."

"It's a nice neighborhood in a town with a low
crime rate," retorted Jackie. "The security here is
perfectly adequate."

"Any robber or—kidnapper off the street—could
be inside this place within minutes." Nico's frown
deepened. "It is unsafe for Esme to be here."

"You sound like Big Daddy Bakkar himself. Except he usually adds 'villains from Imarco, Syria,
Egypt, Israel, Jordan, Iraq'—well, you get the picture,

the whole Middle East—to the list of bad guys who would enjoy breaking in. Not to mention the entire Western world—and let's not leave out Asia and Africa.''

''Rayaz is not a friendly country,'' agreed Nico. ''They prefer to view everybody as potential enemies.''

''A wise philosophy.'' Esme entered the room and stood several feet behind Jackie. ''Rayaz knows that so-called friends are solely interested in our oil supply and care nothing for the country and its people. Which makes them all potential enemies.''

''Imarco has its own prodigious supply of oil but we prefer to use friendship rather than enmity in dealing with other nations,'' Nico countered, speaking by rote.

It was fortunate he could recite Imarconian policy with his mind on autopilot because his body had usurped command at the sight of Esme. His heart slammed against his chest and resumed beating at warp speed, his lungs forgot how to breathe, and his knees felt alarmingly unsteady.

How could he think when all he could do was gaze at her, nearly overcome with lust and longing?

Her luxuriant black hair hung long and loose below her shoulders, her great dark eyes were flashing, and her lips—how he had dreamed of them!—were cherry red, sensuously full and so tempting, he could hardly stop himself from grabbing her and kissing her till they both were senseless.

He had always thought she was beautiful but seeing

her now, after their seemingly interminable separation, drove home exactly how drop-dead gorgeous she really was. And at this rate, he was going to drop dead if he didn't get hold of himself. No heart could beat so hard and so fast and keep functioning.

Nico purposefully looked away to regain some composure. His eyes rested on the Christmas wreath on the door—Jackie's touch, obviously, since Esme shared his Moslem faith. But he remembered talking with her about how much they both enjoyed the warm and joyous festive atmosphere surrounding the Christmas holiday whenever they'd been traveling abroad.

"It is safer to be an enemy of Rayaz than a friend of Imarco, because our country is honest and doesn't feign what isn't real," Esme's voice cut through his musings. "Unlike the ingratiating, deceitful kingdom of Imarco that pretends friendship with everyone but always has the dagger ready for convenient backstabbing."

Nico stood transfixed by her cultured, well-modulated feminine voice—though it would be even more pleasing if she wasn't ripping his kingdom apart.

"Lucky me, caught in the crossfire. Before I'm asked to give my views on your endless national feuds, I'd better practice a little self-serving diplomacy. Come in, Nico." Jackie stepped aside. "I'm going to take an educated guess that those gifts you're bearing are for Esme?" she added drolly.

Nico nodded but stayed where he was, staring at Esme who was not looking at him.

Her attention was fixed on a wooden German music box with plump baby angels circling an evergreen tree with a silver star on the top.

His attention was fixed on her. She wore a loose-fitting silky blue caftan that skimmed over her petite body, concealing her shape. But he knew she was rounded and curvy in all the right places. He had seen her dressed in designer gowns, in jeans, in swimsuits and business suits. Oh, he'd seen her dressed in all manner of attire during their all-too-short courtship and engagement.

Though he had never seen her undressed, not even once.

Again, Nico regretted his kingly restraint which had kept him from making love to Esme during their engagement. If he had…if only he had…

"Your arms must be tired from holding those roses and the big box of candy and bottle of champagne, Nico," Jackie prattled on, as if oblivious to the tension in the room. "And are those theater tickets?" She stood on tiptoe and read the tickets tucked among the roses. "How super! I've been dying to see that play, and those are great seats too!"

"Enjoy the show, Jackie. Along with the flowers, candy and champagne. I will accept nothing from the king of Imarco." Esme turned and walked out of the room.

Seconds later, the volume of music emanating from the next room was turned up, blasting out a tune by a very angry American or Canadian or English female singer. Nico couldn't place the nationality, but the woman's rage was unmistakable.

He muttered an Imarconian curse word. "This is not going well."

"Did you really think it would? Duh, Nico!" Jackie mocked. "You dumped her, you humiliated her, for months she's refused to take your calls, and yet you actually believed you could show up with this stuff—granted, it's terrific stuff and those theater tickets are to die for—but still! You're history, mister. Esme's romantic history. Only a king could believe otherwise."

"I hoped the good old traditional props of courtship might appeal to her," murmured Nico. "I felt I at least must give it a try."

"Well, you tried and failed. Bye." Jackie started to close the door.

"Wait." Nico stepped forward, into the apartment and closed the door behind him. "Here. If you want these, they are yours. Otherwise, throw everything away, I do not care." He loaded the gifts into Jackie's arms.

"I gladly accept! Thanks, Nico, I'll call a friend and we'll go to the play tonight. Meanwhile, I'd better put these gorgeous things in water."

Jackie hurried toward the small kitchen with her booty, leaving Nico standing alone in the room. A moment later, the volume of the music was mercifully lowered, and Esme came out of her bedroom.

"Jackie, is he—"

"Gone?" supplied Nico. "No, as you can see, I'm

still here. Jackie is in the kitchen, putting the roses in water and possibly gorging on the chocolates.''

"Get out of here right now," Esme commanded.

"No."

"No?" Esme repeated, her dark eyes suddenly ablaze with fury. "You refuse to leave?"

"Yes, I refuse to leave." To underscore his resolution, Nico dropped down onto the chintz-covered sofa. His eyes met hers.

Their gazes locked and held for a long moment. Esme was the first to look away.

"I'm going to call the—" she began.

"An idle threat because the phone is in use." Nico tilted his head toward the kitchen. "I believe Jackie is lining up a date for the theater tonight."

"Why don't *you* go with her?" snapped Esme.

"No. Never. Jackie would be the first to agree that we are not each other's—er—types."

"How true. She is a warm, caring, loyal human being and you are a self-important, treacherous dog from Imarco."

Nico clenched his jaw. "Esme, you do not have to spout Rayaz rhetoric to me. I happen to know that you don't believe it and you never have. You think for yourself and you always have. It sets you apart and is one of your most admirable qualities."

"There might have been a time when I believed your glib lies, Nico, but I don't anymore. As for the Rayaz rhetoric, you have made me a true believer of it all. And yes, I think for myself. What I think is that you are dishonest and cruel and you have an ego three times the size of the Sahara Desert to come here, expecting to be welcomed.''

"So.'' Nico watched her closely. "You are saying that you hate me?''

"The king of Imarco is such a quick study. And so perceptive too. His grasp of the obvious is nothing less than remarkable.''

"You really hate me.''

"Yes!'' Esme glowered at him. "Why are you smiling?''

"Nico, are you still here?'' A startled Jackie emerged from the kitchen, carrying the open candy box. She glanced from him to Esme. "Uh, anyone care for a chocolate?''

"Jackie doesn't hate me,'' Nico said calmly. "At best or worst, she is indifferent to me.''

"I used to detest you, back when you pulled that noble Imarco-comes-first crap on Esme,'' Jackie insisted. "But after all this time, it's not worth the time or energy. Esme feels the same way, of course. Even more so. She is *utterly* indifferent to you, Nico. After all, you can only hate someone you still have strong feelings for.''

"Yes.'' Nico stood up. "I agree. The thin line between love and hate is a universal but apt cliché. And in certain circumstances, it's a line that is easily crossed.''

Esme grabbed a brass lamp from the end table. "If you aren't out of here by the count of four, I am going to bludgeon you with this. One.''

"She's just kidding, of course,'' Jackie interjected.

"She's made public service announcements on Rayaz Television against violence, and now she's tweaking her nonviolent image for fun. Good joke, Essy."

"Two," counted Esme, taking a step toward Nico, lamp in hand.

"A joke, hmm?" Nico backed slowly toward the door. "I do not have a single doubt that she means exactly what she said. About hating me and about bludgeoning me." He looked ridiculously pleased.

"You're missing the humor completely." Jackie tried to wrest the lamp away from Esme. And was unsuccessful. "Esme doesn't care enough to hate you, Nico, she hasn't even thought about you in ages. Why would she, when a hot guy like Bashir Murad is desperate to set their wedding date?"

"No!" Nico's smile disappeared, and he narrowed his brows, his dark eyes hard.

"Three!" Esme advanced on him with the lamp, dragging Jackie who was still hanging on to her.

"It's true, Esme and Bashir are the big news all over Rayaz," exclaimed Jackie, sounding more desperate. "Come on, Esme, Nico isn't getting your little joke so you might as well give me the stupid lamp before it accidentally connects with his head and we get arrested for assault."

"Esme is not going to marry Bashir Murad!" decreed Nico imperiously.

"Four." Esme raised the lamp, but Nico grabbed it before she could do anything else.

His hands covered hers as he effortlessly restrained her from using it as a weapon. A moment later, he had taken it away from her and tossed it to Jackie, who caught it with a gasp.

"You are not going to marry Bashir Murad, Esme," Nico repeated. He reached for her.

Esme quickly sidestepped him. "That is one thing we agree on. No, I am not going to marry Bashir Murad. I am not going to marry anyone. I am dedicating my life to my teaching career. I've already informed my family of my decision, and I will not be swayed by either bribes or threats."

"You can imagine how well that went over with the Bakkars," Jackie interjected wryly.

"About as well as our ridiculous engagement did." Esme glanced up at Nico, then quickly averted her eyes. "No, I believe that particular disaster was a far worse blow to my poor parents."

"I will never view our engagement as either disastrous or ridiculous, although the way it ended is a—"

Esme made a sudden forward movement and gave the unsuspecting Nico a hard shove. He was caught off-balance enough to stumble slightly. One more shove, lighter this time, and he was out of the apartment.

Esme quickly slammed the door shut and bolted it.

"This isn't over, Esme," Nico called through it.

"It was over eighteen months ago, Nico. You can't turn back time. Now go away," Esme shouted back. "Forever!"

She leaned her back against the door, gulping for air.

"Esme, you've heard of 'playing it cool'? Of course you have, I've practically taught a course in it," Jackie said dryly. "Well, just for future reference, you didn't play it cool with Nico tonight."

The sound of Nico's footsteps reverberated in the hallway and down the stairs.

"I don't want to see him again, Jackie." Esme's voice broke.

"I doubt he believes that, Esme. You displayed way too much emotion, you showed him how much you still care. First, all those insults and then, when you totally lost it and threatened him with the lamp… Wow! I thought you were over Nico, but tonight you convinced me otherwise. You acted like a woman in love, Esme. No, even worse, a *wronged* woman in love."

"I did not! I am not! Nico can't possibly think that. Oh, why did he have to come here tonight, anyway?"

"If it's any consolation, *he* didn't play it cool either, Esme. Obviously, he's decided he wants you back."

"No." Esme shook her head almost violently. "It can never be."

And to her horror, she burst into tears.

It was a miserable lonely evening with nothing to do and nobody around. Esme again lamented Jackie's allergy to cats which prevented them from having one here. The Bakkars doted on cats and always had them as household pets.

Tonight in particular, she could use some company, whether feline or human.

She stared at the blank television screen. There was nothing on any of the channels worldwide that captured her interest. Since the university was on winter break, she couldn't even lose herself in her studies. She'd passed last term's exams with flying colors, and classes didn't begin again till mid-January.

Jackie had gone to the theater and would probably sleep over at her friend Christopher's place tonight. Esme glanced at the clock, whose hands seemed to move at a glacial pace.

Spending an evening here alone was nothing new for her; she was used to it. She'd even come to appreciate the quiet calm, especially after the tumultuous events her family had endured this past year....

But Nico's visit earlier this evening had changed everything.

Naturally.

Nico was a force of nature who caused change, just like fault lines underground caused earthquakes. He had changed her life too often and in too many ways. Now he intended to do it again? Esme felt a sharp, visceral pain.

Esme wound the music box and watched the little angels circle the wooden tree to the tune of "Silent Night." And she continued to think of Nico. Much to her disgust, she couldn't stop thinking of him tonight.

She was like one of those marionettes that she and Zara used to play with when they were little girls, gleefully pulling the strings to command the figures to do their will. How they had enjoyed jerking those puppet strings!

And now Nico was jerking *her* around. Again! And doing it so gleefully?

It was ironic and depressing that only Nico, a man who was off-limits to her, could arouse her passion, both in love and fury. She had learned that bitter lesson all too well.

Shame coursed through her. Nico might think he wanted her back, but he wanted the innocent girl he had been engaged to, not the woman she was now.

If he were to find out about her behavior in those distraught, crazy weeks after he'd ended their engagement—and inevitably, he would find out—she knew he would walk away from her again without a second thought.

After all, he was king of Imarco, and his bride must be a virgin.

Esme Bakkar no longer was, which made her an even more unsuitable marital candidate for him than her Rayaz blood ever could. Tradition was important to Nico, and marrying a virgin bride was a deeply held conviction in their part of the world. It was one of the very few things both Imarco and Rayaz, each staunchly patriarchal societies, happened to agree upon.

Since the end of their engagement, she had pretended not to care about Nico and been so convincing that her family and friends completely bought her act.

Only Esme herself knew that she had never stopped loving him.

But she would *not* allow herself to be rejected by him again.

That meant never seeing or speaking to Nico Tanefi again, continuing the course of action she had already implemented. She well knew that was easier said than done. Not taking his calls these past few months had been so hard, and each refusal caused her more pain.

Thankfully, by sheer coincidence, Jackie had answered the phone each time Nico called, sparing Esme from the alluring sound of his voice. Otherwise…

As if conjured up by her thoughts, the phone began ringing.

Esme froze. What if it were Nico? There was nobody here to answer the phone tonight but her.

Her stomach turned a triple flip. If it were Nico, she would slam down the receiver immediately without saying a word, she coached herself. That would be playing it cool *and* keeping her vow not to speak to him again.

"Esme, this is Tariq."

She fought a hot pang of disappointment, which was instantly replaced with anxiety. Rarely, did one of her four younger brothers call her here in England, unless something was wrong at home.

Yet in spite of her increasing apprehension, she couldn't help but notice, "You sound strange, Tariq. Different."

She heard him clear his throat. "I have a terrible cold that has settled in my throat. And also, I am—uh—I am very upset."

"Tariq, what's happened?" Her own voice quavered.

"You must come home right away, Esme. If anyone can put an end to this madness, it is you. Mama and Papa and the others might listen to you. It is worth a try. They will not hear a word from Riad or Amir or Ben-Ali or me."

"What madness? What are you talking about, Tariq?"

"The plan to marry off Zara to a—a rug merchant in Yemen." Tariq seemed to choke on the words.

"What?"

"He is a very wealthy rug merchant, and he says he will raise the triplets and provide dowries for them. They are going to send Zara and the girls to him tomorrow night. That is why it's imperative for you to leave for the airport right away, Esme. A plane has been—"

"Yemen?" Esme could hardly take it in. "Tariq, you must have drastically misunderstood. We don't know anyone in Yemen. Mama and Papa love Zara and they adore the triplets. Think, Tariq. *Yemen!* They would never send Zara and the children there, or anywhere, unless she—"

"I think they've all gone a bit crazy, Esme," Tariq inserted quickly. "Including our grandparents and aunts and uncles who support the plan. The entire family is in an uproar. You see, the—uh—um—the

Hassans have demanded land and money and political power from us, claiming that Zara is responsible for the loss of their son. That she should have stopped her husband flying the plane on the night he crashed.''

''That's insane!'' Esme protested. ''Zara couldn't have stopped him. Rez Hassan always did exactly as he pleased. Anyway, the Hassans were the ones who allowed him to get his pilot's license as a teenager. Who bought him his own plane! Tariq, this makes no sense at all.''

''You know the Hassans! After all, they were never very nice to Zara after the triplets were born, saying they were embarrassed she had so many babies at once, especially all girls. I think that clan must have originally come from Imarco. They've managed to keep their origins a secret, but blood will tell.'' He chuckled.

''Tariq, this is not a laughing matter,'' Esme chided him. ''True, the Hassans are greedy, manipulative and coldhearted enough to do anything. But for Mama and Papa to send Zara and the triplets away—''

''To Yemen. I don't know how they met this rug merchant, but he is very old and ugly. Esme, you have to come home and stop this from happening. Zara begs you. She would come to the phone herself, but she is crying too hard to talk.''

Esme felt her head begin to pound in time with her heart. Her poor sister, her adorable little nieces! ''Yes, I'll come, Tariq. I will not let them send Zara and the triplets anywhere. In fact, I am already formulating a plan. I'll call Bashir and the Murads as soon as I land in Rayaz. They will side with us, I know. They're still angry with the Hassans over the Ramadan incident, remember?''

''Who could forget? Rayaz is just one big sand dune of hostility.''

Esme sighed. ''It does seem that way sometimes. Do you have my flight booked, Tariq?''

''Yes. A car is being sent for you and will take you to the jet. Thank you, my dear sister.''

''I'll pack a bag and be ready to go when the car arrives.''

''If I do say so myself that was not a bad imitation of Tariq Bakkar, considering I've never met him,'' said Nico's cousin Hamid, a gifted mimic. ''But I've heard enough Rayaz princelings to know they speak Arabic tinged with an upper-class British accent, no doubt from their years of schooling in England.''

''I thought our hoax was finished when you said 'Rayaz is just one big sand dune of hostility.''' Nico frowned. ''You were pushing it too far with that one.''

''Merely a little joke for our mutual amusement, Nico.'' Hamid laughed. ''But you were not amused?''

The two cousins were only a month apart in age, sons of sisters, and had grown up in the palace together. Since childhood, Hamid's skills at improvisation never ceased to astonish Nico. And sometimes to alarm him as well.

''It's lucky Esme confided all that personal information about her sister and the Hassans back when you two were close. I had to use it because at first, she wasn't buying the story of her parents sending Zara and the children away.''

"Probably because the old ugly rug merchant in Yemen was too far-fetched. It's something out of an old cartoon! If you'd made him a Saudi prince—"

"No, I mean it sounded like Esme didn't believe her parents would force Zara to marry anyone if she didn't want to. Could the Bakkars have more heart than we give them credit for?" Hamid stroked his neatly trimmed mustache with his thumb. "Speaking as myself this time, maybe *they* originally came from Imarco?"

Nico laughed at that. "They would be gravely insulted by such speculation. I believe the Bakkars have traced their ancestry back to the dawn of time and claim that not a single one of them set foot in Imarco, except to retrieve all the things we allegedly stole from them down through the centuries.''

"Politics. Families. They have much in common with land mines." Hamid was droll.

"I can't thank you enough for making this call for me, Hamid," Nico said, becoming serious. "I know it will be a turning point for Esme and me."

"I hope a forgiving nature is among your beloved's attributes, Nico. Because when she finds out there is no crisis involving her sister, that we deliberately scared her to trick her onto the plane, things could get uglier than our fictional old rug merchant in Yemen."

"She loves me." Nico spoke it like a prayer. "She

will forgive me for doing what needed to be done to reconcile us.''

Hamid's dark eyes were gleaming. "*You* are a hopeless romantic, Nico.''

Chapter 3

"Princess, may I take your coat and bag?"

Esme whirled around, nearly cracking heads with the uniformed steward standing behind her. He'd approached so stealthily that she hadn't heard a thing.

They both jumped back with startled gasps.

"I most humbly beg your pardon, Princess!"

"Princess," Esme repeated grimly. She stared again at the interior of the Lear jet. She'd been expecting the usual interior, the small kitchen and lavatory in front and the extra-large seats side by side extending to the back of the aircraft.

What she saw instead was a custom-designed cabin furnished like a luxurious room in an Arabian palace. The silk-covered divans and ottomans were there, plus a few modern pieces, like the huge reclining chairs. Thick exquisitely patterned carpets covered the floor and walls. At the front end was a fully equipped galley with every kind of kitchen appliance and in back hung a dark curtain, concealing whatever might be behind it.

She had flown Air Rayaz all her life and never seen such a plane. She smelled a rat now, a huge broiled one.

"We abolished those titles twenty years ago. Nobody uses them in Rayaz."

The steward seemed to wither under her fierce gaze.

"Except the Hassans and their servants!" Esme exclaimed. "I think I am beginning to understand what is going on here." She turned to face the dark curtain and raised her voice. "So you are cowering back there? How ridiculously immature—and so typical of you! Who is back there? Zayed? Mommar? Kareem? Answer me!"

The ensuing silence heightened her rage. "Well, you are very right to fear me. And just wait until everybody finds out that you've turned one of the planes into your version of a hedonistic rock star's private jet."

The purring engines rose to a roar, and the plane began to pull away from the gate.

"Stop!" Esme stormed toward the back of the plane. "Order the pilot that he is *not* to take off. I will not let any of you Hassan boys use me to extort a single coin from my family."

The steward, looking terrified, chased after her, exhorting her to please take a seat and fasten the seat belt. Esme ignored him.

Reaching the curtain, she yanked it open to find total darkness within.

She blinked, waiting for her eyes to adjust. Gradually, she was able to make out the shadowy outlines of a large bed. Her heart leaped into her throat. This was no time to give in to terror, she must be the one to supply it.

"Are you hiding under the bed? Or in a closet?" she demanded. "You are cowardly, though wise, not to let me find you. But I will. And then..."

The plane picked up speed and the steward uttered a lamentation, frantically citing airline regulations on takeoffs and landings.

"Stop this plane!" Esme ordered, though she realized it was a lost cause. She felt sick with fear but knew she could never show it.

Suddenly, a door opened, flooding the area with light. And Esme found herself facing...

"Nico?"

It was surreal. Was she hallucinating? Was Nico Tan-efi actually standing before her, quite unkinglike in jeans and a burgundy wine-colored sweater? Unkinglike but heartstoppingly sexy.

Esme drew a rattled breath. "Nico," she repeated, incredulous.

"Yes, it is me," Nico said wryly. "You seem more shocked to see me than at the prospect of being kidnapped by the Hassans. Is kidnapping members of other ruling families so commonplace in Rayaz that it is an obvious conclusion to draw when—''

"*You're* kidnapping me?" The full adrenaline rush hit her with the force of a speeding train. "You can't do such a thing! It—it is an act of war!"

The steward uttered a squeak of dismay.

"Leave us, Jamal," Nico ordered. "You ought to take a seat and prepare for takeoff, in keeping with those airline regulations you mentioned. You are most knowledgeable and I commend you."

"Thank you, Your Highness." The steward disappeared, pulling the curtain closed behind him.

Seconds later, the plane lifted off, and the jolt of going airborne sent both Nico and Esme bouncing against the carpeted walls of the cabin before they both landed sprawling on the big bed.

Frantically, Esme pushed down the skirt of her demure gray-and-pink dress that she had donned before leaving for the airport, aware that appearing demure always scored points with the relatives. At the time, she had figured she would need every advantage to win them over to her side.

But she was not facing any Bakkar. Esme's heart raced. And a dress was most impractical for rolling around on a bed with Nico.

Just that simple observation sent sensual frissons through her.

"Perhaps we should have buckled up too," Nico remarked as the plane continued its turbulent ascent. "This is an unfortunately rough takeoff."

"Maybe it's a metaphor for this harebrained, criminal scheme of yours," snapped Esme.

The plane tilted sharply to the right, almost rolling both Esme and Nico onto the floor. They each grabbed hold of the bed's fixed headboard and hung on.

"I hope you don't suffer from motion sickness," murmured Nico, "because this is definitely the flight to induce it."

Esme was tugging at her skirt again. Every time she moved, it rose higher, exposing her thighs. She caught Nico staring unabashedly at her legs and drew up her knees, so her skirt totally covered her folded limbs.

"It would serve you right if I got airsick all over the royal bed in Air Force One, or whatever you call this fancy plane of yours, Your Highness," she added, making it sound more like an insult than a title of respect.

"Since Air Force One is the American president's official plane, I don't use that term or any other one for my plane. And it is not at all like a hedonistic rock star's," he added, a defensive note in his voice.

"Oh, you know that for a fact, do you? Because you now hobnob with rock stars? I feel certain you have not shared that information with the solid citizens of Imarco."

"I assure you that I have never *hobnobbed* with anyone, let alone rock stars, Esme."

"Kindly drop that patronizing tone. At least do me the honor of speaking to me like a sworn enemy," commanded Esme, her tone definitely worthy of a sworn enemy.

The plane lurched again. Both kept their grips on the headboard. As if on cue, they simultaneously turned their heads toward each other.

Their eyes met.

"When you came after me with the lamp earlier this evening, I thought it might be an aberration," said Nico. "But it seems that you really are a warrior. I've always known you were high-spirited, of course, but I never realized how fierce you could be."

"Well, now you know, don't you?"

Nico's lips quirked. "When you were threatening the Hassans, I found myself feeling sorry for them, had they actually been around for you to find. You sounded capable of anything."

"I am. I know how to do moves in karate and judo and akido and boxing. My brothers took the classes and taught me what they'd learned."

"And you've actually put this knowledge to use?" asked Nico with real interest.

"Oh, yes." Esme nodded. "When I was twelve I beat up several of the Hassan brats for picking on little Rashid Murad at a wedding reception. There were other times, I felt compelled to—um—act in the defense of someone who was weaker."

"And you successfully subdued the bratty aggressors every time?" Nico propped himself up on one arm.

The glint of admiration in his dark eyes was unmistakable.

"Yes," Esme replied, warming under it. "Because I also added what my brothers called girly tactics— things like hair-pulling and scratching—to my repertoire."

"Ah, the element of surprise. The unexpected is often most effective." Nico nodded his approval. "As is a reputation for taking action when necessary."

"Among the families, I do have a reputation of being something of a—" Esme almost smiled. "I believe 'firebrand' is the kindest term that has been used. I have heard more disparaging ones. The Hassan brothers and cousins still quake in fear of me from our earlier battles."

"It hasn't occurred to them that they are now fully grown men who are taller and outweigh you by at least a hundred-plus pounds?"

"No, I remain the powerful creature whom the Hassan boys had better not enrage. They are sickeningly ingratiating toward me now. It embarrasses their parents who, needless to say, do not adore me."

"So perhaps that is why our engagement did not provoke quite the riotous disapproval in Rayaz as might have been expected?" Nico grinned. "Maybe you were seen as your country's revenge on Imarco? At least from the Hassans' point of view."

Esme wanted to laugh. She had always been charmed by Nico's sense of humor and felt herself effortlessly beginning to slip under his spell again. Which could not be allowed to happen, she reminded herself.

Nothing had changed since earlier this evening,

when she had reviewed the reasons they could never be together.

Earlier this evening… She sat up abruptly.

"No, no, this can't be happening! Oh, how did I forget, even for a moment? You picked a terrible time to kidnap me, Nico. I have to go home, I have to help my sister. Tell your pilot to land in Rayaz. Never mind, I'll tell him myself."

She hopped off the bed, but within a split second, the plane dipped, flinging her to the ground. Nico leaned over and hauled her back onto the bed.

Forewarned of her fighting prowess, he quickly drew her arms over her head and held them there, securing her wrists with hands as strong as manacles. He swung his legs over her, one between her knees the other atop their pile of limbs.

Esme was efficiently, effectively pinned to the mattress. Her skirt was again hiked high; she could feel the rough denim of his jeans rubbing against her sheer stockings. The sensation, the subtle sounds were almost unbearably erotic.

But for now, her fear for Zara's plight superceded everything.

She began to struggle. "Let me go! You don't understand, I have to save my sister!" Her voice was hoarse and thick as her eyes filled with tears.

"No, Esme, no, listen to me." At once, Nico's tone became soft and soothing, though he did not loosen his grip on her. "My sweet, I am sorry to have alarmed you so. Your sister is fine. She and the triplets are in no danger of being sent anywhere."

Esme went stock-still and stared up at him, her face a portrait of astonishment. "How do you—"

"—know about the phone call tonight, from your brother Tariq? That is, the phone call *allegedly* from Tariq? I was there when my cousin Hamid placed the call, Esme. You have not yet met him but when you do, you will see that Hamid is a gifted mimic. He posed as your brother Tariq over the phone tonight, saying whatever was necessary to get you to come to the airport and onto this plane."

"The rug merchant in Yemen who wants Zara? And the Hassans' demands on my family which pushed them to the breaking point?" Esme was visibly confused. "All of it is—"

"Fictitious. Yes, all of it. Although from what I have come to know of the Hassans, they seem quite capable of what Hamid-as-Tariq invented. And even worse."

"Oh!" Esme began to struggle anew, intensifying her efforts. A white-hot rage streaked though her. She had been masterfully, maliciously duped!

"How dare you? You maligned my family and insulted every Bakkar! Deep in my heart, I *knew* they wouldn't be so heartless, but I was infected by the toxic propaganda you and your cousin concocted! I am sick with shame for swallowing your treacherous poison."

"You have no reason to feel shame, and for the perceived insult, I humbly apologize," Nico soothed. "The whole marriage tale was Hamid's invention and

I agree, it was a tad excessive. Again, I am sorry you were so disturbed by it all, Esme.''

"Your insincere apologies are an insult in themselves. I will not accept them! Furthermore, it isn't only the Bakkars you have reviled, it is also the Hassans. Your terrible cousin accused them of—''

"I make no apologies about the Hassans,'' Nico cut in. "I've disliked them intensely since you told me their reaction to the birth of Zara's triplets. Instead of being thankful for the miracle of three healthy identical babies, they were critical and contemptuous. I find them reprehensible, and so do you, Esme. You had no trouble accepting Hamid's story of the Hassans' fictional nefarious plans. You expected it of them.''

Esme fumed. It didn't help that he was one-hundred percent correct, especially when she still felt like a gullible fool for falling for the scam. And particularly not when the feel of his hard body entwined with hers was insidiously transforming her anger into a wholly different kind of heat.

Which she didn't dare give in to. "You had no right to tell your cousin what I told you in confidence,'' she scolded.

"You have a legitimate point, Esme. Never again will I betray anything that you confide in me, you have my word on it. Meanwhile, Hamid will not repeat anything he knows about Zara and the Hassans.''

Without slackening his hold on her, he slipped one of his hands around both her wrists, freeing his other hand. He gently glided his palm over her cheek, cupping the side of her jaw. He raised his knee until it was almost in direct contact with the soft secret place between her thighs.

"I am not in agreement with all Machiavellian tenets, but in our unique situation, I truly felt the end justified the means," he said softly.

Esme raised her eyes to his. She swallowed hard at the intensity of his gaze. His gentle caress, coupled with the power of his muscular body, provided a dizzying contrast. A seductive one. If she moved her legs just an inch or two, she would be straddling his thigh. A throbbing empty ache within pushed her to seek that tempting pleasure

She felt dangerously close to succumbing to both dizziness and seduction. To experiencing the pleasure. She balled her hands into fists, as if to physically fight the temptation.

"What do you think you will accomplish by—by this, Nico?" She flinched at her breathlessness which revealed so much. Too much.

"I want to spend time with you, Esme. You made it very clear you wouldn't give me a chance to even talk to you, so I had to resort to something else." Nico knew it was time to improvise and hoped he could do as good a job as Hamid. "You see, I, uh, read in an American book given to me by Ryan Fortune that—"

"Ryan Fortune? Isn't he the man the cartel hoped to cheat in the oil deal, but he proved too savvy to fall for the scheme?"

"You know about that?" Nico was surprised.

"Everybody in the Middle East knows about that, Nico. In Rayaz, Ryan Fortune is held in great esteem because he was wiser than the Powers That Be."

"Never mind that they were part of the Powers That Be who tried to scam him," Nico said drolly.

"Keep in mind that *you,* representing Imarco, were also part of the scam that Ryan Fortune outwitted."

Nico smiled, a glint in his eyes. He decided that now was not the time to divulge that Ryan had some vital assistance in outwitting the cartel.

"I also hold the man in great esteem for his wisdom," he said instead. Which was certainly the truth, just not the whole truth. "So I read the book he recommended, and it suggested 'being proactive.' Therefore…"

"Making up vicious lies about my family, alarming me, taking me away and holding me against my will is your idea of being proactive?"

Esme tried to rally her anger which was dissipating at an alarming rate. The more she talked to Nico, the longer she lay with him, the stronger and more urgent her need grew. She'd better fire up her temper again—and fast!

"I am certain neither the American book nor Ryan Fortune would condone this imperious, disgraceful, criminal behavior of yours. Proactive, ha!"

"I hit the target with inspiring accuracy, so to speak." Far from appearing contrite, Nico was smiling his success. "I knew you would do anything for your sister, but I only guessed that if there was family trouble, your brothers would turn to you so the Tariq/

Hamid phone call was a risk. Your response, however, clearly proved I got the dynamics exactly right.''

Their bodies were so close that she physically felt the momentary relaxation he allowed himself. Esme, determinedly thrusting herself into full defensive warrior mode, took instant advantage of it.

''Before you finish congratulating yourself, you should be aware there are other *dynamics* you got exactly wrong.''

As if ejected by a spring she hurled herself up and out of his arms, managing to roll off the bed before he had a chance to react.

''You were wrong to believe I want to spend time with you!'' She flung the words at him as she raced toward the curtain. ''There was a reason why I wouldn't talk to you, why I wouldn't take your calls, a most obvious reason. I have nothing to say to you— and I never will!''

Nico caught her before she could go any farther. He wrapped his arms around her waist, hauling her back against him.

''I don't believe you,'' he murmured, his lips against her ear. ''There is plenty you want to say to me, and I am prepared to listen to every word. If you have to vent your rage against me to get past it, then so be it.''

His voice, low and urgent seemed to echo in her head. The feel of his lips moving against the sensitive lobe of her ear sent shivers coursing through her. The plane dipped again, and Nico's grasp tightened, keeping her from lurching forward or falling.

Rather than feeling imprisoned, she felt herself savoring his protective strength. Esme knew she was in deep, deep trouble but couldn't summon the will to fight any longer. Not when the heat of his strong warm body enveloped her, not when her senses were filled with him.

Her eyelids fluttered shut. The last thing she wanted to do at this particular time was to vent any rage. Nico opened his hand across her stomach, and tongues of sensual fire seemed to radiate from each of his fingertips, streaking through her to every erogenous zone.

Her head lolled back against him, to rest in the hollow of his shoulder. She placed her hands over his, ostensibly to remove them, but somehow her fingers linked with his instead.

"My darling." Nico's mouth was warm and moist against the sensitive curve of her neck. "I missed you so much. I need you so much."

Esme could feel the passion surging through him, sparking her own as hot and fast as a lit match thrown into a pool of gasoline. All her carefully rationalized thoughts and analyses, all her commonsense arguments about why this should never be, why they could never be together, were eliminated in the fiery erotic blaze.

Silently, she turned within the circle of his arms, their bodies rubbing, never breaking contact, as she completed the movement. She lifted her head and saw the hunger, the urgency flaming in his dark eyes.

Her lips parted and her eyes closed heavily as his mouth covered hers.

Nico groaned with sensual bliss. The sweetness of her lips, the soft feminine warmth of her body nestled into his, flooded him with pure primitive male triumph.

All the terrible lonely months without her, all the wanting and not having her, was finally over. He was holding Esme in his arms, he was kissing her, and she was responding to him with a needy hunger that matched his own.

He felt her arms slide around his neck and heard her moan softly as she molded the full length of herself to his body. The feel of her rounded breasts, the taut buds of her nipples hard against his chest, of their bellies pressed together, sent his mind spinning into an orbit where old-time traditions and rules did not apply.

During their brief engagement, he had never allowed himself to hold her like this, possessively, intimately. To kiss her deeply and rapaciously, as he did now, although he'd wanted to. Oh, how badly he had wanted to!

But he had never let himself lose control. Always, he had reminded himself of their stations, their upbringing, the expectations upon them both.

But now…

He didn't think of Imarco or Rayaz or postponing passion till the royal wedding night. Giving up Esme for the sake of Imarco was something he would do only once. Now that she was back in his arms, he was finally, simply a man who was with the only woman in the world for him.

He moved his hand to cover her breast, to fondle the enticing soft mound through the silk of her dress. His fingers traced the lacy outline of her bra and he pressed his palm against the peaked nipple.

Esme drew a ragged breath and her body arched, her hips pressing hard into his. Her spontaneous response shocked her and abruptly, the thick fog of sensuality engulfing her, lifted.

"Nico, I—we—" Her voice, breathy and weak, trailed off.

"Yes, sweetheart," Nico murmured, as if picking up the thread of a conversation she had initiated. "Yes, my love."

He nibbled on the creamy smoothness of her throat, sending a sensual shudder through her. The lure of his masculinity combined with her love for him was overwhelming; her defenses against him were puny and meager in comparison.

Esme forgot everything but the need to yield to him, and to her own desire for him.

She nuzzled the smooth dark column of his neck as she wriggled against him. Her movements allowed him to nudge her thighs farther apart and settle into the notch between them.

Esme quivered at the blatant sexual contact. A jolt of pure pleasure shot through her. It was thrilling and terrifying, like nothing she had ever experienced before.

The sensations increased exponentially, sending her higher, sending her soaring, as he began to unfasten the top buttons on the bodice of her dress. The silk-covered buttons, alternating in pink and gray, extended down the front length of her dress.

Nico stopped unbuttoning when he reached her waist and slipped his hand inside her dress. Esme's heartbeats thundered in her ears as he deftly opened the front clasp of her pale pink bra and cupped one naked breast.

They both sighed.

And then, they were lying on the bed, his hand caressing her breasts, first one and then the other, circling her nipples with his thumb. They were so tight, so ultrasensitive, that sharp needles of pleasure bordering on pain pierced her to her very core.

Esme realized vaguely that she had no recollection of moving from where they'd been standing, by the curtain, over to the bed. And onto it.

Her mind was focused solely on Nico, and the delicious things he was doing to her. A thick syrupy warmth flowed through her, pooling hotly between her thighs.

When he closed his mouth over one nipple, she whimpered his name. His lips drew strongly on the sensitive bud, and shards of arousal pierced her womb. The feelings were somehow both too much and not enough. It was a pardox, a thoroughly addictive one.

She clasped his head with her hands and stroked his thick dark hair, while holding him fast to her breast. She lay still, barely breathing, as wave after wave of exquisite pleasure washed over her.

Her skirt was tangled around her hips again, her legs entwined with his, but this time, she made no attempt to restore her modesty. Opening her eyes a little, she glanced down to see his long nimble fingers working the lower buttons of her skirt. Pushing the silky material aside. Sliding his hand between her legs.

He touched the most private, vulnerable part of her body and made her cry out, her control dissolved by their intimacy.

Her whole body throbbed with need; she felt fantastic and helpless at the same time and reveled in her own responses to him. Never had she felt so feminine or been so aware of the wonders of being a woman.

This was what she wanted, what she'd always wanted with Nico.

"I want you so much, my darling," Nico's low, husky voice aroused her as masterfully as his hands, his mouth. "And you want me."

He gently rubbed her, the wet silk of her panties giving him proof of her desire. As if he needed any more proof, Esme mused dreamily.

"I'll be gentle, sweetheart, I'll make it good for you."

He slid one finger beneath the material to touch the moist downy thatch. "You can trust me, my baby. Give yourself to me."

It was the way she had always dreamed it; Nico making love to her on their wedding night, arousing her, soothing her virginal fears. Except she'd never had any fears about sex with Nico. She had wanted it, she had wanted him.

And he had never tried to do more than kiss her during their courtship or even during their engagement. He had been the perfect gentleman, the king protecting his virginal bride-to-be, even from himself.

Esme's eyes flew open as the sudden insight struck. Nico wasn't going to stop himself tonight, although he still believed she was that virginal bride-to-be he had left eighteen interminable, life-changing months ago.

He was gentling her, wooing her, trying to prepare her for the unknown milestone of sex.

Which was not unknown to her, not anymore.

Emotional pain seared her, and Esme fought back tears. She had wanted her first time to be with Nico. It hadn't mattered to her if she was his wife or fiancée or girlfriend, she had just wanted him to be her lover. But he had always stopped kissing her before passion could build into a fire that burned away all restraint.

And now...

"Nico, stop. We can't do this," she blurted out. She heard the note of anguish in her voice.

So did Nico who completely misinterpreted it. "Esme, darling, don't be frightened."

Esme swallowed hard. He thought she was a virgin, frightened by his masculine demands and her own volatile responses. He expected her to be.

And she wasn't.

"Let me up, Nico," she commanded.

Nico lay motionless, as if frozen, for a long moment, then slowly, removed his hands from her and sat up, sighing deeply.

Esme jerked to a sitting position, her hands shaking as she refastened the clasp of her bra and buttoned her dress. She was excruciatingly aware of him watching her every move.

"You never stopped me before," he said wryly, his dark eyes never leaving her.

"I was always the one to end things between us."

"Oh yes, you ended things between us. You ended things permanently."

Sexually frustrated and heartsick with regret, Esme felt her temper begin to flare. She suddenly, badly wanted to fight.

"Permanence is only temporary," Nico said with a calmness that she envied.

It also infuriated her. How dare he stay calm when her nerves felt like they'd been through a shredder?

"Is that some stupid Imarconian proverb you're quoting? Not only does it make no sense, it isn't true. Which pretty much sums up Imarco *and* its king."

"Ouch." Nico arched his dark brows "So we're back to hurling jingoistic insults, are we? Truth be told, that was not anybody's old proverb. I made it up on the spot," confessed Nico, still sitting on the bed and watching her with hungry dark eyes.

"Well then, all those prizes you won for extemporaneous speaking while on your school debating team were merely gifts handed to you because you were Imarco's future king,'' Esme said snidely as she stood up and combed her fingers through her hair, trying to smooth out the tangles. ''You certainly didn't rightfully earn them if 'permanence is temporary' is your idea of being extemporaneously clever.''

''I am quite proud of all those prizes—which I rightfully earned, Princess,'' Nico teased. ''But it is sweet that you remember my debating team stories.''

''I remember everything you told me, Nico, but most of all, I remember you telling me to get lost. *Permanently*. Anything temporary was not an option.''

Nico winced. ''I did not ever tell you to get lost, Esme.''

''Oh, you phrased it a little differently, no doubt calling upon your prized extemporaneous speaking skills but your meaning was crystal clear. I was a Rayaz millstone around your neck and you were cutting me loose. I had no say in the matter back then, but I do now and I—''

''The tangles are only getting more knotted,'' Nico cut her off midsentence, reaching up to touch her hair. ''Your fingers aren't doing the job. You need a brush.''

Diverted by his touch, Esme remembered to step out of his reach. She caught sight of the thick gold signet ring on his finger. She had never seen him wear it during their engagement.

His eyes followed hers, to Ryan's gift, that magical

totem of true love. Though Nico did not believe the legend, he hadn't taken the ring off since receiving it.

"A friend gave this to me." He rubbed his thumb over the engraved surface. "The double crowns on the ring are similar to a birthmark I have."

"It's most unusual." Esme peered at the ring, interested despite her wish not to be. "You never mentioned a birthmark of any kind."

"I'll show you now, if you wish." Nico unbuckled his leather belt and the first button of his jeans. Then the second.

"No! No, never mind," she said before he could go any farther.

She was sure she heard him snicker softly.

Esme's cheeks flushed scarlet. Where was his birthmark? She could make a few inspired, intoxicating guesses. She caught a glimpse of wiry black hair, exposed by the open front of his jeans, and reflexively lifted her eyes to find him watching her stare at the revealed patch.

"Sure you don't want to see it?" Nico's grin was playfully seductive.

"I'm quite sure!"

It was definitely time to play it cool, as Jackie would advise. Blushing like a shy maiden was not cool. Neither was ogling him or raging over their failed romance, but she'd done all that too. Esme stifled a groan.

"As—as you said before, I need my hairbrush to comb out this rat's nest. There is one in my purse and another in my bag."

"Your hair is not a rat's nest, Esme, it's charmingly tousled. It looks very sexy, like you have been in bed with—"

"Bring me my bags!" She sounded as imperious as any princess accustomed to having others leap to do her bidding.

"Yes, Your Majesty." Nico didn't leap; he slowly slid off the bed, his tongue firmly in cheek. "Your wish is my command."

He smiled at her and then pushed the curtain aside to retrieve her bag.

It took every ounce of willpower Esme possessed not to smile back. She couldn't melt every time he smiled or teased or touched her, not when she knew it could only lead to more heartbreak for her.

"Make yourself comfortable for the night, my sweet." He handed her suitcase and purse to her. "Take the bed. I will be out here in the main room of the cabin."

"But what—where—"

"The kidnapping is proceeding as scheduled, Princess. We are flying to America and we'll be in the air all night."

"America?" Esme gaped in disbelief.

"I remember you mentioning several times that you'd always wanted to take a trip to America, but none of the daughters of the ruling families have ever been permitted to go there. 'Too wild and wicked,' say the patriarchal princes of Rayaz. Do they really believe that Europe, on the other hand, is the bastion of pure innocence?"

"No," Esme mumbled, dazed. "But Europe is closer to Rayaz than America. And older."

Nico laughed. "Well, you will be far away and less accessible in America, which suits my purposes well. So like the storybook genie in the magic lamp, I am granting your wish, Esme. I am taking you to America."

Chapter 4

"Esme, we'll be landing in about fifteen minutes."

Esme woke to the sound of Nico's voice. Though she'd never thought she would sleep a wink, eventually she had, and she hadn't awakened once, until she heard Nico call her name.

Trying to still the sudden roller-coaster pace of her heart, she rolled onto her side to glance up at him. Nico, fully dressed in his jeans and a University of Texas sweatshirt, was standing just inside the curtain. Looking at her.

She smoothed several long strands of hair away from her face, a nervous gesture, a stalling gesture. She cleared her throat. "Landing where?"

"Texas."

Texas? That was truly unexpected.

Esme sat up in bed. Her nightgown was high-necked and long-sleeved, all white cotton, ribbons and lace. The garment was so modest and demure she didn't bother holding up the sheet as a protective drape.

Her dark eyes flicked to the letters of his gray sweatshirt. "And are you trying to blend in by pretending to be a college student here? I feel I must inform you that your disguise isn't working, Nico. You look too old to be a fraternity boy."

"I'm relieved to hear it. A friend gave this to me and since we're in Texas, I decided to wear it. Do you think I could pass as a UT alumni?"

He smiled at her, inviting her to share his small joke.

Esme heaved a sigh. "Nico, what in the world are we doing in Texas?"

"I thought I'd sufficiently explained the kidnapping last night, my sweet. I—"

"I know that part." Esme was exasperated. "Couldn't you have kidnapped me to New York City? That is where I've always wanted to go. Or perhaps Disney World. But *Texas*? I only know Texas from cowboy movies I've seen, and I have no interest in riding the range herding cattle."

"Don't worry, we won't be. We've landed on a private airstrip and we're not in cattle country. I'll drive the Range Rover provided for us to a cottage that a friend has made available. I've been told that it's fully stocked with every amenity."

"Who is this generous friend of yours?"

Nico shrugged. "Nobody you know."

"Because this *friend* doesn't exist," she said flatly.

Nico laughed. "I'm a bit old to have imaginary friends, Esme."

"You refuse to divulge any information, even where we are, and are using this mythical friend to keep from answering any of my questions truthfully. Texas is your idea—or perhaps your smart-aleck cousin's idea—of a joke. Give it up, Nico. I know we aren't in Texas."

"No?" Nico studied her thoughtfully. "Then where do you think we are, Esme?"

"In Imarco, of course. Everything is at the king's disposal, transportation, a cottage, supplies, just as you ordered."

"Your Rayaz paranoia is surfacing, Esme," Nico teased. "Can't you allow yourself to believe that I really do have a generous friend and that we really are in Texas?"

Esme bit her lip. "How long do you intend to hold me prisoner here in your miserable country?"

"The future queen of Imarco should not refer to her realm as miserable, Esme."

"Future queen? Me?" Esme folded her arms and stared at him. The lump in her throat felt as if it had turned into ground glass, but she didn't dare betray any signs of sorrow. She had to brazen this out.

"I thought you simply wanted to spend time with me. Now you say you are—proposing?"

"Darling, of course, my intentions toward you are honorable. I would never defile your good name by compromising you. Perhaps I am—er—rushing things but—"

"You are being proactive, like in the American book?" Esme cut in sarcastically. "Did this book ever mention what to do when being proactive doesn't work? When being proactive backfires?"

"Of course not. Only those books promising the desired results ever get published in America."

Esme lowered her eyes to hide the shine of tears. She had guessed that marriage was on his mind, of course, but hearing him admit it outright delivered a painfully visceral blow.

He was the honorable king who would not defile or compromise her—because she was to be his Virgin Queen. In Imarco and in Rayaz, among other countries in the Middle East, a woman who'd had a sexual experience with another man was considered defiled and compromised.

Thankfully, their countries had moved beyond beheading women for such "crimes," but the stigma remained. Marriage between her and Nico could never be. It was dangerous to let herself even fantasize otherwise for a world of pain lay beyond such dreams.

"I don't know why you've changed your mind and decided you want to marry me, after all, Nico, but my answer is no," Esme said sternly. "I do not want to marry you and I most certainly don't want to be the future queen of Imarco. Now if you will please give me some privacy, I would like to get washed and dressed."

He frowned and appeared ready to protest. But he merely said, "Take all the time you need. We will leave when you are ready."

Nico sat in the luxurious—but not showy and hedonistic like a rock star's!—cabin, waiting for Esme. Last night everything appeared to be falling into place; his kidnap plan, aided and abetted by Ryan Fortune, seemed like a grand success.

Sensual images of making love to Esme flooded his brain, and his body reacted immediately, intensely. He'd spent much of the flight in a state of arousal, thanks to those memories which he did not even try to suppress. They were too wonderful, they were the beginning of his dreams coming true.

Sweet, passionate Esme! She had melted in his arms, responding to him with fiery feminine heat, making him lose control and unleash all the desire and the love he felt for her.

Nico bolted upright. Maybe that was the problem? Despite his attempts to reassure her, had his lack of control—and her own—frightened her? He must not forget that she was inexperienced and unaccustomed to such ardor, on his part and her own. Had their mutual passion induced shame and guilt in her?

He knew how strictly women in his own country were brought up regarding sexuality. One could only guess how much more repressive it was in Rayaz! There was a running joke in Imarco that Rayaz was finally, though reluctantly, coming into the thirteenth century.

He didn't doubt that Esme wanted him. Last night

had given him all the proof he needed. But now Esme, feeling shameful and guilt-ridden, was punishing herself—and him—for their behavior.

Obviously, he needed to turn down the sexual heat until she felt comfortable enough to trust him—and herself—again.

Could he go back to the chaste kisses and light touches that had defined their first courtship and engagement? The unresolved sexual tension had stretched endlessly between them, a delicious form of torture, but they had kept it that way. Unresolved.

Now that he'd experienced a blissful sensual taste of her, a glimpse of what resolving that sexual tension would be like—*pure heaven!*—could he resume their former proper, traditional premarital relationship? Especially while spending time together under the same roof?

Nico clenched his jaw. He would have to, for Esme. He would do anything for her, and if that included sacrificing his urgent needs to match her own readiness, so be it.

"I'm ready to go." Esme was standing beside him, holding her suitcase in one hand, her purse slung over her shoulder.

He had been so lost in thought he hadn't even heard her approach. He rose to his feet, wishing his blatant arousal weren't quite so evident. Jeans didn't hide what the flowing robes worn in the Middle East did.

But Esme didn't look at him. Her eyes were fixed on the door of the aircraft.

Nico took the opportunity to study her. She wore

a plaid skirt and prim, buttoned-to-the-neck white silk blouse, dark stockings and black flat shoes with straps. Her hair was pulled high in a long ponytail.

He blinked. "You look like a schoolgirl."

"I thought I was going to Rayaz to talk my family out of shipping my sister and the triplets to Yemen, remember? This is the way to dress on such a mission. Actually, this is the way my grandparents and aunts and uncles still see me. It's the way my parents like to believe I dress all the time in school in England."

"Ah, strategic dressing. Now I understand."

"Had I known you were kidnapping me for a seduction scene, I would have packed quite differently."

He visibly gulped. "What would you have packed, if you'd known you were going to be with me?"

Esme saw that uneasy swallow, she heard the strain in his voice as he attempted to sound casually amused. His burning dark eyes belied his tone; Nico was hardly the casual type. She had also cast a very covert glance at the bulge in his jeans. And suddenly an idea popped into her head....

Nico was expecting an untainted virgin, the required ideal candidate for queen. Since he didn't seem to believe what she had been subtly trying to tell him—that she was unfit to be a royal bride—then it was time he realized it for himself.

Show, don't tell. That was the mantra of every writing teacher she'd ever had. Why couldn't it be applied to situations other than storytelling?

What if she were to stop telling him, however

obliquely, and flagrantly show him that she was not queen of Imarco material?

"What would I have packed for our secret little idyll, had I known about it, Nico?" Esme flashed a sudden sultry smile. "Nothing but naughty lingerie, baby. You would have immediately realized that I am a bad girl. Very bad."

Nico gaped at her as if she'd grown another head. And Esme continued down the path she had chosen.

"In fact, why bother to pretend anymore? Since we aren't in Rayaz, and I don't have to worry about giving my family a collective cardiac arrest, I think I'll go back and prepare for my first appearance in Imarco. Give me just a few more minutes, sweetie pie."

Esme laid her hand on Nico's chest and rose on tiptoe to skim her lips against his. She had observed Jackie, a veteran flirt, often enough to pick up all the moves.

With Nico, it all came naturally to her. She didn't have to pretend she enjoyed the touching, the teasing kisses, the flirting. With Nico, she not only truly enjoyed it, she loved it.

She loved him.

And since this was the only time she and Nico would ever have together, she might as well make the most of it before he sent her disgraced, defiled, bad girl self away and forgot all about his folly in wanting to make her his queen.

She disappeared behind the curtain again, leaving a bemused Nico staring after her.

The Esme who emerged this time was a completely

different entity than the one who had dressed to please the conservative Bakkars.

She'd gone from no makeup to full-stage makeup. Cherry-red lipstick, dramatically thick sable eyeliner and mascara. Heavy blue eyeshadow and very rosy cheeks. Her hair was still in a ponytail but it was pulled off to one side, the long dark tresses draped alluringly over her shoulder.

She still wore her white silk blouse, but she'd undone the first four buttons and folded down the collar, inventing a plunging neckline. She had also unfastened the lower buttons and separated the sides of the blouse, tying them in a knot just under her breasts.

Her slender midriff was bare, and it was all to easy to catch a glimpse of her lacy bra and cleavage.

She'd also kept on her plaid skirt but had transformed it as totally as the blouse. The skirt was rolled to an eyepoppingly short length and hitched low on her hips, exposing her navel and smooth flat upper abdomen.

When she took a step, her short skirt revealed the tops of her thigh-high black stockings, which seemed to add decadence to her once-innocent black-strapped shoes.

Esme smiled when Nico caught sight of her stocking tops, then almost laughed out loud when he spied her gold belly button ring. She'd been in a rebellious mood that summer day when she had asked Jackie to accompany her to Simon's Body Piercing Parlor.

Until this moment, she, Jackie and Simon the chief piercer were the only three humans on the planet who knew about her belly button ring. Now there were four.

"No more schoolgirl, Nico," she said provocatively. "Well, I guess I could be a slutty schoolgirl. The kind that gets expelled for bad conduct."

Nico opened his mouth to speak, then closed it again.

"Shall we go to this hideaway that's awaiting us?" Boldly, Esme sauntered ahead of Nico, taking care to brush against him as she went. "When we get there, I'll show you my tattoo. And you can show me that double crown birthmark of yours."

She glided past the wide-eyed steward Jamal and walked through the door onto the set of stairs, which had been pushed up to the plane. But instead of the hot climate of Imarco, which she'd been expecting, she was hit by a blast of cold air and—snow flurries?

She'd seen snow in England...but in Imarco?

"You need your coat, schoolgirl."

Nico was right behind her, wrapping the full-length blue wool coat she had worn and discarded upon entering the plane last night.

"I've been advised that Texas is having a prolonged cold spell this winter. If we're lucky, we can get to the cottage before the snowstorm that's predicted for later today."

Now it was Esme's turn to be stunned speechless. Wherever they were, it was not Imarco which, like Rayaz, never had snow. Her thoughts scrambled into incoherence.

"You're shivering," Nico observed solicitously.

"We won't be in the cold for long. Just down these stairs and over to the Range Rover, about a hundred yards from here. See it?"

He slipped his hand around her nape and directed her head toward the Range Rover which was idling nearby.

Placing his other hand on her waist and applying gentle pressure, Nico walked Esme down the stairs and hurried her toward the waiting vehicle. A penetrating blast of icy wind whipped her hair over her face and Esme pushed it back with hands already turning blue from the cold.

Nico pulled her back against him, sheltering her with his body. "It will be warm in the car, sweetheart. Only a few more feet and we'll be inside."

A rangy, freckled young man jumped out of the driver's side and ran around to open the passenger door for Esme.

"Hop in and get going," he advised chattily. "You guys better make tracks to beat the blizzard. Dallas is getting whomped by it right now. You got enough time if you step on it."

"Thank you." Nico handed him several bills. "You've been most helpful."

The boy flipped through the bills and gazed worshipfully at Nico. "Thank *you,* sir! And drive carefully now, y'hear?"

Inside the heated Range Rover, Esme turned to Nico. "This really is America."

Nico grinned. "What finally convinced you?"

"The weather. And the—the 'you guys.' I've never

heard anybody but Americans say that. And they use it for everyone, regardless of sex or age.''

''It can be disconcerting,'' agreed Nico. ''I once heard an American tour guide address a mixed group of senior citizens as 'you guys.' I can just imagine my grandparents' reaction if they and their friends were ever called 'you guys.'''

''As for Grandmama Bakkar and her cronies being called 'you guys'?'' Esme smiled. ''That boggles the imagination.''

She stared out the window as Nico, following the boy's advice, sped down the road to beat the blizzard. ''Nico, is this really Texas?''

''Yep, we guys really are in Texas.''

''Good try, but you don't completely sound American.'' Her smile widened. ''The accent, the usage—somehow it doesn't fit you.''

''I have a whole week to practice getting it right. That's how long I've arranged to be away from Imarco.''

Esme took a deep breath. ''And do you intend to keep me here for the entire week? I left Jackie a note saying that I went to Rayaz. If my family should call me, Jackie will wonder what is wrong.''

''My cousin Hamid is going to pay Jackie a visit today and bring a note from me explaining that the two of us are in America together and asking her to cover for you, should your family happen to call you this week.''

''You asked Jackie to lie to my family, if need be?'' Esme frowned her disapproval. ''Why doesn't

your cousin, the brilliant mimic, call them himself
pretending to be either Jackie or me? He could pretend he is both of us and alternate voices. That would
be fun for him, wouldn't it?''

"He is not quite that brilliant, Esme. Don't hold a
grudge against him, Hamid deceived you at my re-
quest. When you meet him, you will see that he is
both loyal and charming. I am counting on him using
that charm of his to talk Jackie into becoming our
ally.''

Esme remembered Jackie's assessment of her behavior with Nico in their flat last night. *"I thought
you were over Nico, but tonight you convinced me
otherwise. You acted like a woman in love, Esme."*
No, Hamid wouldn't have to exert much charm to win
Jackie's co-operation; she would believe she was doing Esme a favor.

"Esme, I do not want you to be a reluctant captive,
I intend to do everything in my power to make you
want to stay here with me this week," Nico said huskily.

Esme was quiet for several long moments. In all
honesty, Jackie would be doing her a favor, covering
for her during this week with Nico. This was her one
and only chance to snatch a bit of happiness with him
before losing him forever.

Why not take it? pleaded a yearning little voice in
her head.

"I want more than a single clandestine week with
you, Esme," Nico continued. "Much more. At the

end of our week together, we will announce our engagement to our families and our countries.''

Thinking of what could never be made Esme want to cry, and she quickly switched her thoughts to the plan she'd formulated on the plane. To show him that she was no longer virginal queen material, while making a lifetime of memories to treasure.

"Suppose I agree to willingly stay with you this week, Nico? In return, you have to agree not to talk about an engagement. I don't want any pressure. In fact, let's not talk about the future beyond this one week.''

His grin was unabashedly triumphant. "Since you agree to willingly stay, I won't have to pressure you into an engagement, my darling. You will want it as much as—''

"Beginning now, you can't even mention that word, Nico.''

"Fair enough, my precious.'' He removed one hand from the steering wheel and cupped Esme's knee. "Do you really have a tattoo?''

He sounded intrigued, not disapproving.

"Yes. Down the block from Simon's Body Piercing Parlor was Tristan's Tattoos with the widest selection of tattoos in London. Celebrities from all over the world come to Tristan's. His wall is filled with their pictures.''

"I assume he did not add a picture of you?''

"Of course not!'' She was momentarily floored by the very thought. "It would be like driving a stake

through my father's heart. The family knows nothing
about—''

She stopped herself midsentence. She had slipped
into sounding like the Bakkars' very proper daughter.
Time to switch gears into Imarco's never-to-be queen.

''Actually, it's too bad my picture isn't up in Tristan's place. Copies would be faxed all over the Middle East if you tried to spring another engagement to
me upon the loyal citizens of Imarco. And just imagine the gossip at the next meeting of the oil cartel!''

''Didn't we agree not to mention that word beginning with an 'e', Esme?''

She felt his hand slip slowly under her skirt and
follow the path of her black silk stocking. Her heart
slammed against her rib cage, and every pulse point
began to throb.

''Where is it?'' Nico asked huskily. ''This tattoo
of yours?''

His fingertips reached the top of her stocking and
probed the satiny soft skin of her naked inner thigh.
Esme closed her eyes and tried to steady her ragged
breathing.

''Nico, you should keep both hands on the wheel,''
she advised in a voice soft and weak with arousal.

''Should I?'' He stroked her stocking tops, then the
bare skin above it, alternating his caresses from place
to place, stimulating her, making her squirm shame-
lessly in her seat.

''I think we both need to eliminate the word
'should' from our vocabulary this week, Esme. We've
both spent too much time doing what we should. We

need a vacation from all those 'shoulds' in our lives. Don't you agree?''

"You sound nothing like the dutiful king of Imarco, Nico," she reminded him breathlessly.

"And in your current outfit, you look nothing like the dutiful daughter of the Bakkars, Esme," he teased.

Hearing herself referred to as the Bakkars' dutiful daughter was like being doused with a bucket of cold water. Pushing his hand away, Esme sat up straight and tightly closed her legs.

A moment later, she realized that she was not behaving like the slut she must convince Nico that she was. Forget the Bakkars' dutiful daughter, she was the tarnished tramp who would not be his queen.

Playing two vastly different roles was proving to be more difficult than she'd originally thought. How did split personalities ever keep their identities straight?

Quickly, she opened her coat and crossed her legs, taking care to display a tantalizing amount of upper thigh.

"I hope I have shocked you," she said, her voice a silky purr. "I promise to make this week the most shocking time of your life, Your Highness."

"You can try. In fact, I look forward to it, Princess. But I ought to warn you that these days, I am shock-proof."

There was an odd world-weary note in his voice that gave Esme pause. He sounded jaded and cynical, most out of character for Imarco's idealistic young king.

For the first time since he had walked out of her life, she allowed herself to really and truly consider the reason he had given for leaving her, to examine the political circumstances extending beyond her own personal rejection and heartbreak.

"I haven't really kept up with events in Imarco," she said tentatively. "But I did hear your uncle Amman was banished from there forever. That his life is considered to be endangered if he tries to enter any country in the Middle East, including Rayaz. He is a pariah, although I haven't heard why."

"Such information would be kept from a gently reared woman such as yourself. But I can give you a modified version. It is past time that you learned the facts, Esme."

Nico seemed to brace himself before resuming his disclosure. "Amman's supporters learned that my uncle is a vicious sexual deviate. When Amman appeared ready to launch his coup, several of his victims came forward to tell all to my closest advisors."

"That was very brave of them," murmured Esme. "They might have been risking their lives."

Nico nodded. "The junior officers in the army had openly sided with me from the start, but when the information about Amman came out, the senior officers who had pledged loyalty to him, against me, resigned in disgrace."

"And those who didn't resign... I hope you fired them?" Esme's dark eyes flashed.

"As fast as I could sign the order. Currently, Imarco's army is staffed with young colonels and generals whose loyalty to me is unquestionable.''

"And word of Amman's perversion was spread to all, in and out of Imarco?'' guessed Esme.

"Yes. That was the easiest part. As you know, salacious gossip spreads faster than the speed of sound. People are invariably interested in hearing it, believing it and passing it along. Amman left the Middle East, realizing there were too many countries vying to punish him for his deviancy, for betraying our faith. I've been told that the Saudis and the Iranians are still determined to punish him for his sins. Amman will spend the rest of his life watching his back, unable to trust anyone.''

"It is what he deserves," Esme said gravely. "No wonder you are shockproof. I didn't know, and I—I apologize for my tasteless sexual provocation earlier, Nico. It was brazen of me and—''

"Esme, my sweet, I like it when you tease me. Sexuality is not shameful. You can't equate your naughty schoolgirl game with Amman's debauchery. Expressing our love, whether tenderly—or playfully and seductively—is good.''

He took her hand and carried it to his mouth, brushing his lips across her palm.

"I am looking forward to your attempts at shocking me. Don't disappoint me, Esme.''

Chapter 5

Less than an hour later, after the biggest breakfast Esme had ever eaten, and with snow beginning to fall at an increasing rate, the couple stepped inside the "cottage," which actually was a ranch-style house at the end of a long private driveway in what was clearly an exclusive rural neighborhood.

Esme stared in wonder at the fire crackling in the stone fireplace, at the seven-foot tree fully decorated with strings of lights and tinsel and ornaments of all kinds, ranging from whimsical reindeer and elves to exquisite, elaborate bells and stars made of blown glass. There were even two big red stockings hanging on the fireplace with the names Esme and Nico sewn on the tops.

"I think Santa Claus has already made a stop here," said Nico, standing behind her.

He gazed around, smiling at each holiday touch. When Ryan had offered the "cottage" along with the use of the Range Rover, Nico had accepted, grateful for the opportunity for privacy for Esme and himself.

He hadn't expected this special Christmas atmosphere, in addition to everything else Ryan had provided. Nico was deeply touched. His father was a generous, thoughtful man.

His father…

Nico knew in that moment that he had accepted the truth about his identity and was at peace with it. He had been raised by a loving father, Omar Tan-efi, but there was room in his heart for his biological father Ryan Fortune too. Even though Ryan would never know of their kinship, Nico would nurture the friendship which had grown between them.

"Oh, Nico, this is so dear of you!" exclaimed Esme, giving him an impulsive hug.

Nico encircled her in his arms. "I'd love to claim credit but it was my—my friend who—"

"That friend of yours." Esme lifted her face to his, smiling into his eyes. "You are determined to carry on with the charade, are you?"

"Charade?"

"Nico, I know there is no *friend.* You own this place. And you arranged for it to be decorated for a real American Christmas, something that has always intrigued us both. You remembered all our talks about it." She sounded thrilled.

"You think I bought a place in Texas? That I have servants here who—"

"All right, we'll play it your way." Now she sounded downright *jolly*. "Santa Claus is your own special friend, and he is responsible for all of this."

It was warm in the room, with the fire blazing. Esme walked over to a chair and dropped her coat onto it, then gazed at the Christmas tree.

Nico came to stand beside her. "Your eyes are glowing like...well, a child's at Christmas." He slipped his arm around her waist.

"But that is the only childlike thing about you." Slowly, his thumb stroked her smooth bare skin. "This sexy naughty schoolgirl look works for you, Esme." He laughed softly. "It definitely works for me too."

He fingered her navel and the gold ring there. Esme shivered as waves of sensual yearning swept through her. She was alone with the man she loved, who she would always love.

And at this moment, he loved her too. That is, he loved what he believed her to be. Soon, he would know what she really was, and it would be all over between them. She would be back in England, studying and planning for her teaching career.

But right now they were together, loving each other, wanting each other.

She moved into his arms. "This feels so right, Nico."

Her whole body felt on fire, as if the flames from the crackling blaze had ignited inside her, burning to flashpoint. Beneath her silk blouse, she felt her nipples harden into tight peaks that pressed against the lacy cups of her bra. The stimulation was almost painfully intense.

"It is right, Esme." Nico used two fingers to tilt back her head, making her meet his ardent dark eyes. "Darling, all those months without you, I—"

"No." She laid her palm lightly against his lips. "Don't talk about that." She arched her hips against him and daringly used her other hand to cover the full hard length of him, throbbing against the rough denim of his jeans.

"Make love to me, Nico."

"Sweetheart," he whispered. "I want you to know—"

"No more talking. We've already done enough of it. We spent all those hours during our engagement and before, talking." Esme lightly feathered her lips against his. She used the tip of her tongue to trace the sensual outline of his well-shaped mouth.

"At least let me tell you how much I—"

"Later." She opened her mouth over his and he instantly, hungrily took the lead from her, tightening his arms around her and deepening the kiss.

A small moan escaped from her throat as she kissed him back with an urgency that equaled his. His tongue was in her mouth and she rubbed it with her own tongue, engaging him in an erotic little duel.

The kiss went on and on, and passion burned between them, growing hotter, sending them higher.

She rubbed her breasts against the solid breadth of his chest and he immediately responded to her sensual invitation. His palms covered her and she pressed against his hands as he fondled the rounded softness.

She exhaled on a sigh of bliss. Yet as wonderful as this was, it was not enough.

Her nipples were taut and ultrasensitive and needed his attention. She was on the verge of begging him to touch her there when he finally caressed her, unerringly applying a gentle pressure exactly where she wanted it. Where she needed it.

Esme whimpered. He had worked her into a sensual frenzy yet neither had removed a single item of clothing. Desire and urgency flooded her. He was hard and thick between her legs, moving against her, sending shock waves of pleasure through her.

His hands lowered to clench her buttocks, and she rubbed provocatively against him, feeling a void deep within her, empty and aching to be filled. By him.

Suddenly, the simple barrier of their clothes was intolerable. Feeling desperate and daring, Esme slipped her hands under the double thickness of his sweatshirt and white T-shirt, to feel for the first time his smooth bare skin. She glided her hands over his stomach, feeling the wiry hair arrowing downward, then stroked her way to his back and ran her palms down the long expanse of his warm, slightly damp skin.

She was losing herself in him, drowning in the taste and scent and feel of him.

"I need you, Esme," Nico growled. "I promised myself that I would let you set the pace and—"

"You are a true gentleman, Nico, but I need to be

with you now." Esme quivered as he caressed her. His touch sent electricity flowing through her, and she felt the sensual current in her every nerve.

"Since I am to set the pace, I want to speed things up." Her dark eyes shone with humor and desire. "We've already waited too long for each other."

"So you are telling me to pick up the pace?" Nico laughed, a sexy, lusty sound that delighted Esme. "Yes, my princess, I am yours to command. I am ready, willing and able to fulfill your every wish."

Sexual urgency glittered in his eyes, and Esme knew her gaze reflected her own intense need. It was exhilarating to know how much he wanted her, to admit to that she returned his feelings in full measure.

He picked her up into his arms and held her high against his chest.

"I was told this was a cottage but there seems to be several rooms," Nico remarked, carrying her down a small hallway. "Which one shall we choose?"

Three bedrooms opened off the hall, and they peeked into each one as they passed. All were cozily furnished, but the master bedroom at the end had been unmistakably designed to be their destination.

A fire blazed brightly in a stone fireplace across the room from the king-sized brass bed. Pots of red and white poinsettias were everywhere, and a bottle of champagne set in a bucket of ice with two crystal goblets beside it.

"Nico, this is so romantic and so thoughtful." A glowing Esme blinked back emotional tears.

"Santa's elves, remember?" Nico kissed the tip of her nose, then affectionately rubbed it with his nose.

"Don't forget to give those elves a very generous Christmas bonus, Your Highness."

"Consider it done, Princess. And now..." He placed her gently on the thick soft goose-down comforter and stood beside the bed, gazing down at her. "Now where were we?"

Esme rose to her knees and reached for him. "I was doing this...."

Once again, she slid her hands under his sweatshirt, the powerful combination of love and desire making her bold enough to reach for his belt buckle. While Nico pulled off his shirt, she unbuckled his belt and freed him from his jeans.

He stood before her in black silk boxers, his virility so compelling she could only stare, her eyes wide with sheer feminine appreciation.

"My turn." Nico undid the knot she'd tied with her shirt, his knuckles brushing her bare skin. He worked with excruciating precision, taking so long she knew he was deliberately teasing her. Inflaming her.

His technique worked incredibly well. Every inch of her skin tingled in sensuous expectation. She wanted her breasts to be bare, she wanted to feel Nico's mouth on them, to feel the pull of his lips, the flick of his tongue. The erotic memories from last night on the plane were as exciting and arousing as her current anticipation.

At last, he disposed of her bra. Still on her knees,

she moved closer till the tips of her breasts touched the muscular expanse of his chest. Nico's hands glided over her curves, lightly, tantalizingly, and he kissed her the same way. Teasing her, arousing her till she thought she might implode from the heat burning within her.

In pure desperation, she fumbled with her rolled skirt, finally managing to get it over her hips. It lay in a plaid heap and Nico lifted her out of it, laying her down on the bed and then stretching out beside her.

Enthralled and enraptured, she explored his body, caressing him, learning exactly what made him groan with pleasure. When she slipped her hand inside his boxers and wrapped her hand around his pulsing length, she looked, transfixed at the titillating sight.

She was disappointed when Nico removed her hand.

"Esme, it's going to be all over in another second if you—if I—" He paused, panting, as if he'd been running in a long-distance marathon.

"And would that be so bad?" she whispered.

She reached for him again. Seeing Nico so out of control was thrilling; she couldn't resist sexually teasing him.

But he had predicted her move and caught her hands, pinning her wrists on above her head.

"It would be bad," he growled. "Exploding like a randy teenager would be a real blow to my male ego."

"Ah yes, the proud yet fragile male ego that

women have been tiptoeing around for centuries."
She slipped her leg between his and smiled with satisfaction as he stared at her stockings, the silky bands hugging her thighs. They provided a necessary, enticing contrast to her demure white panties.

Nico didn't seem to need any extra enticement, though. His arousal left no doubt of that.

"You have not tiptoed around my ego, Esme, you've run over it with a ten-ton truck—and left tire tracks." He chuckled softly.

"Yet here you are with me, instead of with some vapid simpleton who is all cooing flattery." There was a teasing note of triumph in her voice that she couldn't suppress. She held him close, savoring the feel of his body against hers.

"From the moment we met, vapid simpletons were forever ruined for me." His hands moved over her, stroking her, his lips caressing her till she was shivering with sensation. "I want only you and your sharp little tongue and your sharp little mind and—"

His lips moved from her breasts to toy with the ring in her belly button. And then he lifted his head. "The tattoo? You promised you would show me."

"I think I'll let you find it yourself," said Esme.

He proved to be a detective of admirable speed, and just a moment later located her tattoo of a small multicolored butterfly on the right upper quadrant of her buttock.

"I like it. Did you choose it for the symbolism, the beauty and the freedom of the butterfly?"

"Not exactly. It was pretty and small, and most of

Tristan's tattoos were neither. I didn't want a serpent coiling down the length of my back or a cartoon character stretched across my abdomen.''

"Well, this suits you.'' Nico kissed one tiny wing of the butterfly and then slipped off her panties. Her stockings followed, one by one. "What I do not like is the thought of that Tristan character applying it— or of him seeing you.''

"Tristan is a professional. He says that he treats the human body with objective respect, like a surgeon operating on a patient.''

Naked, Esme lay before Nico. His eyes roamed every inch of her, taking in everything, missing nothing. She was more than a little nervous and self-conscious, and she couldn't seem to stop talking. "Although Tristan claims that he is an artist and surgeons are mere technicians.''

"No more visits to Tristan. No more tattoos,'' Nico decreed, though his smile ameliorated the possessiveness in his tone.

"I didn't need you to tell me that, Your Highness,'' she mocked his imperial command. "I decided on my own that one small tattoo was quite enough.''

"So, as an American friend of mine would say, we are on the same page when it comes to tattoos. And we are on the same page with this, as well.''

He lowered his head to her, and Esme stifled a gasp as his lips trailed down her belly. When he grasped her hips and pressed his mouth to her, her body arched, as if jolted by shock waves. In a way she had been, because the touch of his tongue on the most intimate part of her was nothing less than sensual electricity.

She moved in counterpoint to his erotic rhythm, crying his name as wave after wave of delirious pleasure rocked her. It built and built, until she finally shattered into ecstasy, spinning into a dimension she had never before visited.

Nico held her in his arms, murmuring to her, stroking her hair until she stopped shaking.

She stared at him, dazed. "Nico, that—has never happened to me before. I've—"

His mouth took hers, and her thoughts splintered into nothingness. There was only Nico and his kisses, hot and urgent and demanding, and though she was still lost in the dreamy haze of sexual satiation, she responded with sweet abandon.

She watched him sheath himself with a condom and fought against the abrupt surge of anxiety that swept her.

"And now, suddenly, you are so tense." Nico studied her. "Esme, relax."

When he laid his hand on her thigh, she started violently, as if she'd been stuck with a cattle prod.

"Darling, there is nothing to be afraid of," Nico said soothingly, though his voice was hoarse, and she could see how hard he was fighting to keep control. "I love you."

Esme gulped. Fear was not what she was feeling at this particular moment. Fear would be preferable to this dread and revulsion as she waited for what came next. She had not enjoyed her sole sexual experience during her walk on the wild side after the breakup with Nico.

A whopping dose of regret and guilt hit her with double force. She should not have given her virginity to that nice French restaurateur on their third date; she should have saved herself for Nico, no matter what.

She had been unfair to poor Pierre, whom she had refused to see again after using him—yes, she had used him to relieve herself of her virginity and to get back at Nico—and now she was being unfair to Nico, letting him think she was what he believed her to be.

What he wanted her to be.

What she had to be, in order for him to love her and marry her.

"Nico, I have to tell you that I—" she began bravely, determined to set the record straight and to accept the consequences of her own choices, foolish and headstrong as they had been.

"No more talking." Nico laid his finger across her lips. "You were the one to say we've already done enough of that, and you are right. Now it is time to speak without words."

Slowly, he thrust into her, stretching and filling her. She clutched at him, her clear polished nails digging into his back. It hurt, but she didn't make a sound.

However, Nico was aware and attuned to her every nuance. "I am sorry to hurt you, my sweet." His onyx eyes were solemn and concerned. "I promise it will be better for you. That soon you will want this as much as I do."

Esme sincerely doubted it, but didn't debate the point.

But Nico took his time with her and gradually, almost imperceptibly at first, her body began to accommodate itself to his virile power. She seemed to melt into a liquid silken heat that enveloped his size and strength. She closed her eyes and shivered as he began to move in slow steady rhythm.

A ripple of pure pleasure radiated through her. It was unexpected and exciting, and she wanted to experience it again. She shifted her hips and took him deeper, claiming him as he was claiming her.

They kissed deeply, passionately, adding loving intimacy to the urgency of their physical needs. Their control vanished as they moved together, love and desire sweeping them into a realm of wondrous rapture that seemed to last forever but was over far too soon.

Nico collapsed against her, and Esme held him tight. Their bodies still joined, they kissed and whispered love words, sexy words that neither had ever said to anyone else.

Eventually, he shifted his weight from her but tucked her into his side, spoon-fashion, keeping her close to him.

They lay together in the afterglow of satiated passion, watching the flames in the fireplace leap and crackle over the logs. Neither felt the need to speak.

Right here, right now, they were beyond words.

Chapter 6

Esme was sound asleep when Nico carefully disentangled himself from her and climbed out of bed. She stirred slightly and rolled onto her stomach but didn't awaken.

He gazed at her, drinking in the alluring sight of her naked body as he covered her with the quilt. She was so beautiful she made him ache; so did the memories of the hours before. Esme was everything he could ever hope for in a lover... Passionate and playful. Exciting and tantalizing. Generous and loving.

And she was not a virgin.

He knew because his past included experienced and inexperienced women—and virgins. Esme was sexually inexperienced, but she had given her virginity to another man. She had also neglected to tell him so, keeping that secret from him.

But Esme wasn't the only one who had kept a secret tonight, Nico mused grimly as he wrapped himself in a terry cloth robe. He had not shared the truth of his parentage with her.

Right now, Nico felt as confused as he had on that fateful night when his mother had confessed the truth about her affair with his biological father. He remembered how Nadine had repeatedly assured him that the man who had raised him, Omar Tan-efi, had never, ever suspected anything was awry.

It seemed like ironic overkill that he, Nico, should find himself in circumstances oddly paralleling the Omar/Nadine situation. Their religion didn't include the concept of karmic payback but in theory, it seemed to apply. Here was another king of Imarco, the cuckoo in the nest, so to speak, in love with a woman...who was pretending to be the innocent virgin required as queen?

But was not.

Nico padded barefoot into the living room where the fire was slowly dying and stoked the embers back to life. He lit a cheroot from the box Ryan had so generously provided, and inhaled deeply.

His mother had been adamant that her husband believed his bride was untouched by any man; she'd been equally certain that Omar had never questioned the paternity of his son, born a few weeks earlier, rather than precisely nine months after the wedding night.

Sitting here, watching the tendrils of smoke drift in the air, Nico dispelled his mother's assurances one by one. She had been kidding herself all those years—perhaps to assuage her guilt? He just couldn't buy her version of events, especially not now.

How could Omar not have known that his virgin bride was—well, no virgin? Neither Omar nor Nico were womanizing playboys but both had sexual experience. As royals, as *men* in Imarco, that was considered a necessity for virility, an expectation of manliness.

Nico ground out the cheroot. Imagining the sex life of his parents—all three of them!—made him uncomfortable. Not to mention slightly queasy. But since he had acknowledged the probability that Omar knew he was not Nadine's first lover, he might as well face the depressing possibility that his father also could have doubted his firstborn—and only—son Nico's origins.

Yet Omar had never betrayed a hint of doubt or suspicion to Nico or Nadine or anyone else. He had always been the epitome of a proud, loving father.

Was it because Nadine had given birth to three daughters after Nico, and according to law, girls could not inherit the throne of Imarco? Omar had never made a secret of the fact that he didn't want his brother Amman to rule the country. That meant promoting Nico as his legitimate heir.

Nico thought of the importance of bloodlines in Imarco. It was something of a cosmic joke that the current king of Imarco didn't have a drop of the patriarchal royal family's blood in his veins. He was half his mother's son and half American Fortune.

He closed his eyes and rubbed his temples with his fingertips. Suppose Esme's previous liaison had left her secretly pregnant with her lover's child, à la Nadine? Would Esme try to pass off said child as Nico's?

If it were a boy, he would be first in line for the throne, making the next king of Imarco part Rayazan and part complete mystery.

Esme had mentioned the tattoo and body piercing parlor in England....

What if the future king of Imarco displayed a talent for either of those dubious art forms? A startling image of an intense youngster with dyed purple hair and a headful of pierced rings flashed before his mind's eye. In filmstrip sequence, the heir to the throne brandished a kit with needles and ink, while chasing people around the palace, demanding to adorn them.

Nico awoke with a violent jolt, his heart thundering at breakneck speed.

"Do you want some coffee?" Esme asked, pouring herself a second cup.

She had found a selection of excellent brands, along with a coffee grinder and maker. Santa's elves kept a very well-stocked kitchen indeed.

Esme cast a covert glance at Nico who lay on the long couch, covered by a red-and-green Christmas-themed blanket. An ashtray filled with partially smoked cheroots was on the table beside him. She'd found him there asleep after she had awakened this morning alone in the big comfortable bed.

She had quickly showered and dressed without waking him. The smell of the coffee had done that, but Nico remained on the couch, watching her through half-slitted eyes. He hadn't said a word as she made the coffee and gulped down her first cup. He still had yet to say a word.

"Here. You look like you could use this." She filled a mug with coffee and carried it over to him.

Nico sat up and took the mug from her. "Thank you."

His robe hung open, revealing the bronzed muscles of his chest, and though he kept the blanket draped over his lap, Esme knew he was nude underneath.

"More strategic dressing to please the Bakkars, I see," remarked Nico, after draining half the mug.

"I packed to win the war," Esme agreed. "This dress is the equivalent to a smart bomb."

She smoothed a nonexistent crease from the skirt of her plain ivory-colored silk dress that covered every bit of skin, except her face, hands and ankles. Dainty flatheeled ivory slippers peeked from beneath the hem of her long skirt.

"When I was sixteen, Great-Aunt Saleni bought Zara and me and all the girl cousins these identical dresses and arranged for us to have our picture painted wearing them. The older relatives still sigh their approval when they look at that portrait. My brother Riad said we look like a lineup of vestal virgins."

She looked into Nico's eyes. There, she'd actually said the word, given him an opening to comment on last night. To ask questions, to condemn her. Maybe even to forgive her?

But Nico held her gaze steadily and said only, "Was that a compliment from a proud brother?"

"Certainly not. Riad made it quite clear that he was teasing us, which he loves to do." Esme smiled.

So she had been granted a reprieve. Nico was not going to press her for information. She felt almost giddy with relief. "You know how brothers can be— you are one yourself."

"One who never mocks his dear sisters." Nico's dark eyes gleamed.

"It's too late for revisionist history, Nico. Early on, you boasted how you used to tease your sisters when you were children. Doing things like burying their dolls! Is that dreadful act in some universal guidebook for brothers on How To Torment Sisters? I can't count the number of times Zara and I had to unearth our dolls—literally—after chasing our brothers away with their nasty little shovels."

"Well, my sisters have paid me back—with interest—over the years with their tantrums and their schemes and their endless unsolicited advice. I expect they will continue to do so in the years to come."

Nico finished his coffee and held out his hand to her. The golden double crown imprint on his ring seemed to glow. "Come here."

Esme sat down next to him.

"That isn't close enough." He lifted her onto his lap. "I find that dress you're wearing is inversely erotic. You look so prim and untouchable in it that I am inspired to do exactly what the dress forbids.''

She felt him deftly undoing the long row of silk-covered buttons that extended down the back of the dress. From time to time, he paused to nuzzle her neck, to nip at her earlobe and tease her lips with his.

The heat of his powerful naked body warmed her as he stripped her of her dress and her equally prim and proper white underwear. She felt the steely support of his thighs beneath her, the strength of his arms holding her.

He eased her down, and she felt the smooth leather of the sofa against her back. The heat of sensual pleasure swiftly suffused her body, escalating to throbbing, urgency.

It was hard to believe that she wanted him now more than ever, despite the passionate night they'd spent. Instead of being sated, her need for him had intensified. What she now knew about him, about making love with him, were all the erotic sensual details that she couldn't have imagined before. His taste and scent, the feel of him inside her, filling her, calling out her name in climax. As she had called out his.

Her body arched and shivered as he entered her, and she clung to him, welcoming him with primal feminine urgency. He belonged to her as completely as she belonged to him. They complemented each other in every way, physically, emotionally, spiritually.

"I love you," Esme murmured later, as they lay together on the couch.

She was languid and lazy from their sublime love-making. Gently stroking the relaxed features of Nico's face, she knew he shared her bliss.

"I've always loved you, Nico."

"Even when you hated me?" Nico smiled and caught her hand with his, kissing her fingertips.

"When I *tried* to hate you, when I pretended to hate you." Esme sighed. "I wanted so much to be able to hate you but I still loved you. I always will, Nico. Even after—"

She broke off abruptly.

Nico saw raw pain cross her face, then watched her purposefully don a placid expression. It took only a split second, but he saw it all. And wondered what it meant. Why did she want to put on an act with him? To deceive him?

Was she attempting to deceive him into believing that he was her first lover?

"Even after?" he prompted, a hard note creeping into his voice. "What were you about to say, Esme?"

"I—I forgot what I was going to say." She managed a wavering smile. "Has that ever happened to you? It's maddening to—to suddenly lose your train of thought."

"Don't lie to me, Esme." Nico sat upright, taking her with him. "Don't try to deceive me. You didn't forget anything. Tell me what you were about to say but decided not to."

His lightning-fast change of tone, of mood, his sudden surge of emotion—was it anger or frustration or a combination of both?—that turned his dark eyes steely and his body tense unnerved Esme.

She quickly rose to her feet, clutching the red-and-green blanket around her to conceal her nakedness.

"You are calling me a liar, Nico?" Her voice rose to a squeak.

She felt scared and vulnerable, and for the life of her couldn't summon her warrior alter ego to seize the offensive. This was it, she thought, heartsick. They weren't even going to have one week together, just one night.

Nico had her sexually, he'd realized that she was "used goods" as Mama and Grandmama and every other woman in Rayaz would say, and now he wanted to be rid of her.

He was disgusted with her. So much so, that last night he had been unable to sleep in the same bed with her. Currently, he was regretting this morning's loving interlude on the couch. He must believe it was inspired by lust not love and blamed her for luring him into it.

The signs were all there for her to see, but she hadn't interpreted them until this moment. Nico wanted her gone.

Her lifetime sentence of loneliness, of missing him was to begin right now.

Nico heard the anxiety in her voice and silently berated himself for putting it there. Her huge dark eyes were filled with hurt, and worse, with shame.

He felt like a cad, yet he couldn't seem to stop talking. The words tumbled from his lips.

"Esme, I just want us to be truthful with each other. Honesty is an invaluable part of trust. I have to be able to trust you."

She nodded her head, her eyes downcast. "Ask me anything and I will tell you the truth, I promise, Nico."

"Very well. I will hold you to that promise." Absently, he removed the double crown ring from his fingers and put it on the table. "Esme, I didn't use any protection this last time, here on the couch. You know that, of course?"

"I—didn't think about it. T-till now."

Now, she doubted she would think of little else. She had been unaware of their lack of precautions, too caught up in the moment to give it a thought. She was still too inexperienced to keep track of such details, though Esme knew that would not be an adequate defense for Nico. To men of their culture, an unmarried nonvirgin might as well be a professional hooker.

It felt like her heart was plummeting while her stomach made an upward leap. Perhaps the churning she felt in her midsection was the collision of the two organs.

"If we are very careful from now on, yet you find you are pregnant, we can trace the date of conception almost to the exact hour, can't we?" Nico stood up and reached for his robe, slipping into it.

Pregnant! Esme frantically tried to do some counting. Was this a safe time? When it came to unprotected sex, was anytime truly safe? She was so panicked she seemed to have totally forgotten everything she'd ever learned about female biology. Right now she was so rattled, she was even having trouble remembering how to count. A Tower-of-Babel mix of Arabic, English and French ran through her head.

"Of course, babies arrive on their own timetable," continued Nico. "Sometimes they come early. Why, nine pound babies have been known to be—a bit premature."

Esme stared at him. His tone was as sardonic as his smile. "A nine-pound premature baby? I don't think so."

"But if we have a child born—oh, two or three weeks before the due date charted from this very day—will you claim that it is premature, despite the birth weight?"

"I'm not pregnant, Nico. The timing is wrong."

Her muddled mind had finally put the numbers together. At this particular time, it was very unlikely that she would conceive. Not that there weren't thousands of people walking around whose parents had probably thought the same thing, a dour little voice in her head reminded her. But the odds were in her favor.

"Remember your promise to be honest with me when I ask you this question, Esme." Nico took a step toward her, his dark eyes glittering with intensity. "Would you ever try to pass off another man's child as my own? Would you allow us—you, me, the child in question—to live with that lifelong lie?''

Esme blanched and recoiled, as if he had slapped her.

''Since you are so zealous about being honest, why not come out and say what you really want to, Nico? Skip this cruel game you are playing, I understand the subtext all too well. You think I am a despicable slut, one without morals or even a heart. Only a woman like that would do such a terrible thing as to pass off one man's child as another's. Only a conniving she-devil would be able to live such a lie.''

Tears half blinding her, she snatched up her clothes, taking care to keep herself covered with the blanket.

''We both know that last night I did not come to you as a virgin and because of my dishonor, I can never be your wife. But to accuse me of being capable of vile treachery, like lying about a child's father, is truly sadistic on your part.''

''Quiet!'' Nico thundered. ''I will not listen to any more of this.''

Despicable slut, conniving she-devil, vile treachery. The invectives echoed in Nico's head. She was saying all the things he had never dared to even think about his mother! At least not consciously.

But Esme's every denunciation resonated within him, and he knew they had been in his mind from the moment his mother had told him the truth about herself, about himself.

''I promise that you will never have to listen to me

again, Nico.'' Esme rushed from the room with surprising speed, unhampered by her blanket toga and armful of clothing.

''Make arrangements for me to leave here right away,'' she called before slamming the bedroom door.

Nico followed her but it was too late. She slammed the door in his face and he heard her turn the lock. The king of Imarco was not accustomed to such treatment.

''Open this door!'' he demanded. ''Now! I command you.''

Esme shouted back a curse in Arabic that a sheltered young woman of one of the ruling families of Rayaz or any other in the Middle East never should have heard or known, let alone uttered.

The shock of hearing such a word from her jolted Nico out of his consuming emotional storm. He happened to glance down at his hand and his ringless finger. How strange it looked, without the double crown there. Where was it?

''Is my ring—the one with the double crowns on it—in there?'' he called through the door to her.

''And now you accuse me of thievery?'' Esme was enraged. ''You put it on the table in the living room. I did *not* steal your ring.''

He heard her muttering about the unmitigated gall of any citizen of Imarco daring to ever call anyone from Rayaz paranoid, as he strode into the living room to put the ring firmly on his finger.

Back staring at the closed door again, an image of

a younger, very fierce Esme flashed before his mind's eye. He could picture her kickboxing a few of the Hassan boys into submission—and using that salty swear word while doing it.

His lips slowly curved into a smile. No wonder the Hassans remained terrified of Esme! Such a girl would be beyond their ken.

But such a woman was everything he needed in his queen—brave, tough, willing and able to stand up for herself and those weaker. Esme was smart and funny and would never let him become pompous and overbearing. If he were wrong, she wouldn't hesitate to tell him so; she would be his touchstone. He needed that. He needed her.

And best of all, she loved him and he knew it. She had convincingly shown and told him so. Yet he had reacted to her love...

He was staring at his ring when perception dawned with the force of a sledgehammer.

He loved Esme desperately, but he had alienated her. Seriously. *Again!*

The first time he had chosen his country over her. This time, he had heaped the anger, grief and outrage upon her that he had been carrying around since his mother's shattering deathbed revelations.

Nadine had died soon after her confession, begging Nico's forgiveness, and he had never been able to express his true emotions to her. How could he hurt a dying woman, his own mother, who had been so racked with pain, as well as plagued by a terrible guilt? He had kept his secret—and kept his feelings suppressed.

But they had simmered and smoldered inside him until this morning when suddenly blazing into an inferno that couldn't be contained another minute.

Esme had been the one burned by his incendiary rage. He had lashed out at her, he had hurt her—for something that was not her fault.

She wouldn't believe that though. She was plagued by guilt—being an unmarried unvirgin was nothing to be glossed over in their culture. Esme expected him to condemn her. To hurt her.

Well, he'd fulfilled her expectations. Remorse flooded him.

He could hear Esme in the room, moving about. "Darling, let me in," he coaxed. "I am not angry with you."

"You are furious with me, Nico. At least be *honest* and admit it," she added caustically.

"I can explain, if you will let me." Nico rattled the doorknob. "I want to set the record straight between us and have the whole truth out in the open at last. You see, when you insulted my mother, I took offense as a reflex, but I am calm now and we can talk. Open the door, Esme."

"You're not calm, you're deranged. I never said a word about your mother," Esme replied through the closed door.

"You weren't aware of what you'd said but I—" he began, then frowned. "I can't keep shouting through the door. We must talk, Esme. And if you don't open this door immediately, I'm going to kick it in.''

This time there was no answer from her.

"Esme, open up. Please," he added glumly. Begging did not come easy to him.

Again, no response. Nico heaved a sigh. Now he was going to have to take action. He rammed it with his shoulder, the way the cops did in the movies. The door didn't budge and a sharp shooting pain shot from his collarbone to the tips of his fingers.

Body-slamming a door was a lot harder than it looked in movies—probably because in movies the door needing to be rammed was made of light cardboard. Nico groaned. In his determination to be proactively macho, he'd forgotten that crucial fact.

Discarding drama, he searched for and retrieved a screwdriver from a kitchen drawer. Trust reliable Ryan Fortune to provide necessary tools, along with all the niceties.

Carefully, Nico removed the hinges from the door.

He set the door aside and entered the room just in time to see Esme on her way out the window. Her suitcase was already outside; she had obviously hurled it out moments before.

It was a very short drop to the ground in a one-story cottage. Esme, wearing the Rayaz national costume of loose-fitting, silk, green harem pants with yellow, blue and black silk jacket, and clutching the Christmas blanket around her shoulders for warmth, landed in the snow outside.

It was cold and wet and a shock to her whole system. Her green ballet-style slippers were instantly soaked, rendered useless in the five-or-more-inches of snow. Her harem pants and top were also not designed to withstand cold temperatures, let alone the rigors of snow. She was grateful to at least have the blanket.

"Have you lost your mind?" Nico shouted, leaning out the window. "Get back in here immediately! You'll freeze to death out there."

"No, I won't." Esme held up the keys to the Range Rover that she had retrieved from the nightstand. "Goodbye, Nico."

She grabbed her suitcase and took off.

He let out a yell that would have been a worthy desert war cry in ages gone by. Esme could imagine a terrified tribe of Bedouins running for cover at the sound.

She was certainly inspired to run faster toward the Range Rover that was parked in front of the house. It wasn't easy, running in the snow; she might as well have been barefoot for all the protection her slippers offered.

But Esme didn't stop. At least not voluntarily. With her head start, her destination seemed to be attainable—until Nico tackled her and they both hit the ground with a thud.

They lay prone in the snow, breathing hard and fast. His arms were around her hips in a viselike grip. Her suitcase had gone flying, to land a few feet in front of them.

"You're a pretty fast runner, for a girl," Nico spoke first.

"You're a Neanderthal bully, for a king."

"But I'm king of Imarco. Doesn't that lower the expectations for my behavior?"

"You said it, I didn't." Esme tried to raise herself out of the bed of snow. "Let me go, Nico."

"Not a chance, Esme." Nico hung on to her. "Come back inside with me."

"Not a chance," she shot back.

"Esme, I have nothing on under this robe which flew open when we fell. Portions of my bare anatomy—including a most vital portion—are in direct contact with the snow. As angry as you are with me—and I concede you have a right to be angry—do you really want me to suffer frostbite? Especially *there?*"

Esme shivered. The cold wet snow was inflicting misery on every inch of her own body, and she at least had some covering, however minimal.

The wind chose that moment to gust, and they both shook from the chill.

"It's stupid to stay out here and freeze to death." Esme felt her teeth beginning to chatter. "We'll go inside and change into dry clothes, then I'll drive to the airport."

Nico didn't argue, which did not surprise her, given his half-frozen state. He immediately stood up and extended his arm to pull her to her feet. He got her suitcase too and tried to pick her up to carry her inside.

Esme didn't let him. Still clutching the keys, she

hurried to the cottage. The front door key was easily differentiated from the key to the vehicle, so she was able to quickly slide it into the lock and open the door.

They entered the house and automatically, simultaneously, went directly to the fireplace to warm themselves. Standing in front of the crackling flames, they gradually stopped shaking from the cold.

Nico dropped the thick wet robe and stood there, unabashedly, unashamedly nude. Esme averted her eyes.

"You could put some clothes on, you know," she finally said.

It was becoming more and more difficult to keep her eyes fixed to the flickering flames of the fire, to forbid herself to steal covert glances at him.

"The moment I leave this room, you'll head straight to the car. I know you still have those keys. No, I'm not going anywhere unless you're right beside me, Esme. Even if it means standing naked in front of this fire all day."

"Very well then." Esme folded her arms in front of her chest and stayed in place.

She desperately wanted to get out of her wet clothes but felt too uncertain of herself, of Nico, of this entire situation to do anything but to remain basking in the heat of the fireplace. She casually slipped off first one slipper and then the other. Her feet still felt like blocks of ice.

"I would not be surprised if the drawers in the bedrooms are stocked with winter clothing, like warm socks," Nico remarked. "If we went back there and found them, your feet would no longer be purple."

"You are trying to tempt me, like that serpent in the garden with Eve," Esme said tartly. "Oh, I know all about that. I studied world religions at the university."

"As did I. It's true, I was trying to tempt you, and for a very self-serving reason. I want warm dry socks and clothes for myself."

His frank admission made Esme smile. She quickly caught herself and resumed her stern expression. "I appreciate your honesty, at least."

"Your Rayaz ethnic outfit, while quite fetching, is not made for a romp in the snow." Nico dared to touch her shoulder where the wet silk jacket clung. "I assume you were going to wear this to evoke your family's nationalistic pride?"

"Yes." She did not shrug off his hand. "I would have sung the national anthem in it, to keep them from shipping Zara and the triplets to Yemen. Which, of course, was never going to happen, anyway."

Esme moved away from him, out of touching range. "I only hope you are right about the warm dry winter clothes being available in the other room."

She headed down the hall, leaving her packed suitcase by the door. There was nothing warm enough in it for her to put on right now.

Nico followed her. His gold ring glinted in the light, and he stared thoughtfully at the double crown.

"This ring has a kind of mystical power that makes

true love survive.'' Ryan had claimed the night he'd bestowed it upon his long lost son.

''Of course, you'll have to do your part. Nothing comes to the hapless fool who stands by passively waiting as life and opportunity pass him by,'' Ryan had added.

''Fortunately, you are not of that ilk, son.''

No, Nico silently agreed, he was not.

Chapter 7

Nico and Esme finished their breakfast of Texas French toast which they found in a package in the freezer, complete with instructions on defrosting. They briefly pondered the paradox of toast being both French and Texas, but all that really mattered was that the thick rich slices were delicious. They ate every morsel, drowned in the recommended maple syrup.

In the bedroom closets and drawers, they'd found loose-fitting flannel pants with drawstrings at the waist in a variety of prints and sizes, as well as piles of cotton shirts to wear under an assortment of heavy knit wool sweaters.

Esme matched blue pants printed with tiny yellow stars and a deep blue sweater for herself. When Nico asked for her fashion advice, she coordinated plaid pants and a brown, red and black sweater for him. They put on two pairs of wool socks each.

Sitting in the kitchen, warm, dry and well fed, they turned each other, almost at the same moment.

"I should be leaving for the airport," Esme said quietly. "Are you coming with me?"

"I'll go if you really want to leave here, but we'll fly together to Imarco where we will announce our engagement, Esme."

"Nico." She paused, her eyes filling with tears. "You know I can't marry you."

"No, I don't know that, Esme. We love each other, and we are going to be married. I am a twenty-first-century king who is wise enough to know that you are everything I want and need, for my wife and for my queen, Esme."

"As much as I wish that were true, it isn't, Nico," Esme said wearily. "You already broke our engagement once because my Rayaz background was unsuitable. It still is, from Imarco's point of view. In the future, if more turmoil were to arise in your country, you would have to send me packing—along with any children we might have. My family would consider it the ultimate sign of disrespect and conspire with the other families in Rayaz to declare war against Imarco. We can't inflict such a—"

"I have an impregnable power base now, Esme. You know how it is in our part of the world, once a ruler has achieved that stronghold. I can now promise that I will never send you or our children away, and my country will accept you as their queen. I will make sure that your family accepts me as your husband as well. There will no longer be enmity between our countries, but friendship.''

"You'll be nominated for the Nobel Peace Prize if you pull that off.'' Esme smiled wanly. "But let's be real, Nico. Even if by some miracle, all the political hassles were ironed out, there is that one crucial factor that renders me unworthy of marrying you or any man. My dishonor.''

"I am not a virgin either, Esme. Am I also dishonored? Of course not.''

"You know the standards are different for men and women, Nico.''

"The standards are archaic.'' He took her hand. "But if your parents try to force you into a marriage with Bashir Murad, I will use the old rules to my advantage and tell them that you have given yourself to me and therefore I must marry you. Rather Machiavellian of me, I think.''

"You needn't bother with Machiavellian strategy, you don't even have to be *proactive,* when it comes to Bashir Murad. He and I grew up together, he is like my brother. For years we have laughed at the very idea of marrying each other. Bashir always says that if he had been born a girl, he would have been me, and if I'd been born a boy, I would've been him.''

"I feel a pang of jealousy that he has known you longer and that he knows you so well. But I intend to know you even better, Esme, and in ways Bashir Murad never will. Nevertheless, since he is a dear friend of yours, I shall befriend him," Nico added grandly.

"Never mind Bashir. My family and the Murads know we will not marry. I have other plans for my life, Nico. A child development professor is helping me design a program to educate the special-needs children of Rayaz."

"You shall not only implement it in Rayaz, but in Imarco as well," Nico interrupted, his dark eyes alight with enthusiasm. "You will be known as the queen who advocates a quality education for all children." He leaned across the table and cupped her cheek with his hand. "Maybe *you* will win the Nobel Peace Prize, Esme."

"There is a greater chance of that happening than the two of us marrying, Nico," Esme said sadly. She laid her hand over his. "But let us at least promise that we will always be—" She gulped. "Be friends."

"Friends, lovers, partners. King and queen," Nico added. "I will not give you up, Esme. I know that my behavior in the past causes you to doubt my pledge to have you, but I will do anything—everything!—to make you my wife. I shall begin by telling you a secret, known by only one living person on this earth—me. It is a secret that my mother almost carried to her grave...."

He told Esme what his mother had revealed on her deathbed, about her passionate fling with another man which had resulted in the birth of Nico Tan-efi, raised as the son of King Omar.

"Nico, don't," Esme said quietly, when he was

finished and waiting expectantly for her reaction. "Don't malign your poor dead parents by this story you've concocted to make me feel less ashamed of what I have done. I am touched by your kindness but it is misguided. Disgracing the reputation of your family doesn't lessen my own dishonor."

"You think I made it all up?" Nico was incredulous. "I've already told you I don't subscribe to the dishonor issues. Yet you still believe that I consider you a figure of disrepute and therefore have tried to make myself one? As if to even the playing field or something?"

"Yes. You are noble and sweet but—"

"Misguided," Nico filled in. "Was that the word you were looking for? I am on the verge of losing my temper, Esme. Anyone who would invent such a lie about his parents is a manipulative scam artist. There is nothing noble, sweet or misguided about that. Suppose I tell you that the man who sired me is the Texan Ryan Fortune, the man who gave me this ring."

He held out his hand for her to see the ring. "You know the double crown on the ring matches my birthmark. Well, Ryan has this same birthmark. I have told no one but you about this, Esme. I've decided never to tell Ryan."

"If you are really his son you should tell him so," Esme said. "You owe it to him and to yourself."

"*If,*" Nico repeated flatly. "You still do not believe me."

She stood up and began to twirl a long strand of her hair around her finger, a nervous habit she'd tried more than once to give up. "I—I am not disbelieving you quite as strongly as I did at first," she murmured.

Nico surprised her by laughing. "I am glad to hear it. I processed the news in quite the same way when I first heard it. But to tell Ryan…" His eyes met hers. "You won't really believe me unless I do tell him, will you?"

"Nico, you said you will do anything and everything to make me your wife, then you tell me this so-called secret. I have studied Machiavelli myself. I know his 'the end justifies the means' premise."

"I can see where having an educated queen will most certainly keep me on the right track. All right, I will tell Ryan the truth about myself. We will go to the airport and fly to wherever he is."

A phone call located Ryan at his office in the company headquarters in San Antonio.

"You have something important to tell me, Nico?" Ryan's voice was warm and eager. "I think I can guess what it is. You are certainly a fast worker, my boy. Coincidentally, I also have some news that you and your lovely Esme will find interesting."

Less than two hours later, Esme and Nico were escorted to Ryan's huge corner office in the Fortune TX, Ltd. building, a high-rise on Kingston Street, named for Kingston Fortune, Ryan's father. Nico's grandfather.

Ryan gave Nico and Esme each an exuberant bear hug. He appeared the picture of health—and elated to see the two of them together.

"You are engaged," he guessed before either could say a word.

"Yes," said Nico.

Esme bit her lip, staring from Nico to Ryan. It seemed impossible to imagine the American, who looked like the epitome of the tall Texan, could possibly be even remotely related to Nico, who looked like the epitome of the modern-day young sheik. And yet, here they were with Nico promising to tell his "secret" to his "father."

"Incidentally, I talked to your parents earlier and they told me they were unable to contact you, Esme," Ryan said jovially, "Your friend Jackie told them you were visiting the sick in a London hospital. I congratulated them for having such a kind and benevolent daughter." His eyes gleamed. "And I congratulate you for having such a creative and loyal friend."

"You were talking to my parents?" Esme went from confused to hopelessly baffled. "About me?"

"Sheik Bakkar and I have recently become good telephone pals." Ryan turned to Nico. "We have so much in common, not only as businessmen but as fathers and grandfathers. Through the Bakkars, I've also struck up a solid friendship with the Murads. It seems that all of us—the Bakkars, the Murads and me—are united in our dislike and distrust of the Hassan clan. Rumor now has it that the Hassans were solely responsible for last year's plot to cheat me in the oil deal."

He winked at Nico. "As I told Sheik Bakkar, that

Hassan family is getting a little too big for their britches."

"I am going to guess that you are familiar with the old Arab proverb, 'the enemy of my enemy is my friend,'" surmised Nico. "But why get involved in Rayaz internal matters at all, Ryan?"

"Who me?" Ryan smiled benignly. "I simply thought I should become better acquainted with other members of the oil cartel, that's all. It was serendipitous that my relationship with the Bakkars and the Murads clicked so well."

"Serendipitous?" Esme repeated doubtfully.

"There are few foreigners who have 'clicked' with the Bakkars and the Murads." Nico looked even more doubtful. He cast a quick glance at Esme. "Though they are delightful people, of course. Just—uh—shy with strangers."

"Well, both families are currently caught up in a fervor of excitement." Ryan smiled at Esme. "Your parents wanted to tell you the news themselves but couldn't reach you. I told them I had some contacts in London who would contact you and inform you that your sister, Zara, is getting married to Bashir. He is such a congenial yet compassionate young man. He plans to adopt Zara's adorable little girls. I've been invited to the wedding and hope to attend."

Esme's jaw dropped. "You are joking?"

Nico appeared equally astounded. "At the Christmas party, you implied that would be a logical solution and you managed to make it happen." He gaped at Ryan, awestruck. "But how?"

"Oh, I might have made a little suggestion or two." Ryan shrugged and tried to look modest. "But all the individuals involved made their own choices, of course. It is handy to have Bashir and Zara out of the—I mean, happily engaged, isn't it? Now Esme can get on with her life with you, Nico. I am certain her family will not be averse to your marriage."

"Why, you sly fox, you have somehow made them feel guilty and disloyal toward Esme, as if they have given Zara her doll or something." Nico laughed. "And you have already eased the way for a peaceful resolution between Rayaz and Imarco. Ryan, you are nothing less than amazing!"

"You two have much more in common than I realized," Esme said wryly. "I think it is time that we told Ryan our other surprising news, Nico."

"There is a little one on the way?" Ryan guessed. "Better start with those wedding plans immediately. Papa Bakkar can count backwards to nine months, you know."

Nico and Esme exchanged looks. "Tell him, darling," Esme urged.

Nico took a deep breath. "Ryan, do you remember an Egyptian girl named Jasmine? You knew her about thirty-three years ago and—"

"—she dropped off the face of the earth," Ryan filled in. "Of course, I remember her. She was beautiful and sweet and when she disappeared so suddenly, I was quite worried and tried to find her. And never could. I always wondered what became of her."

"Well," said Nico. "Her name wasn't Jasmine and she wasn't Egyptian…"

"My son," Ryan repeated, for at least the fiftieth time.

His eyes were red-rimmed from the tears he had shed upon hearing the truth. Though he had taken Nico's word without demanding any proven confirmation, his son had insisted on showing him the Fortune birthmark. It was as distinctive and individualized as any DNA test.

"How can I ever begin to make it up to you, Nico? All the years we've missed, all the—"

"You gave me this ring that enabled me to win back my true love," Nico cut in. "And though only the three of us—you and Esme and me—will share the secret, we will act as family forever."

"I am so happy to have you for my secret American father-in-law, Ryan," said Esme, impulsively putting her arms around the older man. "You are Santa Claus and Cupid rolled into one. You are—*proactive!*" she added, her dark eyes glowing.

"A high compliment because that is a quality that Esme greatly admires." Nico stepped in for a group hug.

"Like father, like son," Esme said, smiling affectionately at both men.

The double crown ring caught a ray of sunlight and glowed brilliantly.

THE CHRISTMAS HOUSE
Jennifer Greene

To Lar and Ry:
my real heroes

Chapter 1

Twenty-nine-year-old Jessamine Mitchell heaved a huge sigh. At eight o'clock on Christmas morning, Interstate 10 was more deserted than a skunk site. No surprise. Obviously no one would be driving this early on the holiday if they had any other choice.

On this morning, every blasted year, Jessa replayed the same old mental daydreams of how normal, *regular* people woke up on Christmas…the whole family would race downstairs simultaneously to cluster in front of a lopsided, tinsel-draped tree. Kids would shriek and scream as they tore open packages. Kittens and puppies would pounce on ribbons. Moms and dads would huddle in their jammies, looking bleary-eyed after putting together all those "easy to assemble" toys the night before.

Jessa groped on the passenger seat for another Oreo from the package.

Her breakfast. Maybe as a child she'd fiercely, desperately wanted Santa to show up at her house—just once!—but she'd also discovered there were some outstanding advantages to being family-deprived. There was no one around to scold if she had Oreos and Tex-Mex for breakfast, for example.

There was also no one to stop her from indulging in a foolish trip to nowhere…which was what she figured she was doing this morning. Still, even a wild-goose chase was better than sitting alone on this particular day.

Off to the right, the big Texas sun was just poking over the horizon, spreading a pink-gold glow on the shrubby hills and rolling landscape. Jessa rarely had a reason to drive north of San Antonio. Sure, she knew there were some hotsy-totsy neighborhoods in this direction, but those were hardly her regular stomping grounds, and this sweepy, sprawly landscape was unexpectedly beautiful, besides.

As she crunched down on another cookie, she caught sight of a dusty, rusty tan pickup at the crest of the next hill. Funny, but just seeing another driver was all it took for the loneliness to ebb away. At least there was one other body on the road. And a sole driver, like she was. A guy, judging from the shadow of his shoulders and height, although that was all she could make out in the fuzzy dawn light. For a second there, he looked familiar.

But then she forgot him.

The speedometer on her butter-yellow Cabriolet seemed to be registering 90 miles an hour. It wasn't the first time her speedometer had registered disgracefully high speeds, and normally she was happy enough to skedaddle down the highway when no cop was in sight.

Truthfully, her butter-yellow Cabriolet hadn't started out to be a butter-yellow Cabriolet. It started out to be an '84 Volkswagen convertible on its last legs when she'd bought it for three hundred dollars—and it had been robbery to pay that much. She couldn't afford a cool sports car, but that didn't matter since she never pined for something other people had, anyway. More than one mechanic had warned her that she was pouring good money after bad—as if that were interesting news. She'd already known she was wasting money and didn't care. She'd painted the baby her favorite color, popped a brand new engine in her, and adored the car more than any man she'd ever met—yet.

Still, she eased her foot off the accelerator and slowed down. There was no risk of a cop catching her this morning, but it was bonkers to be in such a hurry when she didn't even know where she was going.

With one eye on the road, she reached over and patted the passenger seat again. Besides the package of cookies, the seat was crowded with the usual debris. Her fringy suede jacket. Her leather shoulder bag. A couple days' mail she'd forgotten to take in.

And somewhere, the small gift-wrapped box that contained a key—and directions.

The key was shaped like a building key of some kind, but Jessa didn't know to what. The typed-out directions led to a location somewhere north of San Antonio, but she didn't know to where. In fact, the entire present was a mystery—but that was precisely why she'd left it until this particular Tuesday morning to pursue. For three hundred and sixty-four days of the year she was independent to a fault, but on Christmas it was hard to be alone. Following through on this strange present from Ryan Fortune had given her something to do on a morning that was traditionally tough for her.

The white sheet of instructions claimed she should take the next exit. Holding the directions and steering wheel with one hand, she reached over with the other to fumble in her purse for lipstick. *Some* might suggest that it was a little late for a woman with a ring in her eyebrow and a tattoo on her fanny to worry about making a positive first impression—and she wasn't. But she also didn't have a clue what she might or might not be getting into. Fear didn't enter the picture. Jessa hadn't acknowledged fear since she was knee-high, for anything or anyone. But a woman alone tended to hone her cautious instincts and carry a few weapons on her.

A little fresh lipstick never hurt anything.

She whizzed off the exit ramp, almost back-ending the dusty, rusty tan pickup in the process. Again, she only caught a glimpse of the driver...and again, she had an ooga-booga sensation that she knew him.

That thought, of course, was pretty silly. The guy's truck windows were too dusty for her to actually catch more than an impression of broad shoulders and height. Certainly she hadn't seen his face, and a pickup truck in Texas was as common as ants at a picnic. So were guys wearing Stetsons. Jessa met tons of people in her job as an assistant buyer, but ten out of ten were the kind of young, urban types who loved trendy clothes. She simply had no reason to run across the kind of cowboy type driving a battered truck, so the chances of his really being familiar were about a zillion to one.

She zipped past him, but then made an effort to slow down. Really, it wasn't her fault that her butter-yellow Cabriolet loved to boogie, but she wanted a look at the unfamiliar landscape. Instead of a suburban look, the homes seemed to be...well, they were so huge and fancy that they seemed to be estates.

She stopped the car at a mailbox, checked the address on her direction sheet—and frowned again as she slowly passed the gated entrance and aimed up a long, rambling driveway. Somebody had to live here. And the last thing she wanted to do on a Christmas morning was intrude on anyone.

Ryan Fortune had told her to explore the directions and the key—her present—any time that it was convenient for her. But this house...

Wow.

The one time she'd seen Mr. Fortune's house, the

Double Crown Ranch, Jessa thought it seemed like a Spanish castle, big enough to house a city…or maybe two. This place wasn't *that* extraordinary, but it still qualified as majorly intimidating. The size of her dreams was the two-bedroom town house she called her own, and considering her background, that was plenty luxurious. This…

Man. She parked in the empty driveway and gingerly stepped out, her gaze taking in the property like a kid with her first glimpse of Santa. The house itself was plopped on top of a tall knoll, built of Spanish white stucco, with black wrought-iron balconies and a red tile roof. No other buildings were in sight. The place had to be three stories—two in plain sight, and one lower level that opened onto a ravine with an Olympic-sized pool in back. She could see a corner of the pool and the rock gardens landscaping it. A big old gnarly cottonwood shaded an old fashioned courting swing. The place was country enough to have a white-tailed bunny scampering in the front lawn…yet urban enough to have a four-car garage.

For a girl who'd never known a father, who'd been living on the streets since she was sixteen—and was damn proud of what she'd made of her life—the house just…bugged her. Undoubtedly, pricey-dicey people lived here. Snobs. Not her kind.

But oh. She could remember dreaming of a home like this when she was a girl. She'd never believed in Prince Charming, never credited the fairy tales, never had patience with peers who whined about how tough they had it. Big deal. She'd had it tough, too. But when she fell asleep at night—well, it wasn't so easy to be tough when the lights were off—and a million times she must have dreamed about a real home. The kind where a dozen kids could spread out and play. Where people laughed and had friends over and invited company. Where people put up trees at Christmas and bought millions of presents for each other and had big feasts, with turkey with an oyster dressing, and rum cake and eggnog and fancied-up vegetables.

Not Oreos and Tex-Mex.

A lump filled her throat. She hadn't felt that stupid lump in years. She was doing fine with her life—more than fine, in fact. She had a great job, her own place and maybe she ran through money, but she was holding her own. She didn't need family. She didn't need a pricey-dicey house. And for damn sure, she didn't need a man. It was just...

Some things brought on that old yearning—especially when she hadn't had a chance to brace herself—and mentally she wanted to curse Ryan Fortune. If the guy wanted to give her something, fine. But what on earth had he dragged her all the way to a place like this for?

She'd never wanted to attend the Christmas party at the Double Crown Ranch two weeks ago. Never had any idea that Mr. Fortune was a billionaire and a big scion in San Antonio society until then—and she wouldn't have cared if *she* had known. She'd only accepted the invitation because he'd called and made such a big deal out of it. Apparently he'd almost died recently from some kind of poisoning and he made out like it would really matter to him if she came to this family shindig.

They did have a little history together, but only because a year ago before, she'd stopped to help him in a car accident. It wasn't the kind of thing anyone would forget. The night had been pouring rain; she'd seen his fancy antique car skid right into a tree and crash, pinning him inside, and suddenly there was the sharp smell of gas in the air. Where Jessa came from, people ran away from trouble. Maybe that was why she never could. As it turned out, though, as frightened as she'd been that she wasn't strong enough to pull him out of the trapped car, someone else had shown up. She hadn't saved Mr. Fortune's life. The other man had.

She understood that's what Ryan Fortune wanted to talk to her about, understood he'd been determined to track her down and give her some kind of gift, but that was never necessary. She didn't need a present, never wanted to take anything—but he'd insisted on giving her the little package with the key. Just kept saying that there was a gift for her at the end of it, and she could pick it up any time that it was convenient for her.

Now, though, staring at the house, Jessa considered climbing back in her car and making a quick exit. Whatever the gift was, she could get it some other time. She couldn't tell for sure if there were people home or not, but for darn sure a family wouldn't want to be interrupted by a stranger on Christmas morning. She...

Hearing a sudden sound, she whipped her head around. Startling her, the dusty, rusty tan pickup she'd spotted on the highway pulled up behind her car. It wasn't surprise at seeing the truck again that made her jaw drop, though. It was the look of the man.

At five feet nine inches, she rarely had to look up to a man, which suited her just fine. This one was tall. Too tall. And way too good-looking, she thought irritably. If a woman went for the mountain-man rough and rugged type, he'd be ideal. His hair was a rich, sun-streaked brown, the skin bronzed, the eyes a golden hazel and compelling as sin.

People rarely guessed that Jessa was a scrapper because she didn't look or dress the part—but she'd had to fight to survive all her life, which was why she recognized that stubborn kind of determination in someone else. This guy had the quality all over him. The bumpy nose. The thrown-back posture. The long, angular face had beautiful bones but a dare-devil chin. Nobody but an idiot was gonna argue with this guy.

Apparently he'd stashed his Stetson in the truck, because he loped toward her, bareheaded. He was wearing boots, worn cords and an aviator jacket that might have been new in the '80s. The curly hair needed a trim. The look in his eyes needed some discipline. The slash of a wayward smile was as wicked a grin as she'd ever seen on a man—and she'd seen her share.

''*You!*'' she let out on a woosh of a breath. She'd

seen him once, last year. And a second time at Ryan
Fortune's Christmas party two weeks ago. But of all
the guys in the universe, Sebastian O. Quentin was
one man that she never conceivably expected to run
across again. "I just can't believe it's you!"

"I can't believe it's you either." Sebastian wanted
to shake his head the way a puppy tossed off rain. Of
course he'd seen the yellow VW on the road. It was
impossible *not* to notice that the woman was driving
like a maniac. And yeah, he'd noticed that the driver
was tall, blond and female, but so were a fair number
of females in San Antonio. It never occurred to him
that the woman was Jessamine Mitchell because their
meeting again was so unlikely.

If there was a human in the universe who was more
his diametric opposite, Sebastian had never met her.
In Texas—unquestionably the land of big hair for
women—this one had a gamine short cut, spiky and
straight. She should have looked butch instead of ul-
trafeminine, but somehow the fringy frame of honey-
blond around her face was sexy as hell. The eyes were
such a sapphire blue that she must be wearing contacts. There was a tiny gold ring in her right eyebrow.
The lipstick was a wicked red. Every finger was
dressed up with a ring. The clothes were as city-girl
as you could get—tottering high heels with no backs,
butter-yellow leather pants that both matched her car
and snuggled down her long, long legs like the drape
of a man's hand.

She was also nothing like the athletic, outdoor

women he tended to like best—but there was something about her. Something that made his heart slam with alarm and his pulse skitter like a nervous buck's. The two times he'd seen her before, he'd tried to analyze the cause of the problem because he wasn't used to a woman getting under his skin that way—but nothing was that clear-cut. The hell-raiser attitude? That soft mouth covered so deliberately with such an outlandish red lipstick? That dare-me look in her eyes?

Again he shook his head, still trying to shake off his disbelief. "What on earth are you doing here?"

She lifted a hand. "Somehow...I think I'm here for the exact same reason you are. Why do I suspect you have a key?"

"Because I do. I got it from Ryan—"

"And he gave it to you the night of the Fortune Christmas party," she finished for him.

Sebastian cocked a leg forward. "I told him afterward that I didn't need any thanks. Or any present."

"So did I. But he almost died recently from poisoning. When he finally pulled through, he just kept thinking about what mattered in his life. It obviously bugged him, that we'd helped him in that accident a year ago and he never found a way to thank us. Still you were the one who saved his life. Not me."

"I think, the point, to Mr. Fortune, was that both of us stopped—when no one else did." Sebastian clearly remembered that night, because it'd been traumatic in so many ways. It had been past ten, dark as pitch, in a relentless, blinding, cold rain. He'd seen the expensive antique car wrapped around a tree.

Seen the slender blond woman—Jessa—soaking wet in some kind of silky dress, all alone, crying and shrieking for help like a banshee. He had no idea how she'd gotten there—there was no time to notice details like her car or anything else. The older man's legs hadn't been crushed, but he was completely trapped in his car, and she'd been frantically trying to pull him out, not giving up for nothing, even though she had to smell the gas, had to know she wasn't strong enough to save him on her own.

At that first meeting, Sebastian had his hands full saving the driver before the car blew up—and it *did* blow. A fire truck arrived with the Jaws of Life, but too late to do any rescuing. Both Sebastian and the older man were safe, flat on the grass, when the gas tank exploded sky-high. And once the gamine blonde realized they were safe, she took off, disappearing into the night, before he had any idea who she was or what her name might be.

She'd made an unforgettable impression on him, though. In spite of the rain, the dark, the danger, his yelling at her to run and call 911, the mud, the old man crying…he remembered the wet dress plastered to her long, skinny body.

The face with those incredible eyes. The fury that she couldn't save the man on her own. He'd wanted to shake her for being so damn stubborn—she'd almost killed herself for a complete stranger. But he'd admired her, too. She had guts to burn. Attitude. And she was sure as hell female to the bone.

Still was.

"And it never occurred to me to ask Mr. Fortune what he'd given you. It was none of my business. I just opened the box later in his study and saw the key. He just told me to follow the directions to find out what the key unlocked, but not to worry, it would wait until I had some free time. No rush."

"He gave me the same instructions." She looked at the house, then back at him, shifting on her feet as if both the house and him made her equally uneasy. "I assume whatever present he had in mind is inside the house somewhere. I just can't understand why he'd make this all so...mysterious. The long drive. To this fancy house in the middle of nowhere. Why on earth didn't he just give us whatever he wanted to give us?"

"I have no idea. But obviously there's only one way to find out." He motioned her ahead of him toward the front door.

Sebastian couldn't remember anything that had seriously thrown him since the death of his parents when he was nineteen. It was as if he'd put up an emotional wall at that time. He'd climbed mountains and rafted over waterfalls without ever losing his cool or feeling fear. He rarely let anything get to him— but Christmas mornings were invariably a little rough. That's why he'd waited until this morning to take this drive. It gave him something to do on the holiday.

On the same token, though, he'd just assumed he'd be exploring the directions and the key on his lonesome. He didn't care what Ryan Fortune had given him. Most likely he was going to give it back, anyway. He didn't need material goods, had no space for them in his '80 Winnebago—for that matter, he didn't need anything from anyone. But he really didn't like surprises that he'd had no chance to brace for.

Jessa Mitchell had thrown him the first night he'd met her. And she was throwing him now.

Dumb, Sebastian chided himself, as he followed that sashaying fanny up to the regal oak front doors. Jessa was no woman who should have troubled him, simply because she was so obviously a fast-lane, big-on-style, urban-type female. He was a hound to her poodle. One hundred percent cotton to her one hundred percent silk. Granite compared to her soft twenty-two karat gold. In fact, he should be kicking back and just enjoying the encounter, since it had to be obvious—to her as well as him—that neither had to worry about falling for each other. It should be fun, being around an attractive, spirited woman who gave off more sexual sparks than a loose electric wire on a hot day—but who didn't represent any threat. And he suspected this strange little meeting *was* going to be fun. It was just…there was something about her.

An unnerving quality.

A specifically *sexy* unnerving quality.

That made him wish he'd climbed a mountain that morning. Or skydived. Or taken the dirt bike into the hills, done some jumping. Or did anything else that was nice and safe—that is, nice and safe on his terms.

At the front door, she hesitated with the key in her hand, and then knocked several times.

"The place is quieter than a ghost, Jessa. There's

no one here. Did you think Ryan Fortune'd give us a key to a house where people were already living?''

Her mouth tipped in a quick smile. "No, I guess that was obvious, huh? But it just seemed impossible that a wonderful home like this was empty. Especially on a holiday like Christmas."

She hadn't asked him how he happened to be alone Christmas morning, but it was one of the things he'd noted about her already. Maybe the two of them were night and day in every other way, but they had that ticklish little factor in common—chasing a wild goose on Christmas morning rather than face being alone.

Finally she turned the key on the lock and stepped inside. He followed her.

Somebody loved this place, because everything looked cared for rather than neglected, but there was no sign of anyone recently living here. For sure there was no Christmas tree, no holiday decorations. A big old *Gone With The Wind*-type staircase dominated the front hall. Apparently there was a full wing of rooms running both sides of the house, because there seemed no end of doors in sight.

Dust motes danced in a patch of sunlight. A scent of lemon wax seemed to be the house's main perfume, faded but still lingering. There wasn't a footprint on the black-and-white diamond floor, nor a speck of dirt anywhere. Furniture was visible through open doors, all of it draped with dust sheets.

Jessa had stepped in, but then stood stock-still, skinny arms wrapped around her chest. "It's so beautiful," she breathed. "What a breathtakingly special place."

He wanted to look at her, not the damn house. Somehow he thought she'd be too tough a piece of work to wax sentimental over a house, but there was something aching in her eyes. Something soft. Something more vulnerable than he wanted to know about her.

Sebastian felt the opposite—a sharp resistance to even being here. He grew up in a home like this. Maybe not quite this upscale, but the Quentins were no strangers to privilege. Even a glance made him feel an old, tired, knife stab in the chest. He didn't like places like this. They just reminded him of his childhood years, when his parents had lavishly given him everything. Love. Attention. Time. Anything he wanted.

For no reason Sebastian had ever figured out, he'd turned into a rebellious, ungrateful teenage hellion. Lots of kids took a wrong turn growing up. Nobody escaped trouble in life altogether. But most kids had a chance to grow out of those disgusting stages. So had he—but not before his parents died. And that sore inside him never quite healed, that he'd lost his parents at a point when he'd been a huge disappointment to them.

His gaze zipped around the front hall, his boots shifting restlessly. Houses like this always made him edgy. His old Winnebago was too small to really call it a home, and that was how he liked it. And right now, he just wanted out—anywhere but to dwell in that emotional closet of old memories.

"Jessa?"

She couldn't seem to stop spinning around, eyes

big, still taking in the old monster place. Yet now she quickly tilted her face up, eyebrows raised in question.

"There's a marble table on the side of the staircase. Looks like two envelopes there."

"Oh!" She promptly galloped over there. "I knew there had to be a clue to the presents here somewhere. Or something to indicate why Mr. Fortune wanted us here..." She scooped up the envelopes, then blinked at him. "Orange? Sebastian *Orange*? That's your middle name?"

He snatched his white envelope. "Orange is a name that goes way back in my family. Actually, it isn't that uncommon. It's just a western name. Mostly from the 1800s—"

"Orange?" she repeated with a grin.

So, he thought. She was a tease. "You've got two choices, Slick. You can forget you ever heard that name. Or you can die young."

"Orange!" she repeated, this time on the tag end of a chuckle.

He sighed, then tore open the envelope. "You might want to read your note. I'm assuming Mr. Fortune wrote us the same thing. Although this is turning out to be pretty damn childish, if you ask me. A treasure hunt with directions. Then an envelope..."

His voice trailed off. For that millisecond, he even tired of looking at her. But the first words of the letter from Ryan Fortune made his stomach turn over.

"I'll be damned," he whispered. "He actually left us this house!"

Chapter 2

Jessa whirled around. "What do you mean?"

Sebastian glanced up from the multipaged letter with a scowl. "I mean just what I said. Ryan Fortune is giving us this house."

"Come on, that's ridiculous. Nobody would give away a mansion like this to two strangers! It's nuts!"

"Nuts or not—that's exactly what he did."

Jessa rolled her eyes. Sebastian Orange Quentin was unquestionably a breathtaking hunk—if you went for the rugged, outdoor type, which she kept telling herself would never apply to her. Still, she'd been enjoying lusting after him until confronted with the sad evidence that he didn't have a brain.

Patiently she used a long red fingernail to open the matching envelope of her own letter. It was time for one of them to get a handle on reality. Jessa didn't know why she felt surprise that she was getting stuck with that job. When something hard had to be done, it always took a woman.

She read the first few lines of the letter. Then sank down on the third step of the fancy staircase. Maybe the universe had obeyed all the usual physics laws a few seconds ago, but now everything was tilting. "He actually wants us to have this house," she said weakly.

"That's what I told you."

"But it's so...unbelievable. I realize he gave us a key, but it still never occurred to me that he could possibly mean to be giving us a house. I just thought he'd stored the gift in some location where it was safely locked away. Because he was eccentric. Or because it was something awkward in size. Never because he actually intended to give us anything like a house, for Pete's sake."

"Well, Slick, it bites to agree with anyone wearing a ring in her eyebrow...but it seems I can't argue with you. Mr. Fortune seemed like such a solid guy. Straight arrow. Good man. Who'd have guessed he had a screw loose?"

The insult about her eyebrow ring almost made her crack a grin. Of course if he insulted her again, she'd have to whack him upside the head, but in the meantime she felt oddly reassured. They were two strangers in an awkward situation. It was going to help a ton if they could talk. Help even more if they could joke together.

Still, the mood to smile didn't last long. Even the

fun of a verbal slanging match couldn't divert her from the crisis at hand. "Really, Sebastian, this isn't funny. The house just can't be ours. No one just…gives away…a fabulous home like this. Cripes, the property together has to be worth a million dollars."

"I'm guessing over two."

"Two milli—oh, my God." Faster than a bullet, memories suddenly zoomed through her mind. One was a tediously reoccurring nightmare. She had to be around seven years old. Her mom had been curled up on the couch, with an empty bottle on the lamp table next to her. Sleeping, Jessa'd understood then. And while her mom had been sleeping, she'd been pulling up cushions and bending over chairs, trying to chase down enough change to walk down the corner and get some fast food. Two bucks would have thrilled her then. Knowing she'd never depend on anyone for two bucks again thrilled her even now.

But two-million dollars was another dimension entirely. Her mind couldn't get around numbers that big. Couldn't even begin. That was so good it was… frightening.

Abruptly she felt Sebastian's big hand at the back of her neck, gently urging her head down between her knees. The sudden, sick dizziness embarrassed her. She gave herself credit for being tougher than rawhide, and certainly she'd never admit to vulnerability in front of a stranger. Even more relevant, she'd die before throwing up on that gorgeous black-and-white diamond floor. "I'm okay," she said impatiently.

"Sure you are. That's why your face was turning pea-green." Still, his hand lightened on the back of her head, grazed her shoulder and then dropped. His gaze on her face, though, was as ruthless as a laser. "I'll let you up, if you promise me you're not gonna keel over."

"I never keel over," she promised him. It was just hard to stop reeling. Mr. Fortune had never once let on the monumental size of his gift. In fact, she distinctly remembered him saying that she should just follow the directions whenever she had the spare time, as if his little present would wait indefinitely.

"Uh-huh. Well, it's a big house. If a glass of water would help you feel better, I'm betting I could scare up one."

"No. But thanks."

He didn't argue, just hunkered down on the stair beside her—close enough for her to grab if she needed someone. She didn't need or want to touch him, but she was again reminded of the dark, rainy night when he'd saved Mr. Fortune's life. Sebastian had come on the scene like a quiet bulldozer. He'd issued orders, taken charge, established himself as boss in half a second flat—but not really in a mean way. He'd never raised his voice. And even though Jessa couldn't stand bossy types—being one herself— there was something reassuring about him. Even if a woman were feeling sick as a dog, he was the kind of man you'd trust to stand by you.

Sort of.

He'd crackled the pages of the letter again and was

reading them intently, ignoring her. Which was fine, except that sitting this close, Jessa could hardly ignore *him*. She kept telling herself that he was a trustworthy kind of guy—and he'd already proven that, the night of the accident—but something about him put her hormones in a dither.

It was simply his appearance, she thought irritably. He clearly hadn't bothered to shave that morning. His hair was thick and rumpled, his chin shadowed with stubble. His jacket smelled of old leather, his skin of soap and wind. The bones were classy—even if he didn't have the clothes sense of a dog, anyone could tell he'd come from class—yet he kept reminding her of a young Harrison Ford. Something about his grin was irreverent. Something about his clothes looked hopelessly untidy and sexy. Something about his eyes made him look disastrously disreputable.

Rusty hormones cranked to life, making Jessa feel edgy and weird. Appreciating a guy's cute butt was one thing, but feeling the live-wire stirrings of desire was another. The former was fun, the latter unsettling. She was frigid and had the references from any number of guys to prove it. More relevant, she'd never seen frigidity as a problem but as a point of pride. It had always been a relief, knowing she was nothing like her mother—the kind of woman who'd let hormones rule both her life and her judgment.

"What a boondoggle," Sebastian muttered, and sifted from the second page of the letter to the third.

"Boondoggle? I never heard that word before."

"My dad used to say it. Means, something that

works out the exact opposite of what was intended. Like when good intentions go completely awry.''

Jessa cocked her head. ''I assume you're thinking about Ryan Fortune's good intentions.''

''Exactly. No question he meant something damn nice for both of us with this house. Only it's sure going to create a major complication in both our lives.''

Once her stomach settled down, she tried to see the house through Sebastian's eyes—as a nuisance of a complication—but there was no way. All her life, she'd yearned for a home...and this one was so much more than she'd ever dreamed of. Plunked down on the staircase, she couldn't see that much...but still, more than enough to fall hard in love. The room off to the right had a two-story stone fireplace and a double set of French doors leading onto a veranda.

It was so easy to picture a Christmas tree in there. Kids racing around. A floppy-eared dog snoozing on the hearth. Adults laughing and talking, catching up the way families—real families—did on holidays. Her mind embellished the pictures, adding heaps of people and heaps of food. Smells wafted from the long trestle table behind the couch, nostalgic smells like pumpkin pie and vanilla and orange and cinnamon. She imagined an empty plate on the hearth, where a cookie had been left for Santa.

''There, you're getting color back in your face,'' Sebastian observed.

''Huh?''

But he'd already bent his head and appeared to be

concentrating on nothing but the letter again. "Mr. Fortune explains a whole bunch why he felt so strongly about giving us this gift. People don't stop to help a stranger anymore. They're too afraid. And it's even more rare that people feel motivated to do the right thing—just because it's the right thing. The way we did."

"I didn't do anything," Jessa insisted.

"You keep saying that. But Mr. Fortune thought your stopping was brave, and frankly, Slick, so do I. You stopped first. Even though you were a woman alone, in the middle of the night. And that old car— you had to smell the gas, had to know that antique was made way, way, before today's safety standards, had to be afraid it would blow up. Yet you stayed with him."

She wasn't used to people praising her. It made her stomach turn over in an unfamiliar way. "Oh, for heaven's sake. Anyone else would have done the same thing."

Those deep golden eyes rested on her face again. "But no one else did, Jessa. Only you and me."

For a second she felt a pull toward him, stronger than a smack of lightning. Mr. Fortune *was* right. These days, most people seemed to feel it was more important to protect themselves than to do the right thing. Jessa knew why she stood up for a darn fool principle...but it was something else to be sitting next to someone else who actually lived by the same weird, outdated principles. Who'd have guessed that two such different people could ever have something so unusual in common?

The thought unsettled her so much that she had to argue. "Would you cut it out? I didn't do anything hard. You're the one who saved him."

"But my stopping was logical. I've got both my EMT and Wilderness First Response certifications, so I was at least prepared to do something in a crisis like that. More to the point, though..." he motioned to the section of the letter he'd been reading "...is that Mr. Fortune's near run-in with death made him realize all the thank-you's he'd neglected to say in this life. All the moral debts he hadn't gotten around to paying." Sebastian glanced up. "But he says you were the hardest one to track down, because you left without anyone knowing your name. You *did* run off awfully fast."

Again, she remembered that long ago night. By the time Sebastian had pulled Mr. Fortune out of his car, she'd heard the scream of sirens in the distance—cop cars, fire trucks, ambulances. She'd been sopping wet and freezing. Still she'd have stayed if there was something else she could have done, but at that point any bystander or extra bodies near the accident were only complicating the situation. "I didn't run off. There was no time or reason to tell anyone my name. I just wanted to get out of the way."

"But that's part of what impressed Mr. Fortune. That you didn't seem to expect a reward or even a thank-you." Sebastian was still scrolling down his copy of the letter. "And once Mr. Fortune finally managed to track you down, that was when he discovered that you didn't have family. Likewise, he'd found out by then that I didn't have any living relatives. That's when he came up with the idea of giving us the house. He says, 'You two are too old to adopt. But I wanted to do something to make you feel like you're part of a family. My family. Honorary Fortunes…''

Her heart started swelling again. You'd think she'd have an impenetrable coat of cynicism after all these years? And usually she did, but this was just such a huge thing to take in. It was like meeting Santa Claus in the flesh when you'd been positive he didn't exist. And then the rest of what Sebastian said sunk in. "You don't have any family either?" she asked quietly.

"I have a couple aunts on the East Coast. A few cousins scattered around. But no one even close to Texas. Originally, though, it was because of family that I got that blasted middle name."

"Hmm. You don't like 'Orange'?"

He shot her a look—the kind of look that had been emergolating teasers since the beginning of time. "The name sounds either New Age or hokey to me, but actually, it's neither. Orange is a plain old-fashioned western name. Been passed down in the family for generations."

"Jessamine was passed down in my family the same way. Only in my case it was totally ironic. I had no family with staying power. Nobody who valued a name or traditions or anything else. Kind of ooga-booga, isn't it? That we both have family names and yet no family?''

''I don't see any ooga-booga. You got a beautiful name, where I got one that every kid in school made fun of.'' He didn't really sound like he was complaining that much, though, only trying to shift away from that subject and back to the letter. ''Mr. Fortune goes on—and on—about how much he wanted to give us something meaningful. A home was the one thing he discovered that neither of us had. I'm quoting him now...'The Fortune family has had its ups and downs through the generations—and then some—but we always had each other. What I know about you two young people is that you both have strong hearts and courage and values. All I want is for you to have something special. I hope the legacy of the house can be used in a way that gives each of you something you need.''

Her throat clogged up with yet another unswallowable lump. For a woman who'd never had a corny bone, she seemed to be suffering from a million sentimental ones this morning. The selfless generosity of Mr. Fortune was part of that, but so was discovering that someone else was like her in the most unusual of ways. No, she'd never had courage like Sebastian. But she knew he was a stand-up kind of man. She knew he spent the loneliest of holidays alone. And now she understood that he also had no one to love.

Sebastian, though, was obviously tuned to a far crabbier channel. ''You'd think Mr. Fortune might have noticed that we don't know each other from

Adam? What on earth are we supposed to do with a house together, split it down the middle of a joist...hmmph!''

''Hmmph what?'' she prompted him.

''Well, it seems he did consider some of those problems.'' Sebastian read on a little further, and then relayed the information. ''He understands we'll need some time to decide what to do with the property. So he paid the upkeep and taxes for a year. Also paid the wages for a groundskeeper—Jesus Monterres—and a guy who's been coming in to housekeep once a week, Arthur Hayes. After that...''

When Sebastian fell silent again, reading the letter without filling her in, Jessa elbowed him in the ribs. ''Hey. After that, what?''

''After that, we can do whatever we want. Get married and live in it—ha ha. Or sell it and split the money between us. Or one of us could live here, and the other gets half the value via a mortgage. Or any other arrangement we want to come up with.'' Sebastian thumbed to the last page of the letter. ''There's a professional appraisal of the house and property here. And a telephone number for an attorney to handle any questions we've got on the setup, the titles and assays and surveys and that kind of thing. However...''

Jessa couldn't believe how much Mr. Fortune had thought of. It seemed like he'd anticipated every problem they could possibly have. But Sebastian seemed so grave that she felt maybe a joke might help lighten him up. ''You don't think we'd make a perfect married couple? Personally I think we're naturals...with a couple of small readjustments, of course. I could buy a pair of combat boots, assuming I could find a style that came with heels. And you could get a couple of tattoos and pierce your ears—or maybe your nose—''

He shuddered. ''You're trying to scare me, right?''

''About marriage or getting your nose pierced?'' she asked blandly. ''You know what Mae West always said. If you have to choose between two evils, you might as well choose the one you haven't tried before. Personally, in your shoes, I'd go for the nose ring, but—''

''You have a sick sense of humor, Slick. I have a bad feeling we're going to end up friends—as hard as that might be to believe.''

Actually, Jessa didn't think that was hard to believe at all. She'd have to get rid of this embarrassing hormonal tug for him, but otherwise she suspected they were already on their way to getting along well. How could either of them be a threat to the other? He was jockey shorts to her thongs, a Great Dane to her natural poodle. ''You started to say something a minute ago about some appraisal thing—''

''Yeah. It's an addition to the letter. A problem.''

''What?''

Sebastian made a frustrated gesture. ''Maybe the cage bars are twenty-two carat, but a cage is still a cage. It's not gonna be easy to get out of this mess. The bottom line on the appraisal indicates the house and property are worth something like two four.''

"Two four?" she echoed blankly.

"Two million, four hundred thousand dollars."

She seemed to lurch to her feet at the same time he did, as if the gigantic dollar figure spring-loaded both of them. Or spring-loaded both their nerves.

Yeah, they'd been discussing this for the last half hour, but suddenly it really hit her.

Ten minutes ago she'd been a woman on a budget. Now she was worth a million bucks.

Ten minutes ago she'd been a struggler. She'd never asked anyone for anything. Never would. But she'd grown up with fear—fear of going hungry, fear whether she'd have a roof over her head, fear she would ever feel safe. And suddenly she had it all. No reason to worry about depending on anyone else, ever again. She was safe, the way she'd only dreamed of being safe. She could taste it. The freedom from want, the freedom from need.

She never intended to touch Sebastian, had no idea she was going to do it. God knew, she was an extremely happily repressed woman, but right then euphoria got the better of her. Her mouth smiled so hard that her lips hurt. The swelled-up feeling on her chest felt like bursting. Dancing around—knowing perfectly well she was acting like a goofball—there was just a single moment when she accidentally raised her hands to him, laughing, not meaning anything, just kind of inviting him into a Texas two-step.

Maybe he was more annoyed than thrilled by their suddenly owning a house together, but he wasn't hardhearted. Either out of kindness or good humor he accommodated her mood, taking her hand and arching her into the giddy rhythm of a dance.

Heaven knew how that sparked Armageddon…but the beginning of a dance mysteriously, magically— miraculously—became the beginning of a kiss instead. One instant he was spinning her around the black-and-white diamond floor, the next she was swept into a stranger's kiss. She didn't know his lips. The cool-smooth texture. The taste of cappuccino and vibrant, virile man. He was so much taller that he seemed to surround her, yet instead of feeling claustrophobic, she felt belled into the power of his arms.

Shivers chased up her bloodstream, not shivers of cold, but shivers of heat. The excitement racing through her heart suddenly whiskered through her blood, turning into a darker excitement, a rush of nerves.

Maybe loneliness was part of the insanity of that moment. Jessa had been lonely so long that she tended to discount the emotion. There were no refunds or returns if you gave away a heart too cheap, better to keep it locked up, never for sale…yet she'd forgotten how powerful it was, how compelling, to find someone else on the other side of that dark abyss.

She didn't like it, though. She'd never trusted surprises, much less the surprise someone who could threaten her nice, secure frigidity. She liked being safe. She'd been in danger too many times as a child. Risk was never fun, and there was a kind of safety that a woman could get no other way than by closing the door on certain feelings. But...somehow this was different.

There was no such thing as a bond with a stranger. Not a real bond. She knew that. Yet she'd watched him save Ryan Fortune's life, so she knew he had honor. Principles. An unshakeable sense of right. And maybe those factors weren't enough to create a *bond*, exactly, but they definitely had the power to make a sneaky, slinky, silly little kiss turn into something else.

Lips met, tasted, tested. And suddenly clung.

Hands lifted midair for a dance step suddenly curled around his wrists, clutched. Not to stop him, but to hold on.

A dance step suddenly became a cocooning whirlwind, where she felt sucked into the magnetic pull of his chest, his skin, the smell and crush of that old leather jacket, the feel of him. God, who could have guessed that a stranger could take her under like this? That she had even a *hint* of this sexy stuff in her, much less how uproariously, euphorically, it was building.

He tugged her into him then. Took charge. Bent down and took her mouth, not kidding this time, not messing around and lollygagging this time, but kissing her the way a woman is always positive a man never will. Like she mattered. Like she was the princess and he was the prince in the fairy tale who'd die for her. Like she was magic and he couldn't, wouldn't let her go. Like he wanted her, with a hunger that stunned him for its power.

Still. A guy had to breathe.

And when he stopped to suck in a little air, she gulped in an extra quota of oxygen, too. But this wasn't over, not as far as she was concerned. She lifted up for another one of those kisses. Sebastian wasn't getting away scot-free until she'd figured this out. Men didn't *do* this to her. She didn't do this to men. Maybe Sebastian Orange Quentin was a daredevil and risk-taker, but Jessa needed a complete analysis of what was happening here, how it was even possible she felt tempted to go stark, raving mad.

Besides. She was having fun.

He lifted her up, as if his spine just wouldn't bow any longer to make him shorter. And she got another of those kisses she'd been looking for. This one was even better, involving tongues and pressure. She could feel the warmth scaling up his skin, feel his heart thundering against her chest, feel her breasts tightening and swelling. So this, she thought, was Christmas. Presents beyond anything you could ask for. An overwhelming sense of belonging to someone else, something else. No tinsel. Just heart. And need, sharper than pine needles, softer than red velvet, welling from the deepest, darkest secret spots inside her.

"Holy—" Sebastian suddenly yanked his head back. His eyes looked smoky brown, confused, agitated. Hot. "Jessamine. I'm sorry."

He couldn't know that no one actually ever called her Jessamine. Anyone who knew her at all seemed to sense that her real name just didn't suit her. She wasn't an old-fashioned woman. She was the new-

breed woman. Tough. Self-reliant. Only for just that
second, she let him get away with it, because she was
reeling pretty hard. She gulped in a breath, then another. "Don't be sorry. I mean…I didn't intend for
that to happen either. It was just…this was such a
shock. The house. The property. Going from poor to
rich in thirty seconds flat. It just blew me away, but
I never meant—"

"Of course you didn't," Sebastian finished for her.
"The two of us are day and night."

"Day and night," she echoed.

"We can't do this," he said firmly.

Jessa had no idea if he meant they couldn't do the
house or couldn't do any more kisses—but either
way, she could see how terribly stressed he was. More
than she was. She had no idea what was making *him*
so anxious, when she was the one who'd felt knocked
on her emotional keester—still, she really didn't want
to cause him a problem. Her troubles weren't Sebastian's. He was a good guy. So she hustled to agree.
"Perhaps…do you think we should call Ryan Fortune?"

There. Some of the steel seeped out of his spine.
"Yeah, I think that's exactly what we should do.
Thank him and everything. But tell him the truth, that
he's been generous, but too generous. Neither of us
wants this place."

Jessa cast one longing, yearning look around. "We
don't want this," she echoed blankly.

"Mark Twain used to say that a gold mine was
nothing more than a hole in the ground with a fool

on the top. This house isn't *free*. Nothing like this is ever free. But I think the real problem is that it just feels wrong to accept something like this.''

It didn't feel wrong to her. In fact, nothing had ever felt so right in her entire life as this house…and her feelings for Sebastian at this exact moment. Yet her eyes searched his, wishing she knew him better.

Something had obviously terribly upset him. It was pretty crazy to assume it was a few kisses from her. Sebastian had doubtless kissed a few million women…so it was something about the gift, the house, that shook him up.

Certainly Jessa realized that the property was an impossibly extravagant present. Still, it didn't seem that terrible to just enjoy this extraordinary moment. Mr. Fortune had made such an incredible gesture. A wonderful gesture. Surely it was just natural to express a little excitement about such a super thing?

"If you think we should call…" she started to say.

"I do. Somewhere in this house there has to be a working phone. Everything else has been left functioning and cared for."

He charged off in search of a phone as if a dragon were nipping at his behind. Jessa stood still, frowning as she stared after him, thinking what on earth was wrong. So he didn't want the house. They'd find some way to come to an agreement about that. But Sebastian seemed tight as a drum, seriously stressed…and he'd sure kissed her as if she were the last life raft on a sinking boat.

This Christmas, she mused, was turning into a confoundedly bewildering holiday.

A silver little shiver danced up her spine. Jessa just had the unshakeable feeling that her life was never going to be the same. Not because of the house. But because of something to do with Sebastian....

Chapter 3

Sebastian found a functioning telephone in the giant living room off from the front hall. He didn't have to look up Ryan's phone number, because that information was included in the letter. As he dialed, though, his gaze wandered around the room, from the striking two-story fieldstone fireplace to the beamed ceiling and gabled windows. There was no guessing what type of furniture was hiding under all the dust covers, but the architecture of everything he'd seen so far was done up Texas style. Big and grandiose.

He might have loved the place if it hadn't been for emotional burrs churning around in his stomach.

A voice answered on the other end of the telephone line. "Mr. Fortune! Merry Christmas, sir…" Instantly Sebastian pictured the wealthy patriarch. The night of the accident, Ryan Fortune had been shaken and frightened, but even then Sebastian had seen the character, the courage and intelligence. Maybe some would fear him, but Sebastian sensed a man worth respecting. Still did. "Yes. Both Jessa and I are at the house right now. And we don't want to interrupt your Christmas, but the house is exactly the reason we're calling—"

When Jessa showed up in the doorway, he immediately lost his train of thought. When she ambled closer, his brain scrambled even worse. How was a man supposed to concentrate around a woman with a ring in her eyebrow? Something about that tiny gold ring made him think of sex. The fuzzy sweater somehow forced him to think about sex. Come to think of it, the city-girl high heels and those big, wicked eyes forced him to think about sex, too.

Sebastian wanted to self-administer a whack upside his own head.

Maybe he was drawn to risk and dares, but not like this. Not like *her*. What in God's name had possessed him to kiss her like that? For that matter, what in God's name had possessed her to respond so willingly to a complete stranger like him? Couldn't she tell the obvious, that he wasn't conceivably the kind of man she could want in her life?

"...Believe me, Mr. Fortune, neither of us can thank you enough...but your gift is overwhelming. We're both appreciative. But there's no way that either of us could accept something like this. It was never necessary..."

His gaze tracked her fanny, as if his eyes were

magnetized and her little rump was an enticing piece of metal. At first she just dawdled around the room, but once she peeked under the first dust cover, the peace was all done. She promptly started yanking off the dust covers. All of them. Fast and ecstatically.

A couple extra long Edelman leather couches showed up, then a teak trunk used as a coffee table, then some more man-sized chairs. More to the point, all her running around gave him electric views of her delectable rump from all angles.

He shifted on his feet, thinking damnation, if he could just keep five solid feet between them, he could get his mind off his libido, but it wasn't that easy. The call to Mr. Fortune wasn't so easy in a different sense. Moments later, he hung up the phone, his mood as glum as a swamp.

"Well?" Jessa asked him. "Did you tell him we couldn't accept the house?"

"Yeah, I told him. But it was like trying to get through to a rock. He sounded real happy that we were overwhelmed, didn't bother him a lick...and there's no way he's taking it back. He said the property is ours. Period. Do whatever we want, but it's up to us. However—"

"However?"

"However..." Sebastian scraped a hand through his hair. "...he wants to have dinner with us. Preferably some night before New Year's. Whenever's convenient for us."

He didn't try giving her any further details. It was obvious she wasn't paying attention. As far as he could tell, a suggestion that the sky was falling in would result in an exuberant "that's great!" from her, nothing more. Once she'd hurled off all the dust covers and made a complete disaster of the great room, she started spinning around, her eyes shining, her lips curved in a beatific expression. Euphoric. Maybe even orgasmic…although Sebastian had to admit, that particular judgmental description might have occurred to him because his mind was still on sex.

"Isn't it fabulous?"

"Isn't what fabulous?"

"The room, you silly." She waved her arms. He swiftly backed away from her—just in case she had in mind hugging him again. Apparently this time, though, she just had in mind motioning to the decor of the room. "Everything's so wonderful! The giant couches! The upholstery, the old gaming table—I don't understand why so many wonderful things were just left here."

"According to Mr. Fortune, the furnishings you see come with the place. All the personal items are gone, like pictures and stuff, but the furniture that was bought specifically for the house wouldn't fit anywhere else that easily. He said he'd tell us the whole story of the house when—if—we agree to have dinner. He also mentioned that some rooms have more furnishings than others, so not to expect the place to be completely livable."

"We really should look at the rest of the place, don't you think? Maybe we'll get some ideas about what to do with the house if we see the whole thing, okay? Do you have time?''

Sebastian's eyes narrowed. Yes, he had time, but no, this wasn't *okay*. Considering the damn woman was ecstatic after just seeing one room, he thought it was a terrible idea to expose her to even a closet in the rest of the house.

Still, what could he say? It was Christmas. So he watched those long legs in the butter-cream leather pants sashaying up the stairs. Oh, man. It was so easy to see she'd fallen in love with the place, and that just kept getting worse. She danced and pranced and cooed every blasted time she opened a new door. She pulled open drapes and zipped off sheets and poked in every drawer and cupboard she could reach. Clouds of dust billowed in the sunlight, making her cough hard once—but it sure as hell didn't dim her excitement. It was "Oh, Sebastian!" and "Look at this!" and "Isn't this gorgeous? Look at that!"

Well, she'd better not kiss him again, that's all he could say.

"Good grief, Sebastian. There's even a kitchen upstairs here!"

"Yeah, I can see that," he grumped. He peeled his gaze off her rump—for the tenth time—and tried to focus on the dad-blamed, dad-blasted, dad-blooming house.

He knew precisely what the house reminded him of. Pain. Memories. Guilt. Still, he struggled to study the place objectively. On this floor, there were five bedrooms—each large enough to contain a couple of beds, maybe more. All three bathrooms had wiggle room enough for even a gaggle of kids. Jessa identified a "linen room," whatever that was. One door led to an all-purpose sort of room, that could easily be used for a study or computer setup. And the kitchen in the middle of the second floor wasn't full-sized, but Sebastian found himself pausing at the round oak table, running his hand over the grain. The table was scarred and scratched, far from perfect. But it was a table meant to be used, not just to look pretty. A beauty to either work or eat on. The plank pine cupboards looked hand-rubbed. There was an older fridge up here, a sturdy stove.

"I couldn't hear you. What'd you say?" Jessa asked him.

"I didn't say anything."

"Yeah, you did. Under your breath. Something about how it'd be blankety-blank perfect for the kids. What kids? You have children?"

"No." He heard the bark in his voice and immediately said more quietly, "I just work with teenagers. That's all."

"Oh?"

He wanted to sigh, heavily and long. He'd heard that avid, innocent "oh" from a woman before, knew there wasn't a prayer in a million that she'd let it go without prying further. "I run a wilderness camp for troubled kids. The camp is connected to a larger residential school program. Basically it works like a one-two punch. I get the kids first, put them through a three-week program, and then they go on to the school. Since there seems no end to troublemakers across the country who want to raise hell and be up to no good, we always seem to be long on kids and short on space..."

Which was probably why his pulse had charged up for a couple of seconds when he saw the second floor kitchen and all the spare rooms. Thankfully, though, a single glance at the last room in this wing—the master bedroom—obliterated any further thought about his monster kids.

The master bedroom, he had to admit, was something. Cedar walls and cedar-planked ceiling. Broad, long windows faced east, and sliding doors led to a balcony overlooking the pool. Honey carpet. Another skylight. A granite corner fireplace. Elegant, simplistic, sexy. Another door led to a private bath. He cocked his head, saw a tub big enough for a man even his size, black tile, black marble, pure glass shower— the glass shower snared his attention for a few seconds. Hell, you could see anything in there. Such as her. Sebastian could instantly envision Jessa in that glass shower. Naked. Sudsy water streaming through her hair, slinking down her back, down her no-butt, no-boobs, down those lithe, long legs...

He rubbed the tense muscles at the back of his neck. Hard.

"It's hard not to fall in love, isn't it?" she asked rapturously.

"Hard to imagine what it costs to upkeep." She was speaking of the house. So was he. But he was thinking that Jessa would cost higher than he could afford to upkeep, too. There was a hunger in her eyes. A yearning. She liked this house. Bad.

"So tell me more about this camp you run. How does it work? Where do the kids come from? What do you do with them?"

At least talking to her forced him to concentrate on something less volatile than either her body or this confounded house. "Well…the kids get referred to the program from all kinds of places—parents, schools, doctors, whatever. They don't have a police record yet, but they're generally aimed at that direction. We're talking truants, drinkers, drug users. The stinkers they used to call delinquents. Lots of attitude, and all of it bad. Ninety-nine percent of the time, they're on a wrong road—and they know it—but they don't have a clue how to turn themselves around… assuming they even want to."

"Sheesh. They sound horrible," Jessa murmured.

"They are."

She tilted her head. "Which makes it downright amazing, Sebastian, that the instant you started talking about them, you got this warm, affectionate tone in your voice." She pointed up with a royal finger. "Do you want to check out the attic before we head back downstairs?"

Man, her perception was irritating. So much so that Sebastian felt relieved. She was a very annoying woman. That sexual zing was bound to go away if he just gave it some time. "We've gone this far. We might as well check out the whole place."

"I thought so, too…and you didn't answer the

other part of my question. About what you specifically do with the kids?''

He stomped up the wooden stairs ahead of her, so he could test how safe the steps were. ''Well…the reason I get the monsters for the first three weeks is because my wilderness camp functions like a detox program—an emotional detox program. The idea is for the kids to sever their ties from all the regular life influences that were giving them trouble—peers, substances, music, Internet, parents, whatever…''

It was freezing in the attic, but still he paused at the stair top, as did Jessa. There was nothing up here but a massive unfinished space. Still, the open area was tall enough to put in ceilings, make a dorm type of sleeping space or a giant living area. Windows on both east and west exposures let in lots of light…and a view to die for. Of course, his delinquents would likely find some way to jump out of windows this high…

''Keep going,'' Jessa said.

''Pardon?''

''Keep talking. You didn't finish what you were saying about your program.''

''Yeah, well, the idea of this three-week wilderness camp is to reduce life to simpler terms. Force the kids to relook at what matters. Food. Shelter. Safety. I don't run a boot camp or anything like a military setup. I'm not a rule lover myself, so I wouldn't be forcing that on kids—but they *are* going to go hungry unless they pull their own weight and find a way to cooperate. I just work at breaking down life…into what matters and what doesn't. So that when they hit the school, they've already started over in a little different place.''

"Cripes, Sebastian. I can't even imagine the patience that takes. I've never been around kids much, much less such challenging ones. You get a lot of teenagers going through this program?''

"Yeah. Too many. Too *damn* many. And part of the problem is our success rate. We've developed a really terrific record for eight years now—almost none of the kids come back. Only what that means, is that our reputation has spread, and more and more kids are trying to get in. We just never seem to have enough space or facilities.''

He felt her eyes on his face, warm, intent, compelling and abruptly pulled himself up short. How on earth had he ended up talking so long? "You ready to go downstairs and check out the first floor now?''

"Sure," she said.

Again she followed him, willing enough, yet Sebastian kept getting this itchy feeling at the back of his neck—the kind of feeling he got before kayaking into unexpected white water, or waking up in a tent to a sudden lightning storm. Normally that itchy feeling was pleasant. He liked risk. An element of danger. Having to test and prove himself...but damnation, not with Jessa.

Something was increasingly wrong. His hormones, yeah, but Sebastian kept sensing something more serious than that. Even though they had nothing conceivable in common, he kept finding it easy to talk to her. Easy to tell her things. Even easy to be with her—as if they had some kind of bond.

It must be Christmas that was addling his brain. Either that or he had a flu coming on, Sebastian decided, but as he clattered down the back stairs to the first floor, it seemed a good idea to twist this encounter around, and find out something about her. "I told you about my work, but what about yours? What do you do?"

"Retail. Clothes. I work at Spritz."

"Which is…?" He'd never heard the name.

She flashed him a teasing grin. "I'm not surprised you haven't heard of it, cowboy. It's an upscale clothing store. Trendy, hip, urban. Expensive. The owner is the buyer, but I'm the assistant buyer."

"Clothes," he echoed.

"Somehow I sense a ribbing coming on. Right off, you struck me as the type of person who believed image was everything, always dress for success and all…" With a deadpan expression, her gaze whipped from his thirty-year-old leather jacket to his favorite pair of jeans, down to the boots that had been worn in before he finished college.

"Are you trying to imply that I look like a derelict, Slick?"

"No, no, never that. But man, what I could do with that butt and those shoulders if I just had your body in my store—and your credit card."

If she hadn't disappeared around a corner, his jaw would likely have dropped ten feet. God knew where the sound of a rusty chuckle came from, but it seemed to escape from his own throat. She *did* have nerve.

An image played in his mind of her dressing him from the skin out...and then undressing him down to skin. Both images made him scratch his neck again, yet for some strange reason, he was getting more comfortable with her. So she was a city woman with material values. Something about her eyes still said "good heart," and at least she had a sense of humor.

By the time he trailed her a few minutes through the downstairs, she'd clearly forgotten about him again. The house absorbed her interest, and unwillingly, it sucked him in, too. There seemed to be rooms on rooms on rooms—Jessa crowing and humming every time she pushed open a new door. She danced around, pulling off more sheets, touching things, waxing on and on about all the great things in the house. Sebastian tried to keep his eyes off her and concentrate on all the things that were wrong with the place.

The whole west side of the house had a view of the swimming pool and hilly grounds beyond. The long, tall living room led into a study, then a dining room, then a kitchen, then anterooms—like a shower and bath, mudroom, laundry and walk-in pantry. Everywhere the furniture was solid and simple. Basic, classic styles. Everything oversized to fit in with the oversized house.

Sebastian's mood clunked back into a low pit. Everything about the place just...hurt. It would just be so much easier if the house had white carpeting and velvet drapes and crystal and junk like that. He'd have no problem walking away from that kind of place.

Jessa had whipped ahead of him, yet by the time he crossed the hall to explore the east side of the house, he found himself slowing down. There was another living room on this side, this one smaller and more formal—what his grandmother might have called "a parlor" for company. After that came an eight-sided turret room, used for a library, the walls all bookshelves in fancy burl pecan—hell, he'd rather be outside than in, any day, but still the room was so special it was impossible not to savor. After that came a room that seemed like a man's retreat—tile floor, pool table, wet bar—and an office followed that.

The kitchen took up the entire south wall of the downstairs. She was a real monster. Walking slowly, Sebastian ran a hand over the wooden table, the tile counters. The tall cupboards were old-fashioned, with glass fronts and trim painted yellow—almost the same color that matched the sunlight streaming in. Three chandeliers hung over the long trestle table, but they weren't la-de-da-type chandeliers, more practical, old brass, tarnished.

Maybe it was the tarnish that got to him. He just couldn't stop thinking that you could feed a whole brood of kids in this place. Between the upstairs and down, there were ample rooms for private counseling, yet lots of space for group projects, too. Rooms for classes, yet also quieter places for individuals who needed to concentrate on individual goals or work. There were rooms to make messes, rooms you could keep presentable for the public, rooms that just allowed for storage space...

"Orange?"

His head shot up—not just because no one had called him "Orange" since his mother was alive. But because he hadn't realized Jessa had wandered into the kitchen, much less how long she'd been standing there, studying him.

She smiled. "Hey, I called 'Sebastian' a couple of times, but you seemed too deep in thought to hear me. I have to remember next time that calling you 'Orange' works like a charm." Her gaze seemed glued on his face, as if she were reading something there that she'd never expected. "Look, let's sit down for a minute, okay? We've seen the place. Maybe not every single nook and cranny, but most of it. And I'd like to ask you something."

"What?" When she sat down, he hunkered in a chair across the trestle table.

Her eyes softened. "You've fallen in love with the house as much as me, haven't you?"

The question astonished him. He thought he'd made his feelings clear. "Jessa, I don't love it at all. I don't want anything to do with it."

Now it was her turn to frown and look confused. "But I've been watching you—the way you looked at everything. I don't understand."

"I just don't...have possessions. Like a house."

"Oh," she said gently, as if trying to cater to the demented.

Sebastian sighed. "I guess that sounded ridiculous, huh?"

"No, no. Everybody runs around thinking, God, please, please don't give me financial security for the rest of my life no matter what you do. I'd hate it."

Darn woman forced him to grin. Again. "Okay, okay, I realize that sounded weird. I just meant—I really don't want the house. Any house." When she continued to look at him with that patient, I-will-be-understanding-with-the-demented-man expression, he sighed. Again. Sebastian wasn't in the habit of telling strangers his life story, but he wanted her to believe him. Which meant she needed to understand. "Look. It's about the delinquents I take care of..."

He'd always called his kids delinquents. For him, it was a term of endearment. And she seemed to figure that out, because a slow smile tipped the corners of her mouth. "Yeah? What about your delinquents?"

"I was one of them once. Came from a house like this. Loving parents. Lots of privilege. Frankly, I was spoiled rotten, so I had no excuse in hell for turning into a pain-in-the-butt teenager, but I did. Now, it's not a crime to go through a bad patch. Everybody doesn't manage to grow up wearing a halo every step of the way."

Something in her face echoed old pain, old memories. "I know. Believe me, I know."

"Do you? Well...the thing was, in my case, my parents were as great as you can get. The kind of family that a kid dreams of having. Understanding.

Loving. Always there. And they died when I was
nineteen.''

Faster than a bullet, her soft hand reached over to
cover his. Just a gesture of comfort and warmth—but
it did just that. Comforted. Warmed. For a man who
normally accepted neither from anyone. ''I'm sorry,''
she said.

''Yeah, well, that was exactly what turned me
around. The 'sorry' word. I was in college when they
took off on vacation for a couple weeks, and it just
happened that they both caught a terrible virus. The
thing was, they died before I saw them again—before
I could say 'I'm sorry.' And it killed me. Losing them
at point when I knew damn well I was a complete
disappointment to them. Ungrateful. Rebellious. A
creep and a half. They were the best parents this side
of the moon. I can't even explain why I was such an
ass, but it wasn't their fault. It was all mine.''

''So,'' she said softly, ''you set out to work with
kids. Specifically pain-in-the-ass kids.''

''Yeah.''

She nodded. ''And this relates to why you don't
want this house—how?''

He frowned at her again. He thought he'd explained. Somehow being around her proved more
confusing all the time—even when she was being
nice.

''I just don't,'' he answered her finally.

''Okay. Got it.'' She glanced at her watch, a shiny
little bangly affair that looked more like jewelry than

a serious timekeeper. "Good grief, the whole morning's gone."

"Yeah, I didn't realize how late it was either." He lurched to his feet. "On what we should do with the house...maybe we should both sleep overnight, think about it, then meet again. "

"That sounds like a good plan. Frankly, I still feel like I'm in shock. Hard to think straight, but I would like to get this settled. If you want to meet with Mr. Fortune, that's fine with me, too, but I'd rather talk this out with you alone at least one more time first."

"Agreed." He thought. "I really can't do anything tomorrow, but how about Thursday?"

She tapped her foot, then nodded. "Okay. I probably can't get loose until around four in the afternoon on Thursday, but does that time work okay with you?"

"Sure." He strode toward the front hall again, but then realized that she wasn't following. When he glanced back, he saw that she'd gathered up her bag and jacket but then just seemed to be standing there. Maybe she didn't mean to reveal so much of herself, but there was this look in her eyes. As if she was inhaling the house, the way a rosebud took in dew. Thirsty. Hungry. Yearning. It bugged him. "Jessamine?"

She swiveled around on those sassy heels. "Jessa," she corrected him.

Whatever. "You can have the damn house. I don't want it. That's what I've been telling you. For God's sake, if you want it, it's yours."

A ghost of a smile softened her eyes. "I think we need to find a solution that works for both of us. Something that fits Mr. Fortune's ideas about his gift. And that means we need to try to find a solution that's fair. Not just for me, but for you, too."

"Yeah, well, I don't care about fair," Sebastian said impatiently. "Look, Slick. I don't need anything like this. I live in a 1980 Winnebago. That's all I have the time to take care of. And I realize figuring out what and how to do something about this place will be complicated, but we'll find a way to do it."

He could see her lips part, knew she planned on arguing with him—again. For darn sure he never intended to touch her, knowing how disastrously that kiss had worked out a couple hours before. But damn. She looked like a waif, standing in the stupid sunlight in the doorway. This city-slick, city-skinny, city-tough scrapper with a pug's stubborn chin. And he reached out, only meaning to connect his hand to her shoulder, because tarnation, it was Christmas. And she seemed alone, like him. And because they'd shared something extraordinary one year ago...and today.

But she whirled around faster than lightning when she felt his fingers on her shoulder. Her face tilted up to his, and there was this Something in her eyes. An awareness. An elemental sexual awareness that seemed to obliterate everything else in the landscape. "We're a crazy pair, aren't we?" she murmured.

"Completely."

"I can't imagine we'd have anything in common.

Something tells me you'd have a heart attack near a mall—''

"You've got that right. And you'd likely get a heart attack if you saw a mouse."

"No heart attack. But I'd shriek loud enough to wake the dead." She chuckled, but then her mouth softened. Not in a smile. But in a soft line that seemed shaped just for him. "We'll find a way to make this right for both of us, Sebastian. That's a promise."

"You've got the same promise from me."

He bent down. Even as he reminded himself that he'd sworn—*sworn*—not to kiss her again, he found his mouth drawn to hers, pulled, compelled as if strings were tugging his lips toward hers...and then on hers. Strangely, it wasn't really a kiss. More like the brushing of his lips to her lips. A promise of some kind, nothing stronger than that, yet desire suddenly ripped through him like a knife tearing through silk.

A few moments later, when she left, when he saw her zooming down the drive in that girl-yellow baby Cabriolet, he felt the air seeping out of his lungs in a long, low gush. He thought my God, that woman was trouble. Bad trouble. Trouble like he couldn't remember any woman being for him.

He had to find a way to sever that strange bond between them before either of them got hurt.

So he would.

Chapter 4

Leaving Spritz in the week between Christmas and New Year's was sacrilege. Heresy. More forbidden than any mortal sin Jessa had ever heard of. Maybe in a big department store, a buyer's job wasn't affected by the holiday madhouse of sales and returns, but in an independent like Spritz, every employee chipped in or was considered a low-down dog.

Jessa had only felt free to ask about taking off early because she never did. Everyone in the store knew she regularly came through when anyone wanted extra time off and Marina, her boss and mentor, immediately gave her permission to leave. Even so, she felt guilty as a thief for sneaking out when the store was swarming with customers…just not so guilty that she changed her mind.

It was important for her to get to the Christmas

House before Sebastian did. The reason she wanted to arrive first was the same reason she'd streaked her blond hair with a bit of green—the same green that matched her holiday-green ankle-length dress. The boots, the eye makeup, the perfume were all, as Jessa saw it, weapons.

When a girl needed defenses, a girl needed defenses.

At three-fifty-five, she was pacing in front of the great room window when she saw Sebastian's truck pull in the drive. One glance at his face through the windshield, and her pulse kicked like a pent-up bronco.

It was a good thing, she mentally snarled to herself, that no one could fall in love this fast, because otherwise Sebastian might have presented a serious problem. Thankfully her mother had taught her—painfully and irrevocably—about what kind of woman risked it all for a tug of hormones. There was no way Jessa would ever choose that road. She remembered her growing up years too well. The bottles. The laughter of strangers in the middle of the night. The morning she'd wakened up to find no one there—no mom, no fake uncles, no nothing. She'd been sixteen. Thirteen bucks in the house, all of it hers. Her mom hadn't left a dime. Or fresh milk.

Jessa tapped her boot, watching Sebastian eye her sacred yellow Cabriolet and then hike toward the door. Typically, he looked like he was fresh from a weeklong mountain climb—hair so long it brushed his collar, worn boots that put a lope in his stride, chin getting a disreputable stubble, jeans so old they hugged his long, muscular thighs. *Okay, so you're cute, buster. You think I care? You think...*

Abruptly she frowned. Her gaze had pounced on him so fast that initially she missed noticing that he wasn't alone. Now, though, the look of the teenage girl who slammed the truck door and stomped after Sebastian made Jessa pause. Possibly there was a reason he was wearing a scowl bigger than Hurricane Arthur on his brow. It was difficult to classify the package he'd brought with him, but in a glance Jessa's first thought was that the girl was a true female hooligan. She was maybe sixteen. Hacked-off red hair had been painted with blue and yellow. Dark kohl circled the eyes. Tattoos ran up her right arm; snake bracelets ran down her left. The pants were so tight they defied walking, and the top was so short that it defied both modesty and risked pneumonia— of course, when one had a navel ring, one *did* feel obligated to show it off—but the afternoon was a gloomy fifty degrees with a blustery wind.

Jessa hustled to open the front door, speculating why he'd brought the girl—but really, she knew. Maybe Sebastian was six feet three inches. Maybe he was brave enough to save a stranger from a burning car. Maybe he'd stand up to do the right thing no matter what.

But Jessa had the definite feeling that he was afraid of her.

And the feeling was mutual.

As chaperons went, though, the redheaded hellion

didn't look too motivated to provide either supervision or moral guidance to two petrified adults. In fact, the squirt looked more prepared to hook from the nearest street corner.

Jessa opened the door, and would have promptly greeted them, but Sebastian was turned toward the girl for that moment.

"You can wander around anywhere you want on the inside," Sebastian told her. "But no going outside. And ask before touching anything, okay?"

"Like who elected you my boss?" The voice dripped sarcasm.

"I figured you'd get a charge out of seeing this place, but if not, you're welcome to sit in the truck. I'll get my business done as soon as I can."

"I'm not sitting in any stupid truck by myself. Besides, I didn't ask to come here. You made me."

"Hopefully next time I won't have to insist that you do anything. But this time—as you already know—I can't trust you alone."

"Like I care what you think of me."

Jessa easily figured out that the teenage horror was one of Sebastian's "kids," and thought it might be a good time to provide a diversion before they strangled each other. "Hi, darling," she said to Sebastian, which certainly made his head whip around. And to the hooligan, she stuck out a hand. "Hi, I'm Jessa Mitchell. What a cool tattoo. I've got one myself, but I'll have to wear something besides a long dress next time to be able to show you."

That popped Sebastian's eyes wide. But the girl's

face was already contorting from a worldly wise sarcastic scowl to the beginnings of a raucous hoot. "Hey, Sebastian. *This* is your friend? Who'd have thought you even knew anyone this cool? I like your hair."

"Thanks. I see you go for a little paint on the tips, too."

"Yeah, when Mr. Repression here isn't having a royal conniption fit. Sheesh. I'm Martha by the way." Martha stuck her hands in her jeans pockets, and emerged with cigarettes. The pack had been crushed more than a little flat. "Want one?"

Sebastian lifted the cigarettes from her hand and ushered them both inside. "Ho-boy," he murmured. "Why did it never occur to me that you two might hit it off?"

"He's not into tattoos," Jessa whispered to Martha. "You should have seen his face when he first saw my eyebrow ring. I thought I was going to have to do artificial resuscitation... I brought a pizza and a six-pack because I knew I was going to miss dinner. If either of you are hungry—"

"You brought beer?" Martha asked quickly.

"Aw, sorry. I meant a six-pack of pop. I was drinking at your age, though," Jessa told her.

Sebastian cleared his throat.

"Did you hear that, Sebastian? Everybody isn't as uptight as you are. God. He has a cow about every little thing."

"Does he? Well...I was on my own when I was sixteen. Nobody to tell me what to do. Nobody to tell me where to go, and what I could eat or drink or anything else."

"You're like, kidding, right? That really sounds fab. Did you run away?"

"No," Jessa said, "actually, my mother ran away from me. Left me with some beer in the fridge, a half loaf of bread, no money and no wheels. I was free, though. And for damn sure, after that, nobody tried telling me what to do. I did exactly what I wanted."

Martha looked as if she were about to make some fast response, but then unexpectedly shut up. She followed Jessa closer than a shadow for more than an hour. Jessa watched her level four pieces of pizza, guzzle two soft drinks and talk nonstop while she galloped around the house exploring. Finally she settled in front of the TV she described as "prehistoric" in the great room.

Sebastian motioned her into the front hall. That was about as far as he dared let Martha out of sight, Jessa figured, but at least it gave them a little privacy to talk. She perched on one of the steps, and Sebastian hunkered on the step just beneath her—where he could keep half an eye on his charge in the other room.

"You got on with her," he whispered disbelievingly.

"I wouldn't say 'got on.' She's about as sweet as a dill pickle. Does she ever say anything nice to anyone?"

"I've only known her for a few weeks—but no, I

haven't heard her say anything nice so far. At least to me."

"And you're stuck with her today—why?"

"Christmas holiday, there are always parents who don't want the kids, and they're stuck being warehoused at the school. Normally Martha wouldn't be my particular problem, except that the couple who runs the school—Jim and Marly—wanted the week off, had family they wanted to see. There's another part-time guy there most of the time, but today I got elected with the baby-sitter job."

"And you like her?" However unlikely that seemed, Jessa had seen the way he watched out for the hooligan. Even when he was talking tough, he was gentle with her. And even when *she* was talking tough, he never lost his patience.

"Right now she's pretty hard to like. But part of what I keep seeing is how hard she works to be horrible." He heaved a sigh. "Her father's brother hit on her for a bunch of years. By the time the abuse finally came out, she was about fifty percent rage and fifty percent bad attitude. Her dad kicked the uncle out of the family, but that was all he did—he didn't prosecute, call the cops, nothing like that."

"So...she feels betrayed?" Jessa probed.

"Hell. She *was* betrayed. And whether the program can work for her long-term, I haven't a clue. We'll have to see. But as far as this afternoon, I just didn't want to leave her alone at the school."

Jessa believed him, but she still thought it was mighty convenient that he'd brought a sidekick today.

The more they talked, the more she felt an unexpected sense of connection with him. She kept getting the wary feeling that he felt it, too.

The hall was suddenly too quiet. The sound of canned laughter from an ancient *I Love Lucy* show occasionally drifted in from the living room TV, but that seemed a mile distant. Neither had turned on a light in the hall, because initially the daylight had been ample, but dark fell early at this time of year. The hall smelled like wax and old lemon oil, and the husky, dusky shadows kept growing, sneaking around them. She couldn't seem to ignore the warm, male scent of him. The look in his eyes. She kept telling herself that they were strangers, but somehow they weren't. And something kept kindling between them that shouldn't have been there…but it was.

It was this house, she thought. This house changed everything. Her life. Her past. Her future. Nothing had been the same since she set foot in the place.

Come to think of it, nothing had been the same since she'd met up with Sebastian Orange Quentin either.

"You had it rough growing up," he said, referring to the chitchat she'd shared with his hooligan.

"Not as bad as Martha. But rough, yeah."

"No wonder you want a home. I don't know if you've come to any more conclusions about this house—"

"I have." She took a breath. "I do love the place, Sebastian. I'm not going to deny it. It'd be a dream to live here. But…"

"But nothing. If that's what you want—"

"But I don't have a 'cause' like you do. I don't need this kind of space for anything. You've got kids who need a home. Kids you care about. And this wonderful place is being wasted."

"No. I don't need it or want it." He galloped right past that whole idea. "I talked to Ryan again. He'd really like to set up a dinner with us tomorrow night. But personally, I think you should go alone. I'll stay out of it. You want the house. I want you to have the house. You and I can work out how to make it happen without anyone else interfering, but I'm guessing you'd like to hear about the history of the place and all—"

"Orange."

There now. Calling him by his old-fashioned middle name was a guaranteed way of getting his attention.

"Read my lips," she said politely. "You're getting the house. Not me."

"You want it. Don't try to deny that."

"I want it more than I can ever remember wanting anything. I love it like I can't remember feeling anything for a place before. But I don't want to see the place wasted, and for one person to live here would be totally wasteful. It works best if you take the house, and that's that." She promptly stood up, determined to cut short any further argument.

"For God's sake. You are the most confounded, stubborn woman—and for no reason. I don't *want* the place. You *do*. This is simple—"

"Yes, it is. It's yours. Period."

"Dammit." He uncoiled from the stairs and reached out, clearly intending to grab her wrist before she could take off on him. Or that's what Jessa assumed he was doing.

She felt his big hands close on her wrist. Felt the tug. Only the tug that mattered came from a pull deep in her belly, not from any hold he had on her wrist, and suddenly he was pulling her close in a different way. His head dipped, and then his mouth soared on hers, sighed on hers, then sank on hers, heavy and thudding warm.

It was like before. The taste of freedom, of letting go. The sound of her heartbeat thrumming in her ears. The thrilling feeling of excitement, anticipation— when damnation, where was all that nice, dependable frigidity when she needed it? And suddenly she had the frantic, petrifying awareness that Sebastian was the reason she couldn't get all that nice, dependable frigidity back. He wasn't anything like the men she'd known. He wasn't like anyone else, and never would be—not for her.

And a kiss that started out in deep water just kept finding more trouble. His arms tightened, his body heated. Her breasts nuzzled against his chest as if they were made to tease him; his erection nuzzled against her belly in a physical mating call older than time. Somewhere, deep inside her, she heard his loneliness. She didn't understand why he was so adamant about not wanting the house—yeah, yeah, she got it, that he felt he had something to atone for related to his parents' death, but she still couldn't get a grasp on the whole problem. The only thing she could seem to get a grasp on was him. She knew all about this kind of loneliness. She knew all about him, from the whisper and whistle of need in the crush of his mouth, the promise of his tongue, the silky way he dove for more kisses.

"Sebastian," she whispered, a question in her voice that she didn't know the words for.

He answered with another kiss, and another. His hands slid up and down her spine, her sides, one palm finally claiming her breast at the same slow-beat heart-soft pace his mouth found the white skin on her throat.

"Sebastian," she said again, trying to think about the house. About Martha. About birth control—or lack thereof. Trying to remind herself that this place had some kind of magic, because she knew she wasn't her normal self around him. Jessa was wary and tough, because she knew what it took to be a survivor...but she didn't want to be tough. For the first time in her adult life, she kept getting the extraordinary sensation that she didn't have to be—with him.

Kisses chained into more kisses. Her hands wrapped around his waist; his hands fisted in her hair. His heart thundered; her heart thrummed. Her nerves seem to pour into his; his need into hers. Yet suddenly she picked up a strange silence that jolted her into at least a semiawareness.

"Orange," she whispered.

Her use of his middle name alerted him. His head

shot up, then around—and there was Martha, stalled in the doorway, arms crossed as she languidly studied them both. "Oh, man, this is more fun to watch than MTV. I had no idea you knew moves like that, Sebastian. I thought you were the most goody-goody, uptight guy in the whole universe. Wait until I get back to school to tell the others."

Sebastian Orange Quentin lifted his head, took in several deep gulps of oxygen and sighed. "Did the two of you wake up today, saying ho-boy, this is a super day to drive Sebastian over the edge?"

Jessa laughed, partly because she loved what he'd done…used humor to diffuse the problematic situation—for the teenager, for her, for them. But it wasn't humor she saw in his eyes, and it wasn't humor she felt. Something kept quickening between them. Sex, yeah. But they were so unalike that you'd think a little chemistry would be easy to handle—especially for her. She'd never let chemistry get the better of her before. Ever.

But either the Christmas House had some kind of rare psychic power—which she didn't believe for a minute. Or there really *was* something different about Sebastian. Possibly, just possibly, this one man had the power to mean something irrevocably different to her. She just wasn't sure if that thought was more exciting…or more frightening.

"Are you sure I can't talk you into a drink, Sebastian?"

"No, thanks." Sebastian smiled at Ryan even as

he lied. The truth was, he'd like four or five double whiskeys. Straight up, and in rapid succession. But since Mr. Fortune wasn't drinking anything alcoholic—and Sebastian figured he needed all the wits about him he could get—he was settling for ice water.

"And how about you, honey? A little Chablis or Merlot? Or would you rather drink something more serious?"

Jessa smiled easily for Mr. Fortune's easy charm, and while the other two were talking, Sebastian tugged—for the fifth time—on his tie. He hadn't worn a tie since the last funeral he'd attended. It had strangled him then, and was strangling him now.

Jessa and Mr. Fortune both looked like they belonged in the ritzy San Antonio restaurant. Jessa was wearing some kind of long, slinky black dress—some might call it conservative, considering that it covered all body parts—but it still tugged and hugged all his favorite ones. The only color in her hair today was blond, no reds or greens. She'd taken the ring out of her eyebrow, her makeup was discrete. Damn woman looked like she belonged in the upper echelons of society and like she needed to be jumped at the same time. But that was assuming Sebastian was noticing her—which he most definitely wasn't. He was doing his best not to look at her at all.

Mr. Fortune, on the other hand, Sebastian was intent on paying attention to.

"I wanted to bring Lily, my wife, but she got caught up in a family thing," Ryan said. "And truthfully, I admit I was just as happy meeting the two of you alone. There were so many things I wanted to say to you the night of the Christmas party, but neither of you could stay long. I should have realized there were too many people… It wasn't going to be that easy to have a quiet conversation. And I do want to tell you both the story of the house.''

The waiter interrupted them. T-bones were ordered for the boys, a Cobb salad for Jessa and a bottle of wine aired on the table even if no one claimed they were going to drink any. The waiter was wearing a monkey suit, in keeping with the formal red carpet/ white tablecloth decor. Sebastian knew which fork was which, and damnation, he was brought up to know how to dress appropriately, too, but who wore a suit to dinner anymore? He'd thought the tie would be enough.

It wasn't, but maybe it was best that they both see him for what kind of a man he really was. An outdoor guy who had no interest in fancy homes or money.

Ryan glanced at him and shook his head. ''Every time I see your face, I remember that dark night in the rain. My legs were trapped. I could smell the gas. Jessa, here, was trying to wrench my shoulders out by their sockets, but I couldn't be budged, and suddenly there was your face. And your asking if anyone minded if you joined the party.''

Sebastian remembered that night, too. At the time he'd thought Ryan was older, not a man just in his fifties. Like a lot of people in this neck of Texas, his coloring was a mix of Spanish and Anglo, but nothing else was common about him. He had to be over six feet, with dark brown hair and dark eyes and skin darkly tanned even at this time of year. He not only looked like the business scion and business patriarch he was, but like hell on wheels to reckon with.

The night of the accident, he'd been different. Vulnerable—the way even a giant would look smaller in a situation where he was the prey. Fear leveled everyone to their lowest common denominator. But Sebastian hadn't realized how sharp and shrewd Ryan was until this face-to-face meeting.

He'd counted on Ryan to be on *his* side. Originally he'd never planned to attend this blasted dinner at all, but then he'd never figured sex was going to be a problem in his life—much less sex with a woman like Jessa. That last embrace was still needling his conscience days later. He'd tried bringing Martha into the situation, believing the presence of the girl would surely kill any hormone or opportunity in a thousand-mile radius. When that hadn't worked, he'd determined that going with her to this dinner was a good idea.

Jessa was going to get that damn house. She wanted it. She valued it. And if he couldn't talk her into it on his own, he'd figured Mr. Fortune for an ally. Fortune would surely take his side when he understood that Sebastian honestly wanted Jessa to have the place.

Only he wasn't getting a chance—so far—to get Ryan on his side.

After the waiter served dinner, Ryan started talking, telling a story, the kind of conversation where neither of them had to respond or participate...and there were times Sebastian felt as if the older man's sharp, clear gaze was boring right into his character. It started when he poured the port for the two of them, but not for himself.

"I told you two why I don't drink wine anymore, didn't I?" he asked them. "About my being poisoned? Someone putting digitalis into my wine, apparently knowing that I traditionally had a glass before dinner every night?"

Yeah, he'd told them that whole story before—and that his near-dying experience was what provoked him into giving them that insane gift of the mansion. But he'd never really mentioned the details, beyond that none of the docs had first believed he had a prayer of surviving.

"The police are still investigating who did it. Unfortunately a man with too much money always makes enemies. That's just life. Anyway, I think you two met Maggie Taylor at the Christmas party—she was the doctor who was determined to save me, come hell or high water. And I believe you also met Nico Tan-efi as well? He never saved my life, but he essentially saved my business and then stood up to protect me when I was so gravely ill."

"You really feel recovered completely now?" Jessa asked him.

"As far as I tell my wife, yes. But I know it'll be a while before I have my strength back completely. The point of my telling you all this, though, was to explain that you four people have a place in my life

that no one else does. Whether you need more family
or not, I think of you as family. My family. Honorary
Fortunes, if you will. I want you to know that you
can turn to me, if you ever need help or advice or
anything else.''

Sebastian watched Jessa's eyes suddenly glisten.
Felt his own tough heart turn over. She came across
as not just a strong woman, but a woman who was
comfortable with her strength and self-reliance…until
family was mentioned, and then her longing for a
home and ties was so clearly revealed.

Mr. Fortune, though, obviously hadn't expected an
answer, because he continued with his story. ''I
wanted to give each of you gifts, but of the four, you
two were by far the most difficult. I easily suspicioned
what Nico would find meaningful. And it was easy to
discover something that Dr. Maggie Taylor wanted.
But you two were something else.''

''I don't—we don't,'' Jessa quickly corrected herself, ''need anything. Sincerely.''

Mr. Fortune smiled, and then just went on as if
she'd said nothing. The massive steak on his plate sat
almost untouched. ''That house isn't about…need. I
won't give you the name of those who used to live
there. It's not relevant. But their story is. There was
a man who had four children, three sons and a daughter. The daughter was the apple of his eye, became
engaged to a good man, fell deeply in love, planned
a wedding. The groom-to-be—her lover—died in an
accident on the way to the ceremony. The daughter
pined so badly that her father thought he was going

to lose her. She wouldn't eat, couldn't sleep, lost all interest in life and became increasingly reclusive. So..."

Mr. Fortune poured more wine for both of them. "So the father bought her that house. A huge house, meant for a family. Way too big for one lone woman. Everyone thought he was being coldhearted, kicking her out of the nest after all she'd been through...but this father was desperate. Something drastic had to be done. So he bought her the house, and he hired a man to live-in as a caretaker—understanding that this was a century ago, when we all weren't so comfortable with the idea of a woman living alone. It wasn't considered safe, then. Or right."

Sebastian caught Mr. Fortune glancing at him, as if assuming he'd understand that, even if Jessa didn't. But then he went on. "The caretaker was, how can I put it? A surly young man. Good-looking, but grumpy, always grumpy. It seems he'd been thrown from a horse a few years before, injured his leg, walked with a limp. He saw it as a weakness, couldn't seem to get over it. Well. He was the worst thing that ever happened to that young woman. She'd try not to eat, he'd dump the food in her lap. She'd try to pine in her bedroom, he'd chop wood and raise a racket outside her window. They fought day and night. Nothing improper about the relationship, mind you, and heaven knew they were of different stations in life. But I'm thinking that father knew what he was doing."

Mr. Fortune motioned to both of them with a fork.

"The caretaker made the daughter so furious that she *had* to climb out of her shell. And the young man was so morose because of his bum leg—yet she wouldn't put up with his self-pity. The bottom line being…"

Jessa jumped in, her voice entranced. She'd clearly already figured out the story. "They got married."

Sebastian blinked. "How'd you guess that?"

"Oh, Orange. It was obvious. And what a wonderful story!"

"Yup, it is." Mr. Fortune dusted off the crumbs from his roll, and folded his napkin. "They had a pack of kids. Not a dozen, but near. Ten, if I recall. Anyway…this all happened years ago, but the point is, I ended up buying the house from the last surviving daughter because she had a problem. She loved the home. Said it would kill her to have to worry about stinkers ever living there, so she wanted me to have it, made me promise I'd make sure that no one lived there who wouldn't treasure a home. Who didn't *need* a home. She wanted people to value it, people who'd understand about love and family and maybe people who'd been lost once upon a time."

"I'm not lost," Jessa said swiftly.

"Neither am I," Sebastian said even more firmly.

"Of course you're not," Mr. Fortune said amiably. "I just thought you might want to hear the history of the house—that it has a whole background of love and caring…and of turning something sad into something special for the people who lived here."

Sebastian cleared his throat. As generous and kind as Mr. Fortune was, this conversation was going to hell in a handbasket. He was getting farther and farther away from his goal—which was getting Jessa in that damn house on her own—and somehow into more hot water instead. "Mr. Fortune, that's a wonderful story...but you don't have to hit me over the head with a frying pan, or Jessa's head either, to get a message across. I hate to be blunt, sir, but if you were trying to play matchmaker—"

"You mean, because the original couple got together?"

Mr. Fortune suddenly roared laughter, although to Sebastian's ears it sounded fake and contrived. Not like the real sound of his laughter at all. But then Jessa nailed his instep with a high heel, obviously trying to communicate that she wanted him to shut up. When his lips parted to say something anyway, her hand swept under the table and clutched his thigh. High on his thigh. Very high. Which was enough to shut him up instantly, just like she wanted, and Mr. Fortune was free to keep on talking.

"No, no, you two. Gee, that's funny—that I could possibly play a matchmaker in anyone's life. But this is a different generation, for heaven's sakes. I only had one house to give away...at least only one house that was a *special* house. And when I realized that neither of you had a regular home or family...well, it just seemed to me that you could work something out. It's not like it was 100 years ago, when people had a stroke if an unmarried man and woman lived together. Just being under the same roof doesn't put either of you under any obligation, now does it?"

"No, of course not," Jessa agreed warmly, and then kicked Sebastian under the table as if his accusing Mr. Fortune of being a matchmaker was a terrible insult.

"You're both adults," Mr. Fortune said.

"Of course we are," Jessa said again.

"And it's a huge place. You two could probably live under the same roof for months and not even run into each other." Again Mr. Fortune smiled. "Unless you wanted to, of course."

Sebastian wanted to put his head in his hands. All this time he'd thought of Ryan Fortune as a shrewd, smart business mogul—but definitely as a good man. Who'd have guessed he was such a wily old coot? And Jessa was buying into his patter hook, line and sinker.

Obviously he couldn't count on Fortune to be his ally. There had to be some way to get Jessa to take the house. And some way he could be sure of keeping his hands off her.

Chapter 5

Mr. Fortune left the restaurant ahead of them. Jessa kissed his cheek and gave him a warm hug, not letting on that she was the least upset until his taillights were bouncing out of the parking lot.

Then, though, she turned a full-voltage scowl on Sebastian. Finally they were alone—give or take the two dozen cars in the parking lot, and the holiday lights winking bright through the whole city of San Antonio. New Year's was only a few days away now. Even thought the night sky was gloomy with bunched clouds and starting to spit rain, the holiday spirit had infested the city. Sebastian was hiking toward their two vehicles, trying to act like he didn't have a care in the world. At least until he realized she was shooting him furious looks.

"What's wrong?"

"What's wrong?!" She raised her eyes to the sky, as if begging for patience. Men! He'd been adorable through dinner. She'd been charmed by his putting on a tie with the jeans, his brushed-back hair, the sexy scent of aftershave. He'd obviously made an effort— considering they were talking Sebastian—and it showed. She'd have jumped him if she'd been the kind of woman to jump a man. Much more upsetting was that she couldn't seem to shake the dreadful feeling that she was catapulting in love with him—deep, hard and fast.

But none of that excused his dreadful behavior.

She gestured. "I can't *believe* you would be so mean to Mr. Fortune after all he's tried to do for us!"

"Mean? Huh? What are you talking about?" Sebastian looked startled.

"Come on, Orange! You all but accused him of matchmaking!"

A streetlamp gleamed on his glossy brown hair when he suddenly turned to her, a wry expression on his face. "Jessa, he *was* matchmaking. You don't think it's an accident that he was talking about the two of us living in the house together, do you?"

"Of course not. It was obvious what he was hinting at. He thinks that if we spend time together, we'll get together. The two adult orphans. Finding each other. How romantic."

Sebastian looked even more confused. "So I just told him the truth. That it wasn't going to work for us. What, you wanted me to lie, just let it go?"

"I certainly did! For heaven's sakes, Sebastian! He

was trying to do something nice. Surely it wouldn't have hurt anything to cater to him, would it?''

"Cater to him?" Sebastian asked blankly.

She threw up her hands. "So the idea of becoming a couple is dippy. You think I don't know that? But what's the big deal? You could have smiled at him. Chuckled. Let him think we're at least considering it. What harm would it have done to just play along for his sake?"

"Dippy," he echoed, as if he hadn't heard anything beyond that first comment from her.

By then she'd reached her car, and started fumbling in her purse for the car key. Naturally she'd worn her black Gucci bag, to match her black dinner dress. And she loved the bag, but it *was* the kind of purse where everything sank to the bottom in a puddle. It was even harder to find the key because she couldn't keep her mind on the problem. She kept sneaking peeks at Sebastian's face. There was an odd expression in his eyes. One of those *male* expressions, where you just knew anything you said was going to be taken wrong. "What, you don't think the idea of the two of us making a couple is a little dippy—if not completely off the wall?"

"Actually, I think the idea of the two of us making a couple is downright ridiculous."

She bristled. Never mind if she'd just said the same thing. Never mind if rain suddenly startled to drizzle down. Never mind if the drip-drip-plop bounced off her nose, her shoulder, her eyelashes, and the night temperature suddenly turned chill. Sebastian looked

no more ready to go home than she did. He leaned
against his truck; she leaned against her car, as if both
of them would rather argue—even fight—than sepa-
rate and go home to their empty places. "I suppose,"
she said, "that just because I have a tattoo and an
eyebrow ring, you think we're too opposite to make
it together."

"It has nothing to do with the ring in your eyebrow. Hell, I've gotten used to that. It's a little confounding, but I've started to think of it as damn cute."
It would have been a compliment, except that he was
glaring at her.

She glared at him right back. "Oh, I get it. We just
come from completely different backgrounds, right?
You came from money. I didn't. You had a fancy
education. I don't."

He cocked a leg forward. "Jessa, that kind of thing
doesn't make a lick of difference to me, never has,
never would."

"Well, then, why *do* you think the idea of us as a
couple is so loony? We're both orphans. Both alone.
Mr. Fortune seemed positive that our meeting at all
had to be some kind of karma—that there had to be
a *reason* why only two people in the entire city of
San Antonio stopped the night he had that accident.
Just you and me. Only you and me. Naturally, Sebastian, I wouldn't marry you if you were the last
man on earth."

"No?"

"Good grief. No. With your taste in clothes?" She
shuddered delicately. "But that's not to say we don't

have a ton of things in common. On the surface, of
course we're completely different. But underneath is
a different story. You've got a chip on your shoulder.''

"The hell I do.''

God. Men. "You reach out to kids, but not to
someone who could be there for you in the night. No
different than me. I've got defenses ten-feet tall when
a man gets too close. You've got the same Keep Off
signs. We're both carrying sores from when we lost
our parents. Both of us are afraid of caring too much
again. Of losing someone who could matter so much
that it could rip up our world, like the last time.''

"Where do you get all this psychoanalysis? I climb
mountains. Skydive. Take on kids no one wants. Risk
it all with everything I do, hold back nothing. You
think that sounds like a guy who's afraid?''

She should have known better than to use the
"afraid" word. Most men were allergic to it, and Sebastian, she could see, reacted even stronger than
most. Oh, God, he *was* afraid. Of losing, just like she
was. Of depending on anyone else, just like she was.
Of needing. Anyone. Ever. "It's not a crime to be
afraid," she said, more gently now. "I was just trying
to suggest that appearances can be deceiving. That we
really are alike in some ways—''

"Well, I'll tell you one thing we have in common," he muttered.

"What?''

"We're both too damn dumb to get out of the
rain." He still sounded mad when he reached for her.

She knew he was going to kiss her. Knew that was really why they'd stood there in the dark parking lot—picking an argument about nothing. Arguing just for an excuse to be together for another few minutes. Arguing because bickering should have kept them from touching each other again...only somehow it didn't work.

Before his arms had even wrapped around her, she was tilting her face toward his. Before his mouth had a chance to slam down, hers was slamming up. And there it was. That extraordinary heat again. That sense of connection she'd never felt for any man before.

Lips met, clung, molded to each other. His took on her shape. Hers took on his.

Somewhere a siren went off. A car door slammed. Two women chattered, high heels clacking past them in the parking lot as they ran through the rain...and yeah, that drizzling rain had started sluicing down now. Colder. Sharper. A clap of thunder rumbled in the distance, loud enough to make both of them snap out of this ridiculous spell.

Yet she couldn't seem to snap out of it. And Sebastian wasn't even trying. His body gave off more heat than a glowing radiator. His hands kept moving, as if he couldn't stop touching her, couldn't get enough. Those soft, deep kisses kidnapped her emotions like nothing else could have. It wasn't loneliness he gave off, but loneliness for her. Need, specifically for her. He stroked and clutched and kneaded as if every part of her were precious, as if he feared she'd disappear if he didn't hold on tight.

Get a grip, her mind kept scolding, but her heart was wildly singing arias. Wearing heels, she was tall enough to walk right into his body, snug against him, rub against him. Even though some of these terrorizing sensations were familiar now, she still had a hard time believing this could be real. Her frigidity was disintegrating in front of her eyes. The coldness she'd been so sure was part of her character, the toughness she'd valued in herself, was disappearing faster than smoke.

Her breasts suddenly ached. The cold rain slivering into her hair, starting to soak her through, yet suddenly felt like an enticing contrast to the wet, hot silk of his mouth. She wanted more. She wanted him. Now, here, anywhere, any way. It was horrible. The damn man was turning her into a shivery, shaky mess, and she didn't appreciate it.

When he suddenly pulled back, though, looking shell-shocked and vulnerable…or as vulnerable as Sebastian was ever likely to look… She saw the harsh self-discipline in his face and wanted to punch him. "Dammit, Sebastian, don't you ever do this again unless you intend to follow through!"

His jaw dropped. "*Me?* You started it."

"I did not!" At that precise second, truth to tell, she couldn't remember who had started what. Nor could she care. What Jessa did know, though, was that this really, really couldn't keep happening. Something was at risk here that had never been at risk for her before. It wasn't a joke or anything she could take lightly. She felt the lick of fear, real fear. Nothing could have cooled her desire more quickly. She lifted her chin. "We need to settle the problem of the house—and this time I mean it," she said seriously.

"I agree completely, but like I keep telling, there *is* no problem. The house is yours. Cut and dried."

"The heck it is! It's *ours* until or unless we figure out something else to do with it." She thought, fast and furiously. "Look, I'll meet you at the house again tomorrow night. The soonest I can get free tomorrow is eight. On a mid-holiday Saturday, it's just too busy at the store for me to break away earlier."

"All right."

But she wasn't through. That lick of fear was still lapping at her nerves from the inside out. "Sebastian, I don't care what Mr. Fortune tried to fix up for us. I don't care if we have enough funding to run the place for a whole year. I want this decision over with. Whatever we're going to do. Before the New Year."

"Yeah, I agree one hundred percent. I hate stuff hanging over me. Eight o'clock, tomorrow night then."

Sebastian slammed the truck door, then watched as his two sidekicks pelted out of the passenger side. This wasn't precisely how two teenage boys ideally wanted to spend a Saturday night, but it was better than jail, which is where Juan and Paulo had been trying their best to end up before he'd caught up with them.

The two had slicked-back hair, a matched swagger

and an identical smirk. "Hey, cool place," Juan said. "Good place to party."

"Now, you know Sebastian don' party," Paulo told his brother. "He never step off the curb. He wan' us to be like saints, perfect all the time, even on a Saturday night." He shot his brother a sideways glance. "You wanna a little weed before we go in, give Sebastian his one thrill for the night?"

"Very funny." Sebastian cuffed both boys as he led them up the walk.

When Jessa opened the door, his sidekicks were standing in front of him like guard dogs. She glanced at the boys, but her face took on the oddest expression—as if she'd been expecting him to bring extra people, when obviously she couldn't have been. And man, if she'd worked all day in that getup, Sebastian figured she needed a serious bodyguard. She was wearing yellow instead of holiday colors. Pale yellow, like the first hint of dawn, a long silky tunic and slacks, with a collar of gold around her neck and earrings that dripped almost to her shoulders.

Paulo and Juan wolf-whistled simultaneously.

Jessa winked at them, but then focused all her attention on him, looking him over head to toe, from the chamois shirt to the gruff-edged jeans to the scrabby boots. It's not like he hadn't prepared for this meeting. He'd brought the best new-age weapons in anyone's arsenal—two teenage boys. And chosen to wear derelict-type clothes, believing she was likely to be turned off.

Something had to work. He hadn't forgotten that

clinch in the restaurant parking lot and didn't intend to. The whole argument between them had been crazy. First she'd argued that the two of them couldn't possibly make a couple; then she'd turned around and acted hurt when he'd agreed with her. First he'd been concentrating on making her see reason, and then he'd turned around and grabbed her in the middle of the dad-blasted rain and kissed her like there was no tomorrow.

God knew what was wrong with either of them, but this insanity had to stop. His spine steeled as he strode forward, still hawking the boys ahead of him. "Juan and Paulo," he introduced them, "this is Jessamine Mitchell. Ms. Mitchell. Boys, once you've said hello, you're welcome to explore inside the house."

"Hey, Ms. Mitchell." Both boys respectfully shook hands, their manner so angelic that Sebastian was tempted to roll his eyes. Jessa even managed to get a couple decent lines of conversation out of them—before they pelted inside at lightning speeds and disappeared from sight.

"I can't leave them alone for long. They'll have the place turned into a tornado in fifteen minutes, tops, unless they're supervised," he said frankly.

"Yeah, they have that look." She glanced at them again, seeming to note the ultracool pants that hung so low they showed off underwear, the bad-news eyes, the basketball shoes that cost more than a month's rent, the swaggers. Whatever most people might conclude about kids decked out with that much attitude, Jessa studied them with more interested than critical eyes. When she looked back at him, though, there was the critical edge. "I could have sworn we only agreed to meet again to be able to talk seriously."

"We did."

"Yet you brought more sidekicks with you this time? Double trouble? You honestly think we'll be able to talk with them around?"

"I brought 'em for two reasons." He closed the door, shook off his jacket, clomped in. "The first one is obvious. I'm having trouble keeping my hands off you, which you already know."

Her eyes shot immediately to his. Maybe he should have guessed that the truth was always the way to get to Jessa. She wasn't worried about being embarrassed. She'd rather face the alligators under the bed than pretend they weren't there. "It seems that I'm having that same problem," she admitted.

He didn't want to hear that. It was one thing for him to have trouble with his own hormones, another to know that she was warm and willing. Worse yet, when he ambled into the great room, he saw immediately how much effort she'd gone to. She'd brought in logs, started a fire on her own in the fieldstone hearth. Drapes were drawn, lamps lit. Two glasses and an expensive bottle of fine aged whiskey were set up on a tray. She wasn't playing hostess, Sebastian suspected, so much as playing house. He was trying *not* to care, trying not to let that strange bond between them keep growing, but the look of everything tugged at him, because all the little details seemed to shout how much she'd fallen for this place, how much she wanted to live here.

"Sebastian?" She poured two short glasses, and edged one toward him. "You said there were two reasons that you brought the boys—so what's the second reason?"

"Their situation's like Martha's. They have no place to go over the holidays—although in the case of the boys, their parents are in South America. Didn't come home, and haven't come home to see them in more than two years now. They're always sending the boys money. In fact, they have no limit on 'stuff'— expensive haircuts, expensive clothes and sports equipment, high-end electronic goodies, all that kind of thing. But there's no one in their lives who gives a damn."

He glanced up when he heard a ka-thud from upstairs, but he wasn't particularly alarmed. It sounded as if a chair had fallen over, but he could hear the echo of the boys yelling at each other. If they were in trouble—or looking for trouble—they'd either be whispering or dead quiet. When he looked back at Jessa, though, she was intently studying his face, as if she'd barely noticed the commotion upstairs. She wasn't touching the glass in her hand either.

"I've seen you several times with a glass of something alcohol, but I can't seem to catch you taking a drink," he remarked.

She swirled the gold liquid for a moment. The color matched the swirls of gold in her short, choppy hair.

"If I were into drinking, this'd be my choice. I love the taste of it," she said frankly.

"But?" He heard the unspoken hesitation in her voice.

"But my mom could drink like a sailor. And did. I never knew who my father was, so it's impossible to know what his personal demons were. But my mom's problems with the bottle were enough to make me scared of alcohol, except for an occasional glass of wine just to be sociable—like when we were out to dinner with Mr. Fortune. I worry about it, though. Just in case the problem's catching. Who really knows? Maybe it's like cooties."

By teasing, she made the subject easier, but he saw the pride in her eyes, realized that it took courage for her to admit a problem aloud. At least to him. "Yet you still bought the whiskey. Still poured it."

She nodded. "Because I thought you'd like it. Because I thought we might talk more easily if at least one of us could be more relaxed. And because I'm afraid of the click between us, too. And because of that click—I just want to be sure not to lie to you. About who I am or where I've been."

"You think I'd be turned off if there was alcoholism in your background?"

"I think—if you have a brain—you'll add it up. A woman with a no-account background. No education. Some worrisome addictions in the gene pool. Nobody you'd want to be involved with."

"Well now, if we're counting sins, I've probably got you way beat. Truthfully, though, the only kind of background that ever mattered to me was character. And it's not like you can get that through a set of genes.'' Sebastian had already tried to concentrate on the contrary sides to her. It didn't work worth beans. He couldn't stop noticing her character. The guts. The honesty. The courage. The kind of woman who'd pulled herself out of a hellish childhood and made it, alone, because she had grit on the inside. "You're exactly the reason I work with my delinquents."

"Huh?"

"Some of the kids have the potential for character. Some don't. Some have no conscience and it's probably too late to build one in…but some, hell, it's in there. The good side. The fierceness of wanting to make something of their lives, just not knowing how, never having a chance."

"Don't you give me a compliment, big guy, or I'll have to smack you. For God's sakes, get a hint here. We've got to try harder to dislike each other."

He never meant to laugh, but damnation, it was funny. Both of them trying to dislike each other. Needing to dislike each other. Hoping they could dislike each other—only blast it, the more they both tried, the more he felt drawn to her.

As if sensing they were both veering toward trouble again, Jessa shifted forward. "Okay now. We've got limited time, so are you ready to talk about the house?"

"You bet."

"Fine. Because I've thought this all through—

again—and keep coming up with the same conclusion. You're taking the place. For your kids.''

The suggestion didn't even raise his blood pressure this time. He took a sip of the nice, devil-smooth, tongue-scalding whiskey and smiled. ''That's nuts.''

She leaned forward, as if intently concentrating as she marshaled her arguments, but that specific posture offered him a view of cleavage. The blouse gapped, revealing no bra, a whisper of scent, and two soft, small rounded bumps—with a white heart on one. The infamous tattoo. A white heart—for a pure heart, he thought. And that damn tattoo wasn't much bigger than her nipple, but it was big enough to distract him. Which, he suspected, she knew perfectly well. It was why she'd worn the blouse and chosen to forget the bra.

And it was one hundred percent effective. He damn near missed what she was saying altogether. ''Come on, Orange. Just think about it. You mentioned several times that your school and wilderness program don't have enough space for the kids you've got— much less enough space to take on more. And that there are more kids who really need the kind of services you're providing.''

Sebastian stayed cool. ''Jessa, your offer is nice. But my job primarily involves working with the kids outside, in a total wilderness program. It has nothing to do with a fancy-dancy place like this. The teenagers I work with are wild. They'd rip up a place like this at the speed of sound. Destroy it.''

She glanced around, but her eyes zoomed back on

his faster than ants on jam at a picnic. "I think this house looks sturdy enough to take a little wear and tear. Maybe you'd want to store the white rugs, buy some plastic glasses, do some practical things like that. But that wilderness program obviously is only part of what you do. You said it yourself—too many kids need a place. Have no one. And I notice you're part of the baby-sitting/parenting time when there's no one else to fill in."

Okay. She was starting to get to him. So he leaned forward, and knocked back a little more of that whiskey. "Jessa, you can't just 'house' kids anywhere you want to. There are ordinances, rules, zoning laws. I haven't specifically checked in this area, but all you have to do is look around the neighborhood to know it has to be zoned for single-family dwellings. It's a posh area."

"Oh." She looked like he'd hit her. "I hadn't thought of that."

"Trust me. It can't be done."

With her heart in her eyes, she looked at him straight again. "All right. I hear you. But if there's a way to get zoning permission, the house and property would be so much better used by you than me. You love these kids. You need the space. You have a cause, something that's important to you. I just have me." When he started to interrupt, she motioned exuberantly around the room. "This place needs bodies. Children. Noise. Messes."

With his heart in his eyes, he looked straight back at her. "Yeah, it does. But you can do all of that.

Start out with the house, find a guy, get married. Then you start making those kids, and they make the noise. Same result, only you end up with a home you're nuts for. It'll just take you a little time to make it all come together.''

For a moment she fell silent, like an army regrouping its forces, but then she hunched forward with a determined gleam in her eye this time. A mean gleam. "I've been thinking about this," she said quietly. "There has to be a reason you won't even consider taking the house. It's about losing your parents, isn't it? You think—you don't deserve a home. You live in a trailer because of that. Because of guilt. You're still trying to find some way to make it up to them, somehow, someway, for being a disappointment to them.''

"That's ridiculous," he snapped. A thundering crash echoed from the upstairs. "Juan! Paulo! Get your rumps down here!" He yelled, but he didn't even glance up, couldn't seem to take his eyes off her face.

"If it's so ridiculous, then deny it.''

"You don't know me, Jessamine Mitchell." He lurched to his feet, too restless and angry to stay still any longer.

She stood up, too, but apparently only to go toe-to-toe with him, arms wrapped under her chest, chin cocked at him like a weapon. "Oh, but I do, Orange. I haven't known you long. But I feel like I've known you my whole life. I know your loneliness. I know your pride. I know that you're the kind of person to stand up, no matter what the risk or what the cost—because I'm just that ornery myself. Sometimes, I think I'm past it. But sometimes, I think I'm still trying to make up for the things I wish I hadn't seen and known as a child.''

Like he needed this? Sebastian had long known that there was no talking to a woman who thought she knew everything. And he wasn't used to anyone scraping that close to the bone—even if she was wrong. Dead wrong. So wrong that if he'd stood there one more second, he'd either have grabbed her and kissed her...or grabbed and kissed her.

He pivoted toward the door, only to see his two favorite delinquents hovering in the doorway, listening to every word, silent like they'd never been silent since the first day he knew them. They could *always* be counted on to make no end of trouble. ''What the hell was the noise up there?'' he demanded.

''Paulo,'' Juan answered happily. ''He's so clumsy, he tripped on his own feet, fell on his butt. We didn't hurt nothin', Sebastian. We were just chasing around. You two can still talk. We won't get in your way. We'll be real quiet. Honest.''

''Ms. Mitchell and I are through talking. Head for the truck.'' The boys did. And he did. But Jessa, being the confounding kind of woman she was, strode right out the doorway with them, talking to the boys ten for a dozen—as if she hadn't riled him up one side and down the other. As if their argument hadn't bothered her in the least. The moonlight glowed on her smile, on the slinky smooth fabric of her tunic and slacks, in her eyes.

But once the boys were installed in the truck with the door closed, she hiked over to the driver's side, starting to shiver in the chill night, but still looking as if she were in no hurry. "We still haven't settled anything, big guy."

"Oh, yes, we have." Sebastian had tried reasoning with her. She was one of those women where logic and reason didn't work, so now he had no choice but to get tough. "You're getting the house. Period. It's all yours. And I don't want to hear another word about it."

"Wrong." She smiled at him, brilliantly, with that sexy pouty mouth. "I will tell you what I want, though."

"What?" God. She was so stubborn she could make any man lose his mind. And be thankful when it was finally gone.

"We both said that we'd like this resolved before the New Year. So...I won't step foot in this place as of January first. But I would like to spend the night here on New Year's Eve."

"You mean you want to have a party?" He didn't object; he just wasn't clear exactly what she was asking.

"No. To tell the truth, I don't like that holiday. Never have. I love to party, but New Year's Eve has always been a night I spend alone. And I'm not living here, Sebastian—you can take that to the bank— but..." Finally her voice faltered. Just a little. "But

I would like to spend one night in the house. If you don't mind."

The only thing he *minded* was seeing her eyes torn up when she looked back at the place. Knowing she loved it. Feeling how much she loved it. Yet what the hell was he supposed to do to make the damn woman *take* the place?

"That's fine," he said, and thought maybe, just maybe, this might work. If she spent a night alone in the house, she might fall even harder for the place, and that might help convince her to live here.

On the way back to the school, his two sidekicks were quieter than church mice, never looked at him, never kicked, never turned up the radio to eardrum blasting volumes. Nothing. "What's wrong with you two?" he asked finally.

"Nothing," Juan said.

But Paulo, as always, had to contribute his two cents. "We think your lady friend's pretty cool. And that you're an idiot. What you fighting with her for?"

"Yeah," Juan chimed in. "You get someone who cares, you be nice to them. You don't fight. We thought you were a smart man, Sebastian. Now, we got our doubts."

Aw hell. When the delinquents started doubting him, Sebastian figured he was in major trouble. Particularly when he was starting to doubt himself. Here, he was thirty-four years old, and he couldn't remember being this confused. Or this despairing. All over a two-million dollar gift.

And the wrong woman.

Chapter 6

Jessa closed up the store on New Year's Eve. All the other employees had been hot to leave early, yet someone always had to stay late because customers invariably straggled in all day. She never minded staying on the holiday eve before, or tonight either. But by the time she got on the road, blustery clouds were scuttling across the sky, blocking the sunset, bringing the darkness in early, and drunks were already weaving on the road.

When she finally pulled in the driveway of the Christmas house, she could have sworn she was whip-tired—yet one look at the place energized her heart all over again.

God, she loved it. Like she'd never loved anything. Like she'd never craved any material thing before either. But her heart just couldn't deny that this house had magic for her, symbolized what a home was and could be, in a way she'd yearned for all her life.

She stepped in, locked the door, then promptly shed her coat, her heels and her panty hose right there in the foyer. Who was to know? Who was to care? She was giving the place to Sebastian. But it was hers tonight, and she fully intended to savor every second.

Within minutes she'd peeled off her red work suit, donned a threadbare sweatshirt and leggings—comfort clothes—and then got to work. She'd carried in a stash of groceries for the night. The stash included caviar, because she'd never tasted it before—and because she wasn't sure she'd like it, she'd also brought the makings for S'Mores and Snickerdoodles. The back seat of her VW had more goodies, a box of candles and bath salts, and then her giant red, down comforter—Jessa may have never had a sleepover as a girl, but she didn't need a rule book to know the essentials. She didn't need others around her either. She never had. Ever.

As she ambled around the house, she could hear the wind picking up outside, starting to creak and moan through the cracks. She loved the sounds. Somehow she'd always been sure that a real home made sounds like that. An old home. The kind of home that had a history of love and families and kids and babies. She didn't do anything important, just touched things, smelled, savored, explored.

And then she carried a plate of fresh Snickerdoodles up to the bathroom off the master bedroom. Lit the orange and cinnamon candles. Turned the faucets on full blast hot. Dumped in the vanilla bath salts. As she stripped down, she thought she heard the rumble of thunder in the far distance, but she wasn't afraid of storms. If anything, the idea of a big, growly rainstorm only made her feel more protected—this house was just hugely safer than any she'd ever lived in before.

Moments later she sank blissfully into the oversized, black marble tub, and leaned her neck back against the cool rim. A decadent plate of cookies was located within an arm's reach, and the room was softly lit by a dozen of the warm, scented candles.

In the midst of all that lolling, lazy decadence, she could feel tears suddenly burning behind her closed eyes.

She could have this house. She knew that. She could have her dream, have the home she'd yearned for her whole life. Ryan Fortune had seen into her heart, had somehow figured out her one vulnerability, and if he couldn't give her family, he'd given the symbol of it. Nothing was keeping her from living here, staying here. Certainly Sebastian had argued over and over for her to take it.

Another grumble of thunder echoed from the outside, still not close, not frightening, but loud enough to make her open her eyes. She stared at the little licks of candle flames, felt the warmth of silky water on her skin, smelled the soothing vanilla perfume—and chomped down on a Snickerdoodle for a good measure.

To a stranger, she had to look like a pampered,

spoiled rich bitch. But on the inside, she could feel
the steel in her own spine. Yeah, she'd have this
night. And enjoy it to the fullest. But she'd only sur-
vived a nasty, rotten childhood by finding a single
guiding principle that had worked to sustain her.

You did what was right. If you had a choice—no
matter what the cost—you did what was right.

Heaven knew, no one in her growing up years had
ever shown any character. Her father had split, the
instant he'd discovered he'd gotten a girl pregnant.
Her mom had been sweet and loving, when she got
around to it, but irresponsibility and impulsiveness
had made it somehow easy for her to walk away from
a half-grown daughter.

Jessa never said the word "sacrifice." It wasn't a
word that went along with her image. She didn't want
anyone thinking she was a goody-goody type, besides. But it was still that secret principle that had
enabled her to work herself up the ladder to a buyer
position in a sleek, expensive store—a position she
should never have been able to aspire to with her
nominal education. It was the reason she'd stopped to
save a man in an accident when no one else did. It
was what made it possible for her to survive on the
streets before she was seventeen.

And it was the reason she had to give Sebastian
this house.

He needed it—more than she did. He wanted it—
more than she did. And maybe it would hurt, but she
could survive without it. But now she knew Sebastian.
Knew him, had kissed him, had felt the overwhelming

love built into the man from his scuffed boots on up to those gorgeous, sad hazel eyes. She'd seen the way he looked at those delinquent teenagers, how he was with them.

Her refusing to live in the house was the only way to force Sebastian to take it. And giving the house to Sebastian was the only right thing to do.

It was a matter of loving him.

And falling in love with him already hurt. But loving him was still the rightest thing that had ever happened to her.

Jessa leaned forward to switch on just a little more hot water…just as a sudden giant clap of thunder shook the whole house. In the next blink, silver cracks of lightning illuminated the whole window, looking like tinsel ribbons celebrating the New Year. And then abruptly, the house lost power and went completely black.

Sebastian slammed his boot on the truck's accelerator. Few people were on the road at 11:00 p.m. on New Year's Eve except for drunk drivers like the jerk in front of him. The dimwit was weaving all over the road. Quickly, carefully, he passed the drunk, and finally had the highway to himself again—alone, except for the increasingly wild storm. The wind was screaming nonstop, and a scissor-slashing rain was challenging the cranky windshield wipers to keep up.

For years now, he'd spent New Year's Eve with his delinquents—whatever batch of current delinquents were at the school. Tonight, though, the weather had cancelled any hope for outside activities, and Sebastian had figured he was in for a long, long night keeping his monsters occupied.

He wouldn't have minded. In fact he didn't mind— until the storm got bad.

And he kept thinking about Jessa in that house alone. She could take care of herself, he never doubted, in city situations. She wasn't dumb, would never walk down an alley in the dark, park without locking her door; she had a wariness around the wrong kind of guy that'd put her in good stead, too. Still, she was unquestionably a city woman used to solving problems in city ways—like yelling for the nearest neighbor, or being able to dial 911. Those choices didn't apply on a country estate where there were no neighbors and the power was down.

He wouldn't stay long, Sebastian promised himself for the fortieth time. Maybe the fiftieth. That he was checking on her at all was stupid. He realized that. It was just a bad storm. There was no reason to think she was in trouble or stranded.

The problem, for Sebastian, was that ever since his parents died, his life had drastically changed. When you lost everything that mattered, you had to find something to hold on to. The despair he'd felt had damn near swallowed him up until he'd found that something. For him it was a principle. He couldn't make things right with his mother and father; that option was gone.

But…a man could resolve to do the right thing, no matter what the cost to himself. When the chips went down, everybody still made mistakes sometimes, but at least you could hold up your head, if you'd never ducked from doing your best. Even if it looked stupid to others. Even if the damn woman could take care of herself and was probably going to be annoyed at the interruption.

He wasn't going to stay.

And for damn sure, he wasn't going to touch her.

He just wanted to make absolutely sure she was okay, and then he was out of there. Out of her sight, out of her way, and with any luck, back in his Winnebago in time to bring in the New Year solo.

The rain sluiced down in a sudden thick, slicing torrent, so bad he almost pulled over. Visibility was almost zero. The road was a river, the night a smudgy blur of water. Jaw set tight, gaze grim, he turned off the highway. He'd be there in five more minutes…at the house that had been nothing but trouble for him from the moment he laid eyes on it.

And the woman who continued to trip him into taking risks from the instant he'd laid eyes on her.

Holding a toothbrush as if it were a microphone, Jessa reached for a towel to rub her hair dry at the same time she belted out at the top of her lungs, "Cry me a river…cry me a river…I cried a river over y…"

She stopped abruptly, exasperated with herself. She rarely sang, primarily because she didn't like to scare children and small animals with a voice that could scratch a mirror, but the house was hers alone tonight, so she could surely do whatever on earth she wanted to, right? The problem, though, was that she kept coming up with songs that were about rain for the obvious reason—outside, the real live storm was raging like her personal drum band. The candles flickered every time another boomer hit. She could towel-dry her hair in three seconds flat, certainly didn't need the electricity from a hair dryer, but at the moment she could neither see nor remember where she'd put her sweats. The power had only been off for a few minutes, but already a little chill was starting to seep into the house. Of course she could quit standing around naked and get a move on, but this singing thing had gotten ahold of her now.

She really didn't care about the storm. It was a nuisance to be without light, but surely the juice would be fixed in a matter of hours. In the meantime, she had the candles, her Snickerdoodles, and somewhere reasonably close, she'd stashed her down comforter and a sack of clothes. If this were her last and only night in this heart-touching home, she was going to relish every single second of it.

As she folded the towel, she caught her candlelit reflection in the foggy mirror, which gave her new inspiration to ham up another rock song—with the help of her trusty toothbrush-mike. She had it now. A true rock-and-roll blues song, suited perfectly to her flat voice. If there were any mice in the house, this should send them running and fast. "Someone left the cake out in the rain! I don't think that I can take it! 'Cause it took so long to make it..."

From nowhere a giant shadow loomed in the doorway, big as a bear, and panting like a horse who'd galloped four miles at Olympic speeds. Jessa smelled wet leather and man and promptly screamed at the top of her lungs—for a millisecond. That was all it took for her vocal cords to catch up with her brain.

She knew that man smell. Knew those eyes, even if it was practically darker than pitch in the candlelit bathroom. Her hand slammed on her chest—until she realized that nothing happened to be covering her chest except for that bare hand. Swiftly she yanked the damp towel off the rack. "Hot spit, you scared the life out of me! For God's sake, Sebastian!!"

"I'm sorry. Really sorry." Sebastian's voice came out in jolty lumps because he was so clearly out of breath—apparently from running up the stairs. "But I was worried about you because of the storm. Saw your car outside. But then no one answered when I knocked, so I used my key, and then I heard you screaming—"

"I was Singing. Not Screaming, Sebastian Orange Quentin."

"Oh. Who'd have guessed—? No, sorry, really sorry, I didn't mean that." He raised two hands in the air in the universal gesture of peace, but the son of a sea dog was clearly struggling not to laugh as he backed out of the bathroom.

She kicked the door closed—but not hard enough, apparently, for it to firmly latch. From the hall, she heard him clearly say, "Just so you know, honey—I never saw anything."

"Don't go there. I'm warning you."

"Okay, okay." Silence. For all of two seconds. Then, "I'm not going to admit I saw that white heart—now or at any other time. But I just have to say, it really shocked me. Somehow I expected a wild tattoo. A big dragon or some militant women's lib symbol, something like that. I never guessed you'd pick a delicate, romantic little heart—"

"That's it. You're dead." Okay. She wasn't dressed, but it was plenty dark, and the towel was knotted tight enough under her breasts. She stomped out with a fist prepared to slug him.

Something stopped her. Certainly not guilt at the idea of whacking him upside the head. He'd deserved it for scaring the wits out of her, and even more for looking her over up and down in that way he had...that way of making her feel wanted. Desired. Needed, as if he had to brace himself not to touch her.

And suddenly she was sick of that problem. Sick, sick, sick of it. So sick of it, that she advanced in the dreary-black hall until she was close enough to poke a finger in his chest. "How many kids did you bring with you this time?"

"None. Hell, Jessa, the storm's dangerous. I wasn't about to let any of those derelict delinquents out in this weather."

So he hadn't brought his chaperones? She poked his chest again. "So then, what are you really doing here? You told me I could have this night in the house alone! It's all I asked for. This one night!"

"I know. And I swear, I never meant to interfere

with that. Only the storm kept getting worse and worse. The power's off through almost all of the city. Lines down, trees down, no phones working. I needed to be sure you were okay, that's all.''

"That's all?"

"Yeah. That's all."

The hell, that was all. Possibly because her chest was heaving, the towel tried to slip. She knotted it tighter to secure it, but her mind wasn't on modesty. Truth to tell, her mind was almost never on modesty, and right then, right there, the only thing on her mind was the creed of her life.

There was only one way to live. By trying to do the right thing, no matter what the costs or risks to yourself. And she knew exactly what Sebastian had risked by coming here tonight. She knew what that risk meant to him...even if he didn't.

And what he'd done for her required payback. Cut and dried. There was no way out. No shirking her doing what she had to do. No pretending she didn't know exactly what the right thing to do was.

So she reached up and kissed him.

Chapter 7

Sebastian struggled to get his head together. So far there were only two things on his mind—Jessa, and making love to Jessa. No other coherent thought was registering at any level of his awareness.

It didn't help that it was so dark in the upstairs hall. The last he'd seen a watch, the time had been pushing around 11:00 p.m., but there was no knowing the time now, and no lights anywhere except for the candles flickering from the master bathroom. She'd been taking quite a sybaritic bath in there. Candles and perfume and girl scents spilled out into the bedroom and hall like a trail of candy to his senses. And he was hot. Not just sexually, but tarnation, physically. When he'd first unlocked the door downstairs and heard her caterwauling, he'd run—literally vaulted up the stairs three at a time, honest-to-God worried that she was either hurt or someone was hurting her.

It never occurred to him that she might be singing. Or that he might find her naked.

Positively, though, Sebastian knew she was mad at him—so why she suddenly reached up to kiss him was a complete mystery. He'd been prepared to hightail it out of the house the minute he could ascertain that she was okay for sure. He'd been prepared for her to be annoyed with him, even. But not prepared, not at all prepared, for that soft mouth to lift up and take his as if she owned it. Owned him.

Aw hell. His mind was still unraveling faster than a skein of yarn bouncing downhill. Worse yet, the more his mind unraveled, the more he loved it.

He'd always been drawn to a "kick." Whether the action was skydiving or white-water rafting, he loved that electric sensation of risk, the kick of adrenaline, the rush to survive. He thought, sometimes, that he specifically needed to do things that made him feel alive…to make him prove that he valued his life, by fighting for it, because he'd felt so valueless in the bitter bleak stretch after his parents died.

This was a risk like that. A risk to survive. In the most basic corner of his heart, he understood that possibly he really might *not* survive…if he didn't fight for her. Because no one and nothing, ever, made him feel alive the way Jessa did.

First things first, though. He had to get rid of her towel, which was easy. The little knot holding the terry cloth secured over her breasts just took a little tug to disintegrate. Other problems were more difficult to solve, though. He couldn't seem to remember where he was, for instance. Or where in the Sam Hill was the closest bed—even though in principle he realized they could only be a step or two outside of the master bedroom. The vaguely sputtering candlelight just wasn't enough illumination to see anything.

But then Jessa pulled on his collar.

Since the lady clearly wanted another kiss, she got one, but that didn't seem to be the sole demand on her mind, because she pulled harder, her bare feet moving back, obviously trying to propel him to move with her. He didn't mind inch-walking with her to a completely unknown destination. Hell, he was taking a risk that cost him eighty percent of his sanity—and for darn sure, one hundred percent of his heart—so fussing about the inconsequential stuff seemed foolish. He concentrated on what mattered. Where her mouth was. Keeping her naked. Finding a place to lay with her. Soon. And not stepping on her bare feet until they got there.

From somewhere in the darkness, he heard a quiet thud. It seemed to be his leather jacket, thunking to the floor. When she tried yanking off his long-sleeved tee, he was temporarily blinded, but what the hey, it was witchy black where she was leading him anyway. Witchy dark and dangerous. She kept pulling, the same way Lorelei lured in sailors, her lips calling to him, her fingertips, her scent, her softness.

His shirt caught for a second, on his watch, but

then pulled free, and those nimble, quick fingers of hers reached for his jeans zipper.

It seemed to Sebastian that a man—even the kind of gentleman of a guy who was determined to do the right thing—was still justified in turning things around when it was his turn. She'd had her fun.

When he threaded his fingers in that short choppy hair of hers, holding her head still, he took a different kind of kiss. He had to concentrate, hard and with a great deal of discipline, to do it right, but he was devoted to the cause. He did his best to pour all of himself into that kiss, tongues, teeth, the silk of lips sliding against lips, promising, reassuring, giving, taking, everything he was—and trying his damnedest to communicate everything he wanted for her.

She gulped in a sudden uneasy draught of air when he finally let her up.

He glanced around and realized that they were just inside the doorway to the master bedroom. The skylight and glass doors of the balcony led in pearls of shadow, hints of shape. The granite corner fireplace and cedar chests never registered in his attention— but the bed did. Maybe it wasn't precisely safe to make love under that big naked window, with the wild rage of lightning and thunder so close.

But then, making love wasn't going to be safe either. Not with her. Not when both of them were about to get real, real emotionally naked. And if she wanted a promise on that, he was more than willing to give it to her.

"Orange..." She bit out his name on a single

hushed breath—and when Jessa used "Orange" instead of "Sebastian," he'd realized for sometime that she was on the cusp of trouble. Either asking for it—or in it. Just then, either way was okay with him.

Still, he took a moment to assure her, "I've got protection. Somewhere. Wallet."

"That isn't what I was going to ask you."

"You mean there's something else that matters? To either of us? At this precise moment?"

She wooshed out the barest breath, then whispered, "No. Nothing else matters but you and me. And what I think..." she sucked in another spare breath "...what I think and believe we can bring each other."

"Yeah. Let's just see. Let's find out for absolute sure." She wasn't so little, but little enough that it was easy to lift her—lift her only for the purpose of drawing her down. The master bed had a nice, big mattress. Hard. There'd been no sheets on it the other day, when he'd first seen it, but something was bunched at one end now. A big fluffy comforter—he promptly guessed that she'd brought it with her to sleep in here. And later it'd be helpful to have a cover to warm her.

Much later.

Somehow, he knew her. Naturally he realized that he couldn't have seen her naked before—but he swore, from deep inside his heart, that he knew the feel of her skin, her lithe lean body, the bump of her hipbone, the vulnerable swell of her breast. Somehow he knew the way her breath would catch, when he nipped, just there. And the way she'd hiss out his name, if he laved a tongue, just here.

When he rolled her beneath him, he knew—somehow, someway—the way she'd fit him, the way her long limbs would wrap just right around him, hugging him, holding him tight. Her eyes were fierce with emotion. He knew they'd be. She didn't hold back honesty. She didn't lie about what she was feeling, what she wanted or needed. And she wasn't about to settle for less than what really mattered.

Neither was he.

Loving her suddenly made everything clear in his life, in his heart. All these years, he suddenly understood the reason why he'd lived in a Winnebago, never seeking a home or a mate—because if he couldn't make his life right, completely right, he had no interest in even playing the game. This was no game with Jessamine. He was unsure how the stakes had gotten so high, so fast, but they were.

It was his worst fear, disappointing someone he loved ever again. That fear had haunted his adult life, but never more than now. He wasn't damn sure he could survive if he disappointed her. Failing her physically as a lover wasn't that terrible a threat, because hell—they could keep practicing that, happily, for decades, until they got it right…assuming he didn't collapse from a heart attack of exhaustion first. But he *was* worried about failing her on the inside. As a man. As a mate.

People had deserted her. She didn't trust easily. He wouldn't either, if he'd been stuck growing up in her shoes. She didn't want to give up, give over, that last cusp of trust. He had the feeling she was used to cheating under the covers, skilled at coming through with the big sigh, the oh-was-that-good, when in fact, she'd held on to that core of herself.

Not with him. He wasn't settling for that. No matter what happened from this moment on, he wanted to prove to her that she could trust him. That he'd be there. That he wouldn't run out when the chips got tough—or right at the point when she needed someone.

Still…

Still…even knowing there'd never be another woman like Jessa for him, never be another night like this, never be an experience making love even remotely like loving her, he was still stunned to watch her climax—and then his—accompanied by lights and fireworks and joyfully crashing cymbals.

Jessa could hardly believe it—how easy it was to get over frigidity. All this time, all she'd ever had to do was meet Sebastian and fall in love with him.

She wanted to savor the moment forever, but unfortunately in those precious minutes after, when they were both still panting noisier than freight trains and Sebastian was holding her as if she were the most precious of jewels…there was a sudden silence outside. The lull in the storm made her want to savor the peace and joy of the moment, but suddenly the world crashed down on them. Lights popped on. Noise and music seemed to blare from several rooms, and a television left on somewhere screeched out cheers and screams and someone lauching into "Auld Lang Syne."

"New Year," she whispered, and wanted to burst out laughing. Maybe the storm wasn't completely over, but the power was definitely restored. The sudden glare of lights might have been intrusive, except that this wasn't an occasion like another. She loved the light. It was a symbol that last year was over. The last part of her whole life was over. This was now. A whole new year…that was starting with a man she loved.

The way he looked at her, Jessa had to believe he saw her feelings in her eyes. She trusted what she saw in his.

"Would you care to comment," he said tactfully, "on what on earth just happened to us?"

"Why, sure." Possibly the light was just a teensy bit too bright. She zoomed out of bed, switched off the overhead, and dived back to Sebastian—tugging the comforter with her. "You're wildly in love with me," she said smugly.

"You think so?"

"I know so." She tucked the blanket around both of them, then tucked a kiss at the side of his neck. "I happened to recognize the symptoms, because I've been suffering from the same ailment myself."

That made him turn his head. His eyes were wary and warm both. "You're saying that you think you're in love with me?"

"It's not a matter of thinking. It's a matter of knowing."

"Um...Slick...you do realize we've only known each other a week?"

"Yeah. That's what makes it so amazing. For twenty-nine years, I've never had a problem walking away. In fact, I don't put myself on the line for anyone. Ever, really. I'm not afraid of being alone, living alone. Or I never was—until I met you."

"Jessamine—"

When he called her Jessamine, she knew she was in trouble. "Now don't get your liver in an uproar," she said lightly. "I wouldn't put your neck in a noose even if you begged me."

"Meaning—?"

"Meaning, don't waste your time offering to marry me. We've only known each other a week, for Pete's sake."

Whether he knew it or not, he was nonstop stroking her back, holding her close as if afraid she'd escape if he didn't. Still, that didn't stop him from rolling his eyes to the ceiling. "Why is it that being with you makes me dizzy?" That wry grin faded fast, though. He asked her, very softly, "So you don't think we belong together? That marriage would be right. You think this was just a one-night type of thing?"

"No way. I'm thinking marriage. I'm thinking that we belong together long-term. And I don't do randoms, ever, Orange, so don't even try going there. But...it's too soon to do certain things."

"As in..."

There now. The storm really was over. Moonlight started to peek through the clouds, on the balcony, through the glass doors, right on Sebastian's face. "As in...I want some time to romance you, big guy. Woo you." She lifted a shoulder in a little shrug. "We need some time to just mess around, don't you think? Get tattoos together. Get silly on wine some night. Fight. Make up. Dress up and go out on a date. Act uncomfortable like real dates do. After that, you can ask me to marry you, and then maybe I'll say yes and maybe I'll say no."

He hauled her directly onto his chest, where her weight could crush him. It seemed like he specifically wanted her weight to crush him, wanted it forever and maybe even longer. "Maybe I won't ask you."

"Aw yeah, you will. You think you're crazy in love now...but it's only going to get worse." She kissed him to soothe the dire warning in her voice. "But in the meantime..."

"Sweetheart, I don't think I can handle any more 'meantimes' from you just now."

"This is different. Remember? We both agreed that we'd settle the question about what we're going to do with this house by the New Year."

He stiffened. So, of course, did she. "Home" was almost as touchy a subject for the two of them as that other four letter word. "Love." She brushed the hair from his brow, rubbed the pad of her thumb along his lip. "I checked this morning," she said quietly. "You were right. This area is zoned only for single-family dwellings. You can't just house a bunch of kids here.''

"I know that. I told you—"

"But there's an answer, actually. A better answer." He was probably going to get sick of her constantly touching him, but just then...oh man, he just felt so good. And he responded so easily, so volatilely to even the gentlest strokes from her. "I've had a couple chances now to see the kinds of kids you take on, Sebastian. They're bad-news hellions."

"I know." His skin warmed under her touch, but those eyes were wary again, worried. "If they were good kids, they wouldn't need places to go. But the thing is, Jessa...I spend most of my time with them out in the wilderness. It's not like I have to live right with them. Or we would. You wouldn't have to—"

"Hey," she interrupted him.

"Hey?"

"Hey, you idiot. Did you think I was going to object to your work? Or interfere with your doing something important to you? Get real." She hesitated, so that had a chance to sink in, then chatted on. "I've only met three of them, of course. But if the twins and Martha are a fair sample of your delinquents...well, I have to confess, I felt an instant kinship. I was a delinquent once upon a time myself."

"So you told me." There now, he was starting to relax again. Except for that one telling part of him.

"I was way, way better at it than them. You can see their defenses a mile away. I was *good*. Rock couldn't get through to me. But, the point is, I don't know as I'd ever been much with good kids. Bad kids, on the other hand…I feel like I might have something to offer them.''

"Jessa, you're confusing the hell out of me. What are you trying to say?''

"I'm trying to say that Ryan gave us a home. And charged us with finding a way to use it that was meaningful for us. ''

"Yeah, and—?''

"We could foster some kids. Not a hundred. Not a school full. But a couple. Three, four, like that. I don't know the specifics about how we could make it work…I mean, I love my own job. And you're gone sometimes with yours. But I think that's what this house needs to be for. People who need homes. Kids who need homes. Kids who've lost the adults who should be in a position to take care of them. We could do that, Sebastian. Love the hell out of them, fill this house up with noise and messes and the sound of kids' laughter.''

He closed his eyes. "Why am I seeing a couple dogs and babies in this picture?''

"It's growing on you, isn't it?'' She bent down to kiss him, but somehow—it seemed to be magic—she was suddenly the one on the bottom and Sebastian was leaned over her. Furthermore, he looked—he definitely looked—as if he had one thing on his mind. And it wasn't talking anymore.

MAGGIE'S MIRACLE
Jackie Merritt

Prologue

There was something about Christmas that reached deep inside of Dr. Maggie Taylor, overwhelmed her most tender emotions and then dragged them to the surface of her normally all-business exterior. During the Christmas season she was a softer, gentler person. Nativity scenes, carols and twinkling lights brought tears to her eyes. A heartfelt "Merry Christmas, Doctor" from any of her patients, but especially from one who was seriously ill, tore Maggie to shreds. She thanked God every day for her parents and always, *always,* added a prayer requesting a cure for her sister Hannah's rare, degenerative blood disease.

Ever since Hannah had been diagnosed, though, Maggie hadn't just prayed for a miracle; she'd dedicated her medical education, her spare time and every fiber of her being into finding that cure herself. It wasn't a high-priority disease with researchers, but there was a handful around the world and Maggie stayed in contact with each of them. There wasn't a paper or article written on the subject that she hadn't pored over for even the slightest advance in knowledge that might aid her own research of the disease. She was so saturated with facts, theories and hope regarding Hannah's condition that she regarded two elements as enormous hurdles to personal success, as far as research went—time and money. Earning a living consumed most of her time, thus time was money, neither of which was plentiful enough.

So, very much like a high-speed windup toy, Maggie had been working nonstop from morning till night for years, either with patients or doing what hematology research she could manage on her limited budget. For certain she had no social life, beyond what her family provided, and even with massive amounts of Christmas spirit coursing through her veins, Maggie usually ignored or made brief, perfunctory appearances at the holiday parties that seemed to begin early in December within Houston's medical community.

This year, though, something unusual had occurred; Maggie had been invited to a fabulous party at the Fortune family's Double Crown Ranch. The invitation had come directly from Ryan Fortune, the head of the family, with a handwritten message: "Please come, Maggie. I believe you will be favorably surprised."

Maggie had not doubted the "being surprised" part

of the invitation. The Fortunes were billionaires, a family whose history in Texas read like an ongoing saga of romance, mystery and adventure. Maggie had met Ryan Fortune—along with quite a few members of his family—when Ryan had been hospitalized for heart failure. She was the physician who had not accepted that diagnosis and had worked day and night to discover Ryan's true condition—digitalis poisoning.

Her tenacity had saved his life, and when she pondered his party invitation she felt good because he hadn't gone home and forgotten her. She had decided to attend the affair, and it had been everything she could have imagined. And the favorable surprise that Ryan had mentioned in his invitation, although she'd generalized the word *surprise* to merely encompass an evening with the Fortunes in their own surroundings, still resided in her apartment. It was a beautifully wrapped gift, and it looked to her like a jewelry box under that lovely paper and ribbon. When Ryan had given it to her, he'd smiled warmly and told her to open it at her leisure.

Every night when she got home from work she wondered if she should open it then or wait until Christmas.

But on Saturday the twenty-second, only a few days before Christmas Eve, Maggie finally decided to open it and get it over with. After getting it from under the tree she returned to her chair, placed a throw pillow on her lap and then laid the gift on it. Its wrapping was a white-and-gold paper with an angel motif and a lacy gold ribbon. She was careful untying the ribbon as she wanted to keep it, and she tried not to tear the paper during removal.

The gift was an envelope-size lacquered box in a stunning Oriental design, about a quarter-inch in depth, very delicate and lovely. Thinking about the thank-you note she would write this very night before retiring, Maggie gently lifted the lid of the box. It wasn't empty, as she'd expected; inside was a Christmas-red envelope. Assuming it was a holiday card, Maggie slid her forefinger under the sealed flap and extracted the envelope's contents. There were two items, neither of which was a card.

She unfolded the smallest. It was a check, made out to her and signed by Ryan Fortune. Maggie stared at the amount in total and complete shock. She counted the zeroes and nearly fainted. The check was for two million dollars.

"This can't be," she whispered hoarsely, too shaken to speak out loud. With trembling hands she unfolded the second item from the envelope. It was a letter.

To my dear friend Maggie,
My recent brush with death made me appreciate life much more than I ever did. I see beauty wherever I look now, and what was beautiful even before my trial now has a clarity that takes my breath away. But more important than the sight of a glorious sunset or the sensation of God's life-giving rain dampening my face is

what I have learned about love. Love, Maggie, in all its shapes and forms is the key to human happiness. Love and family. I recall our conversations while I was still hospitalized but vastly improved (due to your relentless efforts) about your parents and sister. I remember the expression on your face when you talked about Hannah's disease. You made mention of doing what you could to search for a cure. Reading between the lines, Maggie, I realized that a lack of money was greatly hindering your research. This check for two million dollars should help in that regard.

But in giving you this gift I also give you free rein in how you use it. Again from conversations with you I know that you live alone and that there is no one in your life that makes your heart sing. Maggie, whatever else you do, however high you fly in your career, and whatever you accomplish in your medical research, do not forgo the romantic kind of love. Nothing else you could ever do would be as fulfilling, I assure you.

> Your friend always,
> Ryan Fortune

By the time Maggie pulled herself together enough to think with some clarity again, it was too late to phone Ryan Fortune. Actually she felt somewhat relieved to be able to put off the call, as a simple "Thank you" seemed almost ludicrous. Should she even accept a gift of such magnitude? Dare she *not* accept it? It was what she'd been praying for, after all, the means to retire her current employment and apply one hundred percent of her time to research.

Maggie slept badly that night. She kept waking up, at times experiencing overwhelming joy, and at others suffering almost unbearable anxiety. The next day was Sunday and a day off for her. She knew that she would not be able to do anything worthwhile until she spoke to Ryan Fortune, and it was torture to wait for ten o'clock, which seemed to be an appropriate time to phone a man on what could be his day of leisure. Knowing next to nothing about the Fortunes' routines and habits, Maggie could only use her best judgment about telephoning their home on a Sunday.

By ten, though, she had reread Ryan's letter a dozen times, and with her nerves finally settling down, she recognized the sincerity of his gift. To turn it down would be rude and insulting to his spirit of loving and charitable generosity.

After locating her very best stationery, she wrote a heartfelt letter of thanks. When it was addressed and ready for mailing, Maggie felt relieved of the emotional pressure she'd been under since the first sight of Ryan's check. She knew exactly how she was going to spend the remainder of the day, too—making plans to create her own research lab. Her excitement built as she sat with a pad of paper and wrote down ideas and made lists of the equipment and supplies she would need.

And then it hit her. *I can't do this alone! I must*

*find the very best researcher in the field and convince
him or her to work for me.*

That was an extremely unnerving decision, because
the "very best" was Dr. Elliott Sandwell, a man who
had nearly driven her crazy with stupid jokes and an
ego too large to measure when they were both residents at Mercy Hospital some years back. Sandwell
had focused his medical education on research, while
she had gone into patient care. She knew he worked
in the same huge medical complex in San Antonio
that she did, but she hadn't run into him for so long
that she couldn't actually recall when it might have
happened.

As disturbing as the prospect of even asking him
to leave his current job and work for her was, her
determination to succeed in finding that cure would
not permit her to cross off Elliott Sandwell. But what
was the best way to approach him? Since she'd barely
been civil to him at Mercy and he very well could
have a long memory, he might toss her out of his
office without even listening to her offer.

There had to be a way for her to catch his attention
and keep it long enough to have her say, there just
had to be! With a determined thrust of her chin, Maggie vowed to find it.

Suddenly a plan unfolded in her mind. An entire
scenario, in fact. One that had a much better chance
of working than her merely walking up to him and
asking if he remembered her. All she had to do was
a little research on Dr. Sandwell to find out if he was

still single, and if so, what New Year's Eve party he
was going to attend.

To her chagrin, she found out through a dozen or
so telephone calls to various friends a lot more information than she needed. Every woman she talked to
who actually knew Elliott was more than willing to
discuss the "gorgeous Dr. Sandwell." Apparently he
was the same skirt-chasing Lothario he'd always
been, cutting a wider swath through the female pop-
ulation of the San Antonio Medical Center than Sher-
man had in Georgia!

"Obviously you are still a disgusting cad," Maggie
muttered between calls, recalling again the harem of
gaga-eyed females he'd juggled at Mercy.

But at least he wasn't married, which was an important part of her plot to get his attention. The one
piece of information she could not obtain from anyone was which one of the many New Year's Eve
parties being planned for that night would he be at-
tending. No one, however, doubted that he'd be at
one of the bigger bashes.

She would find him, she told herself. One way or
another she would find him on New Year's Eve.

And if her plan worked, if all the pieces fitted together as she hoped, she'd have his attention. Boy,
would she have his attention!

Chapter 1

New Year's Eve

Dr. Elliott Sandwell enjoyed parties; he particularly liked those affairs held during the Christmas season. It seemed to him that his pal and gal friends were more upbeat in December than at any other time of year—he certainly was—which made for a lot of laughs and some truly merry times. Elliott's friends were almost a hundred percent associated with the San Antonio, Texas, medical community, so he kept seeing the same faces at most of the holiday functions to which he was invited.

The New Year's Eve gala he attended this year was being held in the home of a renowned physician. The house was spectacular even without holiday decorations, but with all of the twinkling lights it seemed to be a place of utter enchantment. There was live music, tables and tables of food and an open bar. Elliott was wearing a tuxedo, as were the other men, and the ladies were dressed to kill. Holding a scotch and water, he stood near a massive fireplace and surveyed the crowd. The buzz of conversation and laughter came close to overriding the four-piece band's valiant efforts. Elliott had already said hello to nearly everyone there and had spent time kidding around with quite a few of them. He'd eaten choice morsels from the array of goodies on the food tables, danced with some of his female friends and now he was waiting for midnight. According to his watch—which was never wrong—it was 11:40 p.m.

At that very moment he saw her, a woman he *didn't* know who was dazzlingly beautiful in a redsequined dress that emphasized every alluring curve of her strikingly perfect figure. Elliott felt as though his heart had suddenly skipped a beat. Who was she? Had she just arrived? He couldn't stop gaping. The lady's long golden-brown hair was in a casual arrangement, some of it up, some of it trailing down the back of her neck and kissing her shoulders in a seductive manner.

Elliott began making his way through the happy throng toward the gorgeous mystery woman. She was talking to two men with silly grins on their faces. At least Elliott thought they looked like a couple of saps, and it was apparent to him, another male, that neither of them had brought this delicious-looking person to the party. They were trying to make time with her, which was a clue that she'd come alone.

That possibility startled Elliott; in his experience women who looked like that did not normally attend parties unescorted. But he rarely traveled alone, either, and here he was without a date tonight. Intentionally, as it were, which was really quite unusual for him.

He was almost there, only about ten feet away from the trio, when he came to a screeching halt. At that range the lady was familiar. He racked his brain, knowing he'd seen her before—possibly even *met* her before—but where? When? *Good Lord, if I've forgotten a woman like her, then I must be starting to lose it!*

Try as he might and frustrating as it was, he couldn't place her. Her face was drop-dead gorgeous, with every feature enhanced by makeup that had been applied subtly but with an artist's touch. Elliott gulped as his gaze traveled down her creamy throat to the deeply cut bodice of her dress, which displayed just enough cleavage to make him and any other man in the room who got close enough for a peek break out in a sweat.

To dampen his throat, which had become desert dry, he threw back the rest of his drink and set the empty glass on the tray of a passing waiter. Telling himself that if she was familiar to him, then he just might be familiar to her and that her memory might be less faulty than his, he walked boldly up to the trio and smiled.

After a look at the two men—both of whom he knew—that clearly stated "Get lost!" he said in a deliberately low and sensual voice to the ravishingly beautiful woman, "It seems like an eternity since we've seen each other. How are you?"

Maggie knew at once that he didn't recognize her. He was the same too handsome, self-centered, cocksure, conceited egomaniac that she'd known him to be at Mercy Hospital when they were both residents there, which was no surprise. But she needed his experience and exceptional brilliance in hematology research, which was her only reason for dressing like a Christmas tart and crashing a party to which she had not been invited. Actually she'd gone to three other big bashes before this one tonight, looking for Dr. Elliott Sandwell, and it was extremely satisfying to her that he was now standing before her with a drooling look in his remarkable blue eyes and pretending that he remembered who she was.

She gave her departing companions only a brief glance and then held up her hand for Elliott to take. "I'm quite well, thank you. And you?"

Elliott couldn't tell if she recognized him or not. Holding on to her hand, he looked deeply into her lovely blue-gray eyes.

"Your beauty lights up the room," he said softly.

She laughed throatily and gently disengaged her hand. "Why, thank you, Doctor."

He smiled when he felt a lot more like frowning. She knew him, all right, and what an insult to her it would be if he had to say, "For the life of me I can't remember your name."

"Did you just now get here?" he asked.

"About ten minutes ago. I had other... obligations," she said in the most breathy voice she could devise.

Elliott considered himself far too sophisticated and experienced with women to be totally knocked out by one, but this lady was in a league all her own. He wanted her as he'd never wanted another woman on such short acquaintance, and telling himself that they'd known each other at some point in the past was not an acceptable excuse or explanation for the sexual palpitations harassing his body. There was a spinning in his head and a churning in his gut. Since he hadn't consumed enough scotch to cause those symptoms, his deductive mind could lay the blame on only one thing: the luscious lady standing mere inches from him.

He cleared his throat and continued the conversation. "Your obligations were other parties?"

"Actually, yes." *Other parties to drop in on to find out if you were there, slick. I had suspected this dress and hairdo would get your attention, but couldn't you at least have remembered my name? You really are the same self-serving jerk you always were, aren't you?*

"And you're here alone?" Elliott asked in the softly sensual voice with which he'd been speaking to her. It was the kind of voice a man used with a woman when he wanted to spin a cocoon of privacy around the two of them. Since she didn't put more space between them or say something to send him on his way, he deduced her enjoyment of the sexually stirring moment as being comparable to his.

Just then he heard his host at the microphone. "Folks, it's almost midnight. We'll start the countdown in exactly one minute."

Startled, Elliott took a look at his watch. The last twenty minutes had rushed by. What was her intention, to see in the New Year and then vanish? He couldn't let her get away without learning her name and making some sort of arrangement to see each other again.

"The approach of a brand-new year is emotionally moving, don't you agree?" she murmured.

"This one is."

"Why…why is that?" Maggie whispered, a little afraid of what he might say. Her charade tonight was not a frivolous whim, and while she'd ardently hoped to draw Elliott Sandwell's attention, she certainly hadn't thought that seeing him again might affect her. Now she wasn't sure that she'd gotten his attention in the right way. The look on his face was far too admiring…and he still didn't recognize her!

The crowd was chanting—five…four…three… two…one—and then everyone shouted, "Happy New Year!" Balloons floated from the ceiling, and amongst the confetti and ribbons couples began kissing.

Elliott put his hands on her upper arms and slowly drew her forward. He saw surprise in her eyes, but she didn't back away. He brushed her lips with his and whispered, "Happy New Year, beautiful." Before she could return the traditional phrase, he kissed her again, this time taking her mouth in a kiss of utter possession. His tongue slipped between her lips and he bent her slightly back so that their bodies would unite from chests to thighs.

Maggie was suddenly so physically inflamed that she was practically senseless. She hadn't factored this into her plans, and she had to put a stop to it. Dizzily she turned her head to break the kiss.

Her voice cracked when she spoke. "I know you don't know who it is that you're kissing. I'm Dr. Maggie Taylor, and I looked you up tonight to offer you a job. Whatever salary you're making working for NTL Research Labs, I'll pay you double."

The din of "Auld Lang Syne," laughter and voices just barely penetrated Elliott's astonishment. Holding Maggie as he was, close to his heart and looking into her eyes, his stunned mind repeated what she'd just said to him. He remembered her now, and it pained him that he'd been so easily tricked by her transformation from wren to flamingo. And why on earth would she ask him to quit his present job and go to work for her? What, in heaven's name, was going on?

Anger began edging his system. This whole thing had to be some kind of prank, and he didn't remember Maggie Taylor as a prankster. To the contrary, when he'd known her before she had rarely smiled at gags, let alone laughed. If she'd ever instigated anything that could remotely be called funny, he hadn't been in on it. She'd been aloof and unfriendly and all business, and every horny intern who'd tried to make time with her had learned that her icy exterior wasn't just skin deep.

"Let's go someplace and talk," he mumbled. Releasing her from his embrace, he took her by the arm and began steering her through the crowd toward the front door.

Maggie's heart was pounding furiously. Something told her to dig in her heels and tell him to knock it off, that she wasn't going anywhere with him. His unexpected kiss had wreaked havoc on her nervous system. She hadn't been kissed that often in her lifetime, but one didn't need massive amounts of experience to recognize the symptoms of overpowering sexual desire. Sexual awakening, in her case. It was a dizzying fact to comprehend, but her libido had come alive in Elliott Sandwell's arms! Running out of here—by herself—seemed only sensible.

But there was a voice in her head that told her to grow up. Her plan was working; she definitely had his attention and wasn't that what she'd set out to attain tonight? As far as leaving the house with him, they certainly couldn't talk seriously in this melee of party noise, could they?

Outside he asked flatly, "Where'd you park your car?"

Maggie was breathing in fresh cool air and beginning to feel more like her normal clear-thinking self. It seemed almost miraculous that she'd not only gotten Elliott Sandwell's attention but he was obviously willing to discuss the offer she'd gasped out after that earthshaking kiss. It was time now to forget that foolishness and get back to business, she thought, and then was taken aback by the touch of sadness she felt because she was in no position to think of that kiss as anything *but* foolishness.

"Car?" she echoed. "Are we going somewhere? Why not sit over there in that lovely little garden? There's plenty of light out here, what with the Christmas fixtures adding to the permanent yard lights."

"It's not exactly the middle of summer," Elliott drawled with some sarcasm. "Aren't you cold? You don't even have a shawl. Come on. Let's go and sit in your car."

"I don't have my car."

He frowned at her. "How'd you get here?"

"Taxi. I don't know this area of the city very well, and I wasn't particularly keen about driving around by myself on New Year's Eve."

"Well, hell," Elliott muttered. "I don't have my car, either. I came with a friend." Taking her arm again, he steered her back through the front door and into the house. Then, to Maggie's surprise he brought her to a chair and said gruffly, "Wait here. I'll only be a few minutes."

Maggie sank to the chair calmly enough, but in about five seconds she was livid. How dare he order her around like that? He'd *told* her to wait there instead of saying something polite and gentlemanly like, "Would you mind waiting a few minutes while I…while I…"

While he does what? Borrows a car from someone? Finds the friend he mentioned and... A woman! Of course! Somewhere in this wriggling mass of happy humanity is the lady who was naive enough to accept a New Year's Eve date with Elliott Sandwell!

Maggie felt like groaning out loud. She really should leave before Elliott got back, maybe with his date on his heels and telling him what a jerk he was. Maggie knew that she would never live down a scene of that nature.

But instead of bolting through the front door, which wasn't very far from where she sat, she took a breath and told her fluttering stomach to settle down. Her mission came first, before anything else, certainly far ahead of personal annoyances. Besides, Elliott Sandwell's love life was none of her business, so why should she concern herself with the disdainful way he treated his paramours?

Maggie had splurged for tonight, paying prices for her dress, accessories and hairdo that would have been unthinkable before receiving Ryan Fortune's gift. It would not happen again. That money was going into research, not into fancy clothes or even a new car, which she could use, as hers was ten years old and not altogether dependable. Regardless, spending so much money to catch Elliott Sandwell's eye was a serious reason for Maggie to stay in that chair, even though she wondered now why this had seemed a more surefire way of getting his attention than simply phoning him.

She knew the answer to that at once, because a

shudder rippled through her body at the mere thought of cold calling Elliott and requesting a meeting. At least tonight he'd approached her, even if her one and only attraction had been the sexy red dress hugging every female curve she possessed.

Crossing her legs, Maggie nervously wiggled her foot in its red satin high heel. What on earth was taking Elliott so long? His date for the evening obviously wasn't taking her brush-off like a lady. Maybe she was giving him a large, loud and colorful piece of her mind, *which* he richly deserved, the cad, Maggie thought with sarcastic inflection.

Suddenly there he was, right in front of her, and in spite of her sarcasm and disapproval and all of the judgmental emotions Elliott Sandwell evoked within her, Maggie's heart skipped a beat. There was something so sensual about his handsome features that just looking at him took her back to that unforgettable kiss he'd laid on her.

"Come on," he said brusquely, overlooking completely, much to Maggie's dismay, any attempt to apologize for his long absence.

She got up, but didn't immediately snap to. "'Come on' where?" she demanded to know.

"I have a car. It's waiting for us."

"A car is *waiting* for us. Rather considerate of it, isn't it?"

Elliott grinned. "A joke, Maggie? Are my ears playing tricks on me or did you really make a joke?"

How dare he ridicule her serious nature? "Didn't you know that I do stand-up comedy in my spare time?'' she snapped, and swept past him to head for the front door.

"Hold on there!" Elliott caught her by the arm again. "Our considerate car is waiting by a side door."

"Oh." She shook off his hand but followed along as he dodged merrymakers through a series of rooms. Then they were in a quiet part of the immense house and finally at an outside door.

Elliott opened it and Maggie stepped through it. There, parked with its engine running and a uniformed driver apparently awaiting their arrival, was a gorgeous white stretch limousine.

"Couldn't get a taxi," Elliott said with a touch of amusement in his voice. "But I think this will do, don't you?"

Maggie cleared her throat. All she had in mind was some conversation, which could have taken place in one of those silent, unused rooms they'd passed through just now. Would she be a fool to get in that limousine with a man whose racy reputation with women would make a novel?

On the other hand, if he actually accepted her offer and they worked together every day, he had to know the ground rules. She was not going to be chased around her desk, or work with one eye on him so he didn't sneak up on her from behind. She might as well kill two birds with one stone, and it really didn't matter where their discussion took place, did it?

"It will do," she said coolly, and marched over to the limo. The driver was faster than she and had the door opened and ready for her to enter the vehicle when she got there.

Elliott was right behind her, and when the door was shut Maggie instantly got the impression of total and complete privacy. The darkly tinted glass between the front and back of the car was up, and the engine was so quiet that Maggie could barely hear it. It was posh and luxurious, with intriguing amber lights indicating various accoutrements, and under other circumstances Maggie knew she would be enjoying herself. With Dr. Elliott Sandwell enclosed with her in this sexy co-coon, however, Maggie couldn't even begin to relax.

''Ah, this is nice,'' Elliott said. He turned his head to see her. ''Are you comfortable? Too cool, too warm, too anything?''

''I'm fine,'' she said stiffly. The limo was moving, leaving the grounds, pulling into the street. ''Where are we going?''

''Where would you like us to go?''

He's using his bedroom voice on me! Oh my God! It occurred to her then that she was behaving like an adolescent on her first date. First of all, this wasn't a date, and while her sexual experience would just barely fill a thimble, she was long past adolescence.

''Actually, I'd like to go home,'' she replied. ''You and I can talk on the way. Shall I give the driver my address?''

''Sure, go ahead.'' Elliott pushed a button and the glass partition soundlessly glided down.

Leaning forward, Maggie recited her address and asked, ''Do you know where that is?''

"No problem, ma'am."

"Take the scenic route. The lady and I have something to discuss," Elliott said before closing the partition again. Turning to Maggie, he asked, "Do we really have something to discuss? I mean beyond the fact that you're ravishingly beautiful tonight."

"I hardly think my appearance would make much of a conversation."

He said, "Beep! Wrong answer. Sweetheart, I could talk for an hour on your appearance tonight. Would you like me to prove it?"

She drew an exasperated-sounding breath. "Good Lord, no. And to answer the only sensible question you've asked me tonight, yes, we really do have something to discuss. You did hear what I said when...right after...I mean..."

"Right after our kiss?"

"Must you sound so smug about that?"

"Honey, you've got to admit it sizzled."

"So damned what?" she snapped. "Look, I didn't get into this car with you to talk silly about a kiss that didn't mean a thing to either of us."

"A kiss that hot means nothing to you? Hmm, too bad. Something tells me that we could make beautiful music together."

"Oh, for crying out loud. Is sex all you think about? Time hasn't changed you an iota, has it?"

"Sex is not all I think about, Maggie, but when I'm with a sexy woman wearing a take-me-to-bed dress, it's pretty hard *not* to think about it."

He'd called her ravishingly beautiful a minute ago

and now sexy. Coming from him those were compliments of the highest order, and she tried but couldn't fault herself for the blossoming warmth in the pit of her stomach. Not that she'd do anything about it or let *him* do anything about it. It was time, in fact, that she got back to business.

"I'm going to completely ignore anything you say that isn't related to my offer. May I present it now?"

"May I present *my* offer? Bet it'd be a whole lot more fun than yours." When he saw her icy glare, he gave up. "Okay, okay, go ahead and get it over with."

Maggie drew a breath. "I'm in the process of opening a hematology research lab. I've leased the space and ordered the necessary equipment and supplies, some of which have already arrived. I figure the lab should be up and running in a week to ten days. But I've been realizing that creating an efficient little lab is the easy part of successful research. I could stumble along on my own, of course, but I want fast results, which demands that I hire some exceptional help. Everyone says you're the best researcher in the field, and the best is what I need." Maggie went on to identify Hannah's disease, then added, "I intend to find a cure before it kills her, and I'd like your help in attaining that goal."

Chapter 2

"Are you government or privately funded?" Elliot finally inquired. Hearing that Maggie's sister was terminal, unless someone came up with a cure in time to save her life, moved him deeply. Still, questions began stacking up in his mind.

"Neither. It's my money...*all* my money."

"What'd you do, win the lottery?" he asked dryly.

"No, but let's just say that I came into quite a lot of money and leave it at that, okay? Now, as I said in the house, I'll pay you twice what you're making now."

"I'm making pretty good money, Maggie."

"Come to work for me and you'd be making more. Plus, no one other than me—so I can keep up with what you'd be doing—would be looking over your shoulder. As long as you stayed focused on Hannah's disease, you'd have free rein with new experimentation and ideas.''

Elliott was becoming very intrigued. ''Free rein'' was much more enticing than additional salary. And the prospect of working in a small, private lab without a board of physicians and businessmen that had to okay every new idea he had was downright exhilarating.

''Do you need an answer this minute, or could I think about it for a day or two? Also, I'd like to take a look at your lab before giving you an answer.''

Maggie nearly swooned with excitement. He was considering her offer. *Seriously* considering it!

''Of course you may have some time to think it over. I wouldn't expect anything else,'' she said, and the husky quality of her voice told them both just how affected she was by his courteous reception of her offer. ''I'm grateful that you didn't say no without giving it a chance.''

''I never say no to a beautiful woman without giving her a chance.''

His silky tone of voice destroyed Maggie's gratefulness, and just like that she was back to resenting his seemingly unending quest for sexual gratification. *Tell him that you will never be fair game for his womanizing so he might as well not waste his breath. Do it now so that he factors your no-nonsense attitude into his decision.*

It was suddenly difficult to breathe. She felt choked on words that should be said but simply wouldn't come out of her mouth because of a fear that he might change his mind about considering her offer if she started laying down rules so soon. She had every right to demand respect from a man, but Elliott had rights, too, and he just might exercise one of them by walking away from her deal.

"Let's see what's in here," Elliott said, and he opened the door of a small refrigerator. "Well, what a surprise. A chilled bottle of champagne." He took out the bottle. "Good brand, too. You know, we never did toast in the New Year. Isn't it bad luck to omit that from your New Year's Eve celebration?"

"Not that I've heard," Maggie said dryly. She watched as he located some lovely crystal tulip glasses in a tiny cupboard and then deftly opened the champagne. When the cork popped he caught the overrun in a glass, which he then handed to her. She didn't want any champagne, and his assumption that she would drink with him was galling.

Nevertheless she accepted the glass, not realizing that the expression on her face could have curdled milk. Elliott almost laughed. *Now, that's the Maggie Taylor I remember.*

But she wasn't totally the Maggie he remembered. Not in that dress, she wasn't, and what about the hot and hungry way she'd participated in their kiss? He'd really like to get her in that mood again and see where it went.

Ignoring her icy demeanor, he held up his glass. "Best champagne in town, Maggie."

It was on the tip of her tongue to tell him to shove it up his nose but that would end their relationship before it got started. So all she did was smile faintly and say, "Really?"

"Yes, really," he said with a teasing half grin.

Maggie felt the knot in her stomach growing. First of all, she rarely drank anything alcoholic, and doing so now with this particular man seemed utterly stupid. She needed a clear head to keep up with Elliott Sandwell on his worst day, and he'd already taken advantage of her inexperience with men in general by kissing her senseless at midnight.

Nevertheless, to avoid even the slightest hint of dissension she kept smiling—albeit weakly—and when he touched his glass to hers and said, "Here's to a happy, healthy and prosperous New Year, Maggie," she took a tiny sip of the champagne. Its taste was surprisingly delicious, and as though she doubted her own opinion about that, she took a second sip.

"Told you it was the best champagne in town. Was I right or was I right?" Elliott said.

"I'm sure you're rarely wrong about anything," Maggie retorted.

"Doesn't happen often," Elliott agreed with a grin. After a swallow from his own glass, he said, "You sure have changed."

"No, actually I haven't."

"Would you have worn that dress back then? I don't think so, Maggie."

"You only knew me when I was on duty at the hospital. You and I never socialized so you have no idea what I wore or what I did during my free time."

"I used to wonder what you did, you know."

"I doubt that."

"It's the God's truth, Maggie. One of the things I itched to do was to take the pins out of that frigid little bun you used to twist your hair into."

"Frigid? You thought my hairdo indicated frigidity?"

"Sure looked like it. Everyone thought so."

"You mean the *male* residents thought so. You were the most ungodly bunch of jerks, drooling over the pretty nurses like pubescent boys who had just discovered the appendage between their legs."

"Hey, you're talking about the appendage I love." Elliott's eyes were twinkling. He truly relished this kind of banter with a sexy woman. "Most women kind of like it, too," he added. "Which is only natural, of course, since men and women were physically designed to fit together. Ergo, it takes both a male and female to make up one unit that is whole and complete."

"Ergo, my left foot! What do you do, lay awake nights and think up weird things to say to a woman, hoping to shock her into hopping into bed with you?"

"Surely you don't think that whole-unit theory is mine. Honey, it's ancient philosophy. Obviously you need to do a little more reading." Elliott raised the champagne bottle. "Hold your glass steady and I'll refill it."

She put her free hand over her empty glass. "No, thanks. I don't want any more champagne, and where in hell are we?" She put her face close to the tinted window on her side of the car to peer out. "Oh, we're almost to my block."

"What'd you think I was going to do, spirit you away to never-never land? Maybe some other time, but not tonight. You're not quite in the right mood for that trip."

She wanted to slap his smug face, and to say out loud the nasty names she was calling him in her head.

But she needed him in her lab. She needed his scientific genius with experimentation, his brilliance in figuring out sequences of steps that just might produce a desired result.

She knew now that working with him was going to be a nightmare. He was cocky and conceited, even worse than he'd been. If he accepted the job, she would have to remember that she was just another woman to him, another conquest to boast about, should she be stupid enough to be taken in by one of his lines or come-ons.

The limousine came to a smooth stop at the curb in front of her apartment. Maggie quickly put her glass in Elliott's hand and said, "Call me when you decide."

"I can't call you without a phone number, Maggie."

"I'm in the physician's directory, same as you. Oh, never mind, I have some cards with me." From her exquisite little evening bag, she pulled out a business card and a pen. "I'm writing my home number on the back." Holding out the card, she saw him put both glasses back into the tiny cupboard.

When he took her card she said dryly, "If you can't reach me at one of those numbers, then I've been abducted by aliens." To her surprise he laughed, and it gave her a good feeling that she'd said something that would make the great Elliott Sandwell laugh with such genuine relish.

But then he ruined the whole thing by saying, "Maggie, my sweet, is it possible that you might actually be fun?"

Elliott spent New Year's Day in a medical library, reading everything he could find about Hannah Taylor's disease. The most recent information, Elliott discovered, was coming out of Sweden, published by two medical doctors, Leon Patric and Clara Hedwig.

By that evening his brain was full of data but craving more. He would like to rid the world of all disease, but that fantasy was so huge that his scientific mind would not permit it to linger. Ridding humanity of just one affliction would give meaning to his life and chosen career, and Maggie's job offer could be an opportunity to accomplish exactly that. Despite his serious outlook on the subject of research in general, it was exciting to envision himself in a small laboratory—properly equipped, of course—and actually making headway with a cure for Hannah Taylor's degenerative disease.

But something had started nagging at him about midafternoon, and it continued to rag him after he got home. Exactly how much money had Maggie come into? Research could be moderately costly or run sky-high, but even low-budget experimentation didn't come cheap. It would be foolish for him to quit the good job he presently had if Maggie was functioning more on emotion than cash.

He finally sat down with the card Maggie had given him and dialed her home number, thinking that was the most likely place she would be on a holiday. He was disappointed to get her voice mail, and he left a very brief message.

Maggie hadn't thought to write her parents' phone number on the back of the card she'd given Elliott, nor did she realize the oversight throughout the pleasant day she had spent with her family. Hannah had been living with her and Maggie's folks for several years now. Most of the time Hannah was too weak to do very much, and it had broken her heart when she'd had to quit her job. Currently she was in an up cycle of the disease and feeling quite well. All day the Taylor clan had enjoyed wonderful food and the kind of upbeat and often funny conversation that can only occur among a loving family.

Around eight the elder Taylors left their daughters alone in the den. As was their habit they retired early and watched television or read in bed until they got sleepy. Hannah usually did the same, but with Maggie there she was happy to stay up and talk.

"This has been a great holiday season," Hannah said. "Don't you think so?"

"I do, yes." Maggie hadn't told her family about Ryan Fortune's check. She'd thought about it a lot, and while she was consistently optimistic with Hannah about her illness, and Hannah knew that Maggie was doing everything possible to improve her sister's health through research, Maggie had ultimately decided that it would be cruel to raise Hannah's hopes too high. She was going to do everything in her power to succeed in her little lab, but what if she didn't? Someday she might be able to go to Hannah with wonderful news, but that could be just a beautiful dream. It was best if she kept some dreams to herself.

Maggie realized that Hannah was studying her rather intently. Smiling at her sister, Maggie asked, "Do I have egg on my face?"

"I was just thinking of how pretty you are."

"Right," Maggie quipped. "I'm a raving beauty, I am, I am."

"You could be, Maggie," Hannah said gently. "Why don't you wear makeup?"

"I don't have time to fuss with makeup and fancy hairdos, Hannah." Today she'd brushed her golden-brown hair back from her face and tied it at her nape with a piece of red Christmas ribbon. Her own words, *fancy hairdos,* made her think of what Elliott had said last night about her "frigid little bun," and she inwardly winced. What an insulting term that was, and it hurt to think it had been passed among her peers during her Mercy term. It wouldn't surprise her at all if Elliott had been the first person to apply the degrading description to the sensible hairdo.

"But it's such a shame, Maggie. You never do anything just for fun, and you must work with some nice unmarried doctors. Don't any of them ever ask you out?''

"Hannah, today was fun," Maggie said quietly.

"Today was wonderful, but don't you need a man, Maggie? Mom and Dad would love to see you happily married, you know."

The direction of this conversation made Maggie uneasy, for it instantly brought Elliott to mind. He was far too good-looking, which, of course, was the reason a lot of women gushed like schoolgirls simply from hearing his name. And why an overbearing, egotistical, cocky personality made a man even more attractive to some women—even those who were extraordinarily intelligent in other matters—was a mystery to Maggie.

Well, she was immune to Dr. Sandwell's questionable charms, she told herself haughtily, then flushed hotly from head to toe at the memory of his midnight kiss on New Year's Eve. It was disturbing to realize that she wasn't nearly as immune to the man as she would like to be.

Noticing that Hannah was waiting for some kind of reply to her question about Maggie needing a man, Maggie shook her head. "Maybe someday, Hannah, but I'm too wrapped up in my career to even think about men right now."

Maggie drove home in a pensive mood. Tomorrow she would work on her lab again. There was equipment and supplies to put away, and she also had to make some decisions about office furniture. If Elliott refused her offer, would she look for someone else? In other words, if she couldn't have the best, did she want anyone?

Sighing heavily, Maggie parked her car and went into her apartment. Inside she headed straight for her bedroom, undressed and got into her nightgown. She had the bed turned down and was all set to retire for the night when she thought of checking her voice mail. Instead of lying down, she sat on the edge of the bed and used the nightstand extension telephone. She learned that she'd had one call…from Elliott!

Instantly on edge because he'd called, she listened to his terse message then put down the phone, sat there and worried. Did his calling so soon mean that he'd already made up his mind about the job?

It was almost eleven. Was that too late for her to call him now? But she knew that if she didn't, she wouldn't sleep all night wondering what he'd decided. Besides, she told herself, late-night calls weren't that unusual for doctors, never mind the fact that Elliott wasn't a practicing physician.

"Oh, damn," she mumbled, annoyed with her wishy-washy concern for the man. Why should she care if he'd happened to go to bed early—undoubtedly an unusual event for a man with his reputation—and her call woke him?

Unless he didn't go to bed alone!

The visual that thought created in her brain took her by complete surprise and was so painful that it actually stole her breath. Deeply shaken, she had to question her powerful but ludicrous reaction to something that had been none of her business in the past and should be none of her business tonight. Certainly the nervy kiss that Elliott had laid on her at the party last night hadn't affected her normal good judgment, had it?

"Impossible," Maggie said out loud and waspishly. Actually she was mad as hell that such a thing had even occurred to her. Did she care how many women Elliott Sandwell slept with? Good Lord, no! As for that midnight kiss, he'd just better not try anything like that again, damn his arrogant hide!

Squaring her shoulders she reached for the phone and dialed the number Elliott had recited in his voice mail message. Three rings later she heard his phone being picked up.

"Yeah...hello," he said a bit thickly.

"Sorry if I woke you, but I figured I'd better return your call tonight. I only got home a short time ago."

Elliott thought of her as she'd been at the party, stunningly beautiful and sexy enough to stop traffic and he immediately visualized her out on the town again this evening, wearing, of course, something comparable to that sinfully seductive red dress he'd seen last night.

She sure had changed from the "frigid bun" Maggie he'd known at Mercy, he thought with a peculiar resentment that made him wonder why her metamorphosis from caterpillar to butterfly should bother him in the least.

It didn't, he told himself, and he sat up in bed and said gruffly into the phone, "It's fine that you called tonight. I did some heavy-duty thinking all day and I have a few questions that need answers before I can make any kind of decision.''

''But you're seriously considering my offer? I hear something in your voice...'' Excitement had assailed Maggie so abruptly that speaking without tripping over her own tongue was difficult.

''I'm considering it, yes. But here's my dilemma. My present position is just about as long-term as I want to make it. You said that you'd come into some money, which you're using to fund your lab. Maggie, I have to know how much money you're talking about. If it's, say, twenty or thirty thousand, then you'd be out of business in a month. To be perfectly honest, you wouldn't even be able to get started, because the equipment that hematology research requires costs more than that. Are you grasping what I'm trying to get across?''

Maggie was irked that he would think she was too dense to understand what he was talking about. ''Let's get something straight, Elliott. I'm no Wall Street wizard when it comes to finances, but neither am I a complete moron. Believe me, I have a lot more money than twenty or thirty thousand.''

''How much more?''

''I don't think you have a right to ask me that.''

''I have every right. You asked *me* to quit a damn good job so I could work for you. Should I just ignore the possibility of your lab going belly-up in a few months because of short funding? No way, Maggie.

I'm either going to know the whole ball of wax or you can write me off. It's your call.''

She hated the idea of telling him anything at all about that money—she hadn't even told her family about it, if for very different reasons—but she hated much worse the thought of his walking away if she *didn't* give him an explanation. Still, his unethical brass galled her. *My money is none of his affair, damn it!*

''Did you demand that your current employer explain its financial situation?'' she asked frostily.

''Maggie, NTL Labs has been in business for over thirty years. I hardly think you can compare what you're trying to do to a company with that sort of longevity and a sterling reputation, to boot.''

She couldn't argue with that. In truth, her whole defense against revealing financial facts to Elliott or anyone else was deteriorating rapidly. If he meant what he'd said—and dared she doubt it?—she had no choice but to tell him the truth.

''I have two million dollars,'' she said without a dram of warmth in her voice. She resented this conversation and couldn't pretend otherwise.

On his end of the line, Elliott's jaw dropped. ''Where in hell did you get that kind of money?''

''From a friend. It was a gift.''

''A male friend?''

''As it happens, yes.''

Of course, Elliott thought. A rich male friend who was funding his sweetheart's hope of finding a cure for her sister. It was probably his money that had paid for that obviously expensive dress Maggie had worn last night.

Elliott felt suddenly deflated, as though some invisible pinprick had let the air out of his balloon. Something had, he realized uneasily, and it wasn't invisible at all. It was a combination of intense disappointment and Maggie herself, who wasn't even close to the shy, reserved young woman he remembered.

He drew a long breath. "Well, with the proper management, that amount of money should support a limited-goal lab for quite a long time."

She knew what he meant by "limited-goal lab" because the entire project was going to be focused on just one disease, but she wasn't quite sure about his reference to "proper management." Or perhaps the resentment she was feeling was over his gall in even hinting that she might not be managing her money well.

And so she said coldly, "Explain your interpretation of proper money management, if you don't mind."

"I don't mind at all, but maybe you don't need financial planning. I mean, when that two million is gone maybe your benefactor will replenish your bank account."

"Well, of course he won't!"

"He won't?" Elliott was puzzled. Obviously he hadn't figured out the whole score of the "Maggie and Wealthy Boyfriend" operetta. "If you're positive that's the case, then you definitely need some money management. I'd be glad to help you out with that, if you'd like.''

"You'd be glad to help spend my money?"

He missed the sarcasm in her voice. "Well, I guess you could put it that way," he agreed amicably. "You're going to have major expenditures at the onset of the project, but then things should settle down and you might even be able to budget your monthly costs. Of course, you'll want to be earning as much income as possible from that portion of your money not needed for immediate expenses.''

Maggie was thinking that he was much too interested in her money. She had deposited that enormous check in an interest-bearing account at a large bank. It was incredible to realize that if she never touched the principal, she would earn more money than she made in a year working as a physician. But she had to touch the principal; she'd already spent a shocking sum on necessary equipment—with more still to buy—and she hadn't yet furnished the offices.

"Well," she said coolly, "dare I ask if this conversation helped any with your decision?"

"It helped a lot."

"In that case, are you prepared to give me an answer tonight?"

"Not quite. I'd still like to take a look at the space you leased for your lab, and there's something that *you* should consider. If I did leave NTL I would have to give them at least two weeks' notice. They'd prefer a thirty-day notice, but I could probably get by with half of that.''

Maggie's heart began beating faster. He was getting close to saying yes! She could feel it in her bones. "I have no problem with that," she said, sounding much calmer than she felt. "In fact, I expected it."

"Do you have any free time tomorrow to show me the lab?" he asked.

"I'll be there all day." She recited the address. "Come by anytime."

"It'll probably be around noon."

"Fine. I'll be expecting you. Good night." Putting down the phone, Maggie saw the unsteadiness of her hand. Since she felt shaky all over, it didn't surprise her. But if just talking on the phone with Elliott made her tremble, how on earth was she going to work in close quarters with him day after day after day?

Chapter 3

Maggie worked steadily all morning. Deciding the most user-convenient spot in the lab for the equipment and supplies she unpacked occupied the forefront of her mind, but behind every thought was some discomfiting anxiety she couldn't dispel with the most resolute of intentions. It was caused by the upcoming appointment with Elliott, which was almost too silly to admit when she knew she would do almost anything to have him on her research team.

The truth was that she feared Elliott's reaction when he saw her today as she really was, wearing jeans, tennis shoes and just a touch of makeup. Her hair was down, but shortly after eleven she thought of the insulting term Elliott had applied to her bun, and she was glad she remembered it again because the memory bolstered her courage. So much so, in fact, that she deeply regretted going through all of that torment prior to New Year's Eve just to appear to run into Elliott by accident. She simply should have picked up the phone and called him. If he hadn't remembered her, so what? What she'd done, she thought with no small amount of self-disgust, was make herself look like a woman he could kiss on a whim, which he'd done and done thoroughly. Since he had no other recent face-to-face impressions to influence his opinion of her, he would arrive here today with that same misconception, which could be the primary cause of the butterflies in her stomach.

"Well, we'll just fix that, mister," Maggie muttered, and rushed to get her purse and take it into the bathroom. Within minutes she had brushed, twisted and pinned her hair into its usual workday bun. She was about to wipe away the light blusher from her cheeks and the faint lipstick on her mouth when she heard the buzzer. Apparently Elliott had arrived.

The door was glass, and Elliott saw Maggie coming to unlock it for him. Her hairdo took him by surprise and he wondered if she'd purposely arranged that bun today. He vowed on the spot not to mention it or to let on in any way that he'd even noticed it. But what a waste of beauty, he thought, recalling how she'd looked at the party. She had an incredible figure, but she was back to hiding that fact today with baggy jeans and an oversize T-shirt.

She was one very confusing lady, he thought just as she opened the door and said, "Hello. Come in."

"The buzzer's a good idea," he said. "Was it already installed when you took possession?"

"No, I had it put in. Knowing how lost I can get in work, someone could rap his or her knuckles raw on the locked door and I wouldn't hear it. Also, I'll probably be working some late nights, so it's a safety precaution, as well. Did you notice the alarm system?"

Elliott was inside, so she shut the heavy door and it locked automatically. "Yes, I did. Another good idea." He began looking around. "How many rooms?"

Elliott was wearing lab clothes, white cotton shirt and pants. Maggie recalled how gorgeous he'd looked in his black tuxedo on New Year's Eve and then had to admit that he looked almost as good in working whites.

She regrouped her thoughts, taking them far, far away from Elliott Sandwell's looks. "There's this small anteroom and three others...two that I'm planning to use for the actual research and the third for an office. There's a rest room, of course. Come on, I'll give you the tour." She led the way to the two rooms slated for research, and Elliott took a look at the equipment and supplies she had placed in each, on counters and in cabinets.

They discussed various pieces of the scientific equipment she'd purchased and then he said, "You didn't suggest my doing this, but I went ahead and made a list of items that I feel are necessary for even

a small lab. Maybe you'd be interested in seeing it.''
He took it from his shirt pocket and held it out to her.

Maggie had a sudden yen to tell him, ''Thanks, but
no thanks.'' And maybe to add that since she hadn't
asked for his help in equipping the lab—which he'd
obviously noticed—then he should have concluded
that she didn't need or want it. After all, she was no
stranger to hematology research, even if she wasn't
in his league.

The point she would like to emphasize right up
front was that if he took the job he would be working
for her, and regardless of his advanced experience in
the field, she was still going to be the person running
the show.

It took almost superhuman effort to keep her mouth
shut on that subject, but her laying down the law before he'd actually said yes to her job offer really was
putting the cart before the horse. She plucked the list
from his hand, tucked it into a front pocket of her
jeans then brought him to the third room. ''This will
be the office.''

Elliott nodded his approval. ''Seems ample. It all
does. Maggie, do you think your sister would sign
some release forms so I could speak to her doctors?
I'm assuming, of course, that she's dealing with spe-
cialists.''

Maggie's breath caught. He was going to say yes!
Why else would he want to discuss Hannah's condition with her doctors?

''Her primary physician is Dr. Worrick, though she
sees at least four other doctors for various ailments

related to her disease. I can't imagine her refusing to sign releases, so I'll give you a yes answer to that question.''

"Worrick's a good man.''

"Hannah has always had good doctors. That's never been her problem,'' Maggie said quietly.

Elliott sensed how distressing the subject was to Maggie. They would, of course, have to discuss Hannah's history many times and in intricate detail if he came to work for her, but there was no need for that today.

Leaning his shoulder against a wall, he gave Maggie a long look. She felt like squirming under such intense scrutiny, especially since her temperature seemed to be rising at an alarming rate. But she vowed to fall over dead before letting Elliott Sandwell know that she was no more immune to his good looks and powerful chemistry than any other woman.

To show him just how unaffected she was, she, too, leaned casually against a wall, choosing one across the empty room from where he stood.

Elliott realized that he was thinking a lot more about her sensual mouth and how it had felt when he'd kissed her than he was about the subject at hand. He gave his head a small shake to clear it, pushed away from the wall and began walking around the room.

Maggie's pulse was racing. She could tell that he was on the verge of giving her an answer, and she all but held her breath until he finally stopped pacing and looked at her again.

"I'll turn in my resignation to NTL this afternoon, but there's no way I can get out of a two-week notice. Although I normally work much longer days, technically my shift is over at six in the evening. What I'd like to do is grab some dinner and then come over here. Should make it by seven. Does that meet with your approval?"

Her jaw dropped and it took a few seconds for her to gather her wits. "Yes…yes," she finally managed to utter, absolutely astounded that he'd accepted her offer in such an offhanded way. She'd worried this moment to death and he'd handled it with complete self-control and an admirable suavity. It flashed through her mind that Elliott Sandwell had everything that any woman could want in a man—charm, intelligence, good looks, wit and sex appeal. Oodles of sex appeal. *Mountains* of sex appeal.

"I…I'll notify my accountant to put you on the payroll as of today," she said shakily.

"Fine. Do you have an extra door key, in case you're not here at seven?"

"Oh, yes, of course." She had to think where she'd left her purse, and when she remembered she dashed for the rest room. With trembling hands, she dug out a key and hurried away. Elliott was waiting in the anteroom. She walked up to him and put the key in his outstretched hand. Breathlessly she explained the alarm system, how to set it, how to shut it down.

Although Elliot appeared perfectly calm throughout her little speech, she wasn't and any attempt to conceal how emotional she was over this incredible business liaison fell flat. Her voice trembled when she spoke and her eyes were a bit watery.

"I don't know how to thank you enough," she said huskily. "At least I can't think of a way right at the moment."

Elliott gave her a cocky wink and grin. "Maybe we can work on that together."

He'd startled the misty emotions from her system. "Work on what together?" she asked blankly.

"Oh, this and that," he said nonchalantly. "By the way, don't put a desk for me in the office. I'd like about a six-foot table in the biggest lab room for my computer, and shelving above that for my books and such." He glanced at his watch. "Got to go. If you're still here at seven, I'll see you then. If not, I'll see you whenever. Bye for now."

She barely had time to stumble over a simple goodbye before he was gone. For a few seconds she could see him walking away through the plate glass front door, then he was out of sight.

Truthfully she didn't know whether to laugh or cry. Her emotions were in shambles. Unquestionably she was grateful he'd said yes to working in her lab, but his acceptance wasn't entirely comforting, either.

Perhaps she shouldn't be thinking of herself at a time like this, but dealing with Elliott on a daily basis wasn't going to be easy for her. She remembered avoiding him and his weird sense of humor at Mercy, which would be impossible to do from here on in. She'd made this particular bed herself—granted, out of necessity—and she would have to sleep in it no matter how aggravating Elliott became. God knew the man could drive her up the wall.

The next few days were hectic and Maggie was extremely busy. However much there was to be done, though, Maggie made certain that she left every day before Elliott arrived.

Actually, she wanted to strangle him and was afraid that she just might try it the next time she saw him. The very first night that he'd shown up for work he had moved every single piece of lab equipment from where she'd placed it to a different spot. She couldn't detect even one small benefit from the rearrangement and had moved everything back to its original setting.

The next morning she furiously gritted her teeth when she saw that Elliott had reciprocated and everything was again where he wanted it. The only difference was that morning she found a note from him. Written first on the paper was a quote.

"He that has much to do will do something wrong."

Samuel Johnson

Maggie:

Do you want this lab arranged for your convenience or for mine? Considering the generous salary you're paying me, I would think you'd want me functioning at my very best level. Try to control your urge to control, okay?

Elliott

His message infuriated her. *Try to control your urge to control.* How dare he? This was her lab, damn him!

Angry or not, she hadn't touched the lab equipment again. The day would come, of course—and very soon, actually. Just as soon as she got everything else organized to her satisfaction—when she would be working with the same equipment that Elliott was using now. Constantly butting heads with him over one thing or another was a dismal prospect, but Maggie knew that she was not going to take any guff off of him, either.

So, she fine-tuned her office, even adding a comfortable sofa for naps during those long, long days that she anticipated would be more normal than not, once she got back into her own research.

One evening she took a handful of medical release forms and drove to her parents' home to see Hannah. After a cup of coffee, some homemade cookies and a family chat, Maggie took her sister to the den.

"Another researcher is working on your case, Hannah, and he needs your signature on these forms so he can get information from your doctors." Maggie hadn't missed the dark circles under her sister's eyes; Hannah was again entering a "down" cycle, and how many more of those could she take?

"Another researcher?" Hannah echoed listlessly. She signed the releases with barely a glance, another sign that she wasn't feeling well.

"A very good researcher," Maggie said gently, recognizing that her own heart was breaking a little more each day over Hannah. "The best in Texas, I've heard from many sources."

"That's nice."

Hannah was so uninterested in research or anything else that Maggie gave her sister a warm, loving hug and took her leave. All the way home she had to keep a tissue handy to sop up the moisture that kept blurring her vision. When she was finally within the perimeter of her apartment complex, she didn't immediately get out of her car and go in. Instead, she sat there gripping the steering wheel and thinking about the path her life had taken.

She was in her final segment of medical school when Hannah became ill. At first her doctor thought she had a severe case of the flu. In brief, it had taken two years, a barrage of tests and a small army of doctors to finally diagnose Hannah's rare, degenerative blood disease. It had been a blow that had sent the Taylor family reeling, Maggie included.

One result of the shock was losing her sense of humor. She'd always been on the serious side, but after Hannah's diagnosis it took more than a little joke to make Maggie laugh. She'd known that her peers had deemed her a hopeless prude, but with Hannah almost constantly on her mind, Maggie hadn't given too much time to other people's opinion of her solemn-faced behavior. She'd worked hard, studied hard and avoided the clowns—especially Elliott Sandwell—whenever possible.

The question, of course, was just how amusing would she have found Elliott's shenanigans—which had seemed to keep everyone else in stitches—if the sense of humor she'd been born with hadn't completely vanished.

Then there'd been Elliott's good looks for her to deal with. Oh, yes, she'd noticed. Her libido hadn't been working all that well at the time, but any woman with eyes in her head couldn't have missed Dr. Sandwell's devilish grin and movie-star handsomeness.

Maggie frowned when she realized that Elliott Sandwell was even better looking now than she remembered. His features had matured. He had a touch of gray in his dark hair. And could anyone who'd ever met him, man or woman, doubt his masculinity when he seemed to exude it from every pore?

Maggie felt suddenly breathless. What in heaven's name was she doing, sitting in her car in the dark and thinking about Elliott's long lanky body and piercing blue eyes? Making a wild grab for the door handle, she gathered the release forms and her purse and then jumped from the car muttering under her breath. Was she demented? She had to work with the man, and the only thing she should feel when Elliott came to mind was gratitude that he'd accepted her offer, just as she was so very, very grateful for Ryan Fortune's generous gift. Ryan Fortune's unexpected and almost unbelievable generosity had turned her world upside down. It had also changed her, giving her a confidence she had never before possessed. Without that great new feeling she knew that she would never have worked up the courage to approach Elliott on any level. And now he was working for her, starting on research that could save Hannah's life.

Although he couldn't possibly know that he was on Maggie's exact wavelength at exactly the same moment, Elliott—still at the lab—was also thinking about Maggie's two-million-dollar gift. In fact, it became uppermost in his mind and he closed a book from which he'd been copying important data to a notebook that he kept very much like a diary. At least he dated his entries, along with noting the source of the information, just in case he wanted to look it up again.

Leaning back in his chair, Elliott locked his hands behind his head and stared into space with a slight frown between his eyes. *Maggie said that a male friend gave her the money. What kind of guy hands out a gift of that size without getting something in return? He's rich, of course, and the two of them must have been close. Extremely close. Why is he no longer on the scene? Does he live in San Antonio? Is he someone with a recognizable name?*

So, Sandwell, if you're theory is correct, then Maggie's not nearly the little Puritan she'd like everyone to believe she is. Think about that for a minute. Think about how she looked on New Year's Eve, and how she let you kiss her. She kissed back, too, don't forget that.

But getting back to her source of financing for this lab, if she doesn't invest wisely she'll run out of funds within a couple of years. And it will be sooner than that if she doesn't keep a tight rein on expenses. Does she realize that? Does she have anyone advising her, preferably a professional? She didn't like talking about her money when you brought it up before, but she won't like it if this lab goes belly-up, either.

You have no choice. You have to at least ask her if she'd like the name of your financial planner.

With that decision made, Elliott reached for another book to peruse for data on Hannah's disease. Letting his mind wander had broken his concentration, however. Instead of absorbing information, he thought of Maggie again. *Every damn time I see her she's a different person. At Mercy she was all business and as stiff-necked as they come. On New Year's Eve she was the kind of sexy siren that every man dreams of meeting. Or she was at first, anyhow. God, she was beautiful! Doesn't she know how truly beautiful she is? Even dressed the way she was the other day right here in the lab. That bun has to go, though.*

Someday, Maggie girl, I'm going to take your hair down, and you want to know something else? I'm betting I can make you like it!

That thought was followed by a visual so unnerving that Elliott gave up on any more work tonight. After turning out the lights, setting the alarm system and making sure the door was locked, he walked to his car, got in and drove home.

It was immensely disturbing to realize that when he went inside his house he was still thinking about Maggie and still feeling unnerved by an imagination he couldn't seem to control.

Chapter 4

As Maggie set the signed release forms next to Elliott's computer on the table he preferred over a desk, her gaze wandered. The newly installed shelving above the table was laden with medical books and manuals. A notebook lay open on the table, and she bent a bit to see the writing better. It was a collection of data pertinent to Hannah's illness, she saw, very similar to notebooks she kept for her own use.

Maggie was suddenly saturated with gratitude so strong and overwhelming that her emotions went awry and caused tears to fill her eyes. There was something quite miraculous about it all, and yes, Maggie could get very emotional about it. With a bit of a poignant smile tipping her lips, she wiped her eyes. She could feel in her bones that a wonderful day was in the making, and it was time she got it underway.

Leaving Elliott's personal workspace, Maggie made several trips to her car and carried in the boxes she'd brought from home that morning. This was the day she'd been looking forward to since receiving Ryan's check—the onset of her own full-time research. The lab was finally equipped, furnished and supplied, and from now on she could give her complete attention to finding that cure.

Still influenced by the intense gratitude she'd experienced a short time before, she unpacked the boxes in her office—all the notes and records and books she'd kept through the years while running herself ragged, squeezing time for research out of days that were already heavily scheduled with patient care. The incredible sense of freedom she felt now had a joyous quality, but she didn't have time to stand around and bask in anything frivolous. That was a pleasure to be saved for the day when some experiment or idea clicked. For the day when she knew without a doubt that she or Elliott, or the two of them together, were finally on the right track.

Caught up in sorting and deciding what should be kept or discarded, Maggie didn't hear Elliott come in. In fact she was completely unaware of his presence until she heard him drawl, "A special occasion, as I live and breathe. Your hair is down."

She jumped a foot, then glared at him leaning so nonchalantly against the woodwork in the doorway and spoke sharply. "Don't sneak up on me like that!"

"I didn't sneak. I unlocked the door and came in. What're you doing?"

"Working. What're *you* doing?" He wasn't supposed to be there in the daytime yet, was he?

"I figured you'd be here. I had a little free time at NTL, so I took advantage of it to come over here to talk to you." Elliott left the doorway and sat in the chair in front of her desk.

"Talk about what?"

"Well, I didn't plan to open our conversation with a compliment, but you look terrific with your hair like that." He smiled.

She didn't smile back. "It seems to me that the state of my hair has always taken up far too much of your time, Dr. Sandwell. Why don't you worry about your own mop, or one of your girlfriends' hair, and leave mine alone?" All she'd done after her morning shower was brush her hair back from her face and secure it with an elasticized ribbon. She'd chosen a blue one that matched the comfortable blue dress she'd put on, but that was as fancy as she'd gotten, which, in her estimation, was pretty darned ordinary.

"Testy, testy," Elliott chided with a devilish grin. "Sounds like you've got something against compliments, which couldn't possibly be the case when your preferred evening wear is something red, revealing and sexy, designed solely to attract attention."

Maggie's cheeks got pink. He hadn't yet figured out that he alone had been her target that night, but he was getting too near the truth for her comfort.

"That…that dress was a mistake," she mumbled.

"Why do you say that?"

"Could we please talk about something else? If talking is what you came for, you must have a topic in mind."

Elliott chuckled. "I do, but let me say one thing before getting to it. One of these days, or nights, I'm going to have the pleasure of seeing you in that dress again."

Maggie's jaw dropped and her eyes got huge. He could put her on the hot seat faster than anyone she'd ever known, and she didn't like the feeling. Anger could very easily get the better of her right now, she realized, because she was thinking that if she didn't need his expertise in the lab so badly, she would first rip his monumental conceit to shreds with some razor-sharp words and then show him the door.

"I don't...think so," she mumbled, terribly disconcerted because only minutes ago her gratitude for Elliott Sandwell's chosen career which had ultimately led him to her little lab had been enormous, and now she'd like nothing better than to slap his smug face.

"Wanna bet?" The devil himself was in Elliott's blue eyes, and it was obvious even to Maggie that Dr. Sandwell was enjoying himself.

At her expense, of course, but showing him the door was out of the question, and besides, she really shouldn't let his silly flirting upset her. *Play it cool, for heaven's sake!*

"I'd really like to get back to work," she said with as much dignity as she could muster. "What did you come here to say?"

Elliott studied her pretty, flushed face for a few moments and wondered what was really going on behind those lovely eyes. Without question she was the toughest-to-read woman he'd ever known. One would think that if a woman bought a dress like that red one—and undoubtedly paid a pretty penny for it—she'd be thrilled to wear it. Especially when she looked in it the way Maggie had.

He gave up on understanding Maggie today and said, "I got to worrying about your financial status again. Two million's a lot of money, but it could dribble away awfully fast without the proper management."

Maggie stiffened. He was far too interested in her money. Was all that cash the reason he'd come to work for her? Her stomach suddenly felt as though it contained a lead weight. Would Elliott attempt to woo her into a romantic relationship with compliments and flirtatious remarks just to get his hands on her money? Did she know him well enough to doubt it?

Nonsense! How would he get a cent of your money if you didn't give it to him, which you're certainly not going to do? Yes, some women make foolish, regrettable mistakes because of men, but that is not going to happen to you. In the first place, no amount of masculine charm will ever lure you into a romantic relationship. Romance is simply not on your agenda, especially romance with a man of Elliott's reputation.

"I am not going to discuss finances with you," she said flatly. "I thought I made that clear when the subject came up before."

"Maggie, I'm only trying to help. Do you have a financial planner?"

"Yes. Me."

"Not good enough, babe. Here's the name of my advisor." Elliott laid a business card on the desk.

"*You* have a financial planner?" There was doubt in her voice.

Elliott heard that doubtful note but ignored it. "You bet I do, and he's good, Maggie. I'd like you to meet him. One of these days when you have a few extra minutes, give him a call."

"I rarely have 'extra minutes.'" This conversation was making her nervous and resentful. He had no business butting in. As she saw it, the biggest threat to her financial stability was wastefulness, such as spending money the way she had for her New Year's Eve getup. But she couldn't regret that shopping spree, not when it had resulted in her landing the biggest fish in the medical research sea. At least in the San Antonio area.

She changed the subject. "I put the signed releases next to your computer."

Elliott nodded. "Good. Thanks." He eyed the business card he'd placed on her desk, then lifted his gaze to her face. "You're not going to call Jerry Hunt, are you?"

"Is that his name?" Maggie felt an urge to say without kindness, "Would you mind your own damned business and leave mine alone?" Instead she breathed deeply and said with hardly any inflection at all, "Please don't press me on that. Not today, at least. This is a red-letter day for me, my first as a full-time researcher, and I'm quite excited about it and don't even want to think about other things, let alone money.''

She was "quite excited"? Elliott couldn't see one single trace of excitement on her face and certainly not in her eyes. He wondered if she even knew what real excitement felt like, the kind that sizzled and broiled in a person's body and made them look and act giddy.

Oh, yes, he thought then, she had seemed pretty excited over their New Year's Eve kiss. But then his eyes narrowed slightly as he thought that she could have been playacting.

That idea was surprisingly unpleasant for Elliott, and he tried to push it from his mind. It bothered him that she wouldn't even consider talking to Jerry—or any other financial advisor, apparently—but maybe he could convince her of the sensibility of taking better care of her money once he was working with her everyday.

Elliott got to his feet. "Congratulations on finally attaining your red-letter day. See you sooner or later…I suppose.''

Fear suddenly bolted through Maggie, fear that he would change his mind about working for her. She rose from her chair. "You suppose?''

"I only meant that we've been like two ships passing in the night.''

"Yes, but you'll be here in the daytime very soon now…and I'll be here…and…'' Maggie walked around her desk with the intention of seeing him to the front door. Her newly gained confidence wasn't so deeply embedded that she didn't need reassurance now and then, she realized uneasily. One tiny hint from Elliott that he might *not* be working in her lab was devastating to her hopes and dreams, which in turn drained her confidence.

Elliott was positive that he heard a touch of panic in her voice. Timing his steps so they would reach the door of her office at the same time, he stopped walking and put his hand on her arm to stop her. She looked at him questioningly, and he said softly, "Obviously you find it hard to believe, but I am a man of my word, Maggie."

She stared into his deep blue eyes and felt a wave of heat run rampant throughout her system. "Yes...of course you are," she said huskily.

"Now you believe it, but you didn't a minute ago." Elliott moved closer to her. He raised his free hand to her other arm, and when she didn't protest the advance, he slowly urged her forward.

She knew he was planning to kiss her, and God help her she also knew she should do something to prevent it from happening. But she couldn't seem to make her body do anything but ache for...for something! For this man's kiss? What was wrong with her? Elliott Sandwell probably couldn't count the number of women he'd kissed...and slept with, as well!

Regardless, when he lowered his head and his face moved closer and closer to hers, she moistened her lips with a flick of her tongue instead of shrieking in anger, or simply backing away from him.

Elliott gently placed his mouth on hers, and he actually felt the tiny gasp she expelled ripple through her body. Her excitement excited him. Her soft lips against his excited him. He teased her lips with the tip of his tongue until she parted them. He felt her hands slide up his chest and caress the back of his neck. His pulse went wild and his kiss became hungry. Her participation fueled the flames of his desire, and he had not the slightest doubt that *her* desire was equal to his own.

He ran his hands up and down her back while one kiss melted into another. Cupping her buttocks he pulled her hips forward so she would feel how aroused he was. They weren't inexperienced kids, and for Elliott there was only one logical conclusion to so much passion between two consenting adults.

"Baby...sweetheart..." he whispered hoarsely between kisses that were becoming hurried and urgent, and he began working up the skirt of her dress.

Dazed by an onslaught of unfamiliar but totally delicious feelings, Maggie just let it all happen. It was as though she'd entered a wonderland, a dream world, where everything was sensation and need. She loved the crisp hairs on the back of his neck, and she kept stroking him in that sensitive spot. And oh, yes, she most certainly felt the hard length of his arousal pressing into her abdomen. It was a sensation she never wanted to end. His kisses were the kind that women fantasized over, and Maggie couldn't seem to get enough of them.

It was when his hand crept inside her panties that the full realization of what she was doing struck her hard and without the least bit of compassion.

She tore her mouth from his and gasped, "Stop...stop."

Elliott heard her, but he had just reached his target, and he couldn't resist gently caressing the core of her sexuality. Her responsive moan was music to his ears, and he whispered, "Are you sure you want me to stop?"

She wasn't sure at all, not with his hand and fingers doing such incredible things and her own body growing weak from the sweet torment besieging it. But somewhere in her nearly stupefied brain sensibility still reigned. She needed Elliott in her lab, not in her bed! This must stop now, and never be repeated.

"Please...no...we...Elliott, we...can't do this." She grabbed his hand and pulled it from under her skirt.

Her stammering response denoted confusion to Elliott and seemed to just beg him to at least try to rekindle her passion. His was certainly still burning. "We can't? Why not?"

"Because..." Escaping his arms, she nervously straightened her clothing and tried to calm her speeding heartbeat. "We just can't, that's why not."

"You mean that *you* can't. Or you won't." Folding his arms across his chest, Elliott leaned against the wall. "Your rich boyfriend is still in the picture, right?"

"My rich boyfriend?" She was on the verge of an adamant denial when it occurred to her that her having a boyfriend could always be used as an excuse to keep Elliott at arm's length. He'd proved today that he thought of her as fair game, and she could not spend their time together playing house instead of working. Never mind that he'd just made her feel more like a woman than she ever had in her life. Never mind that she would like to lie down on the carpet for him. Those things didn't matter; Hannah's life did.

She hated lying and avoided looking into his eyes when she said, "You're right, of course. I believe in one-on-one relationships, and so does my, uh, friend."

He was studying her intently. Something was amiss—Why wouldn't she look at him?—but he could only guess at what it might be.

"You're completely faithful to each other? Sounds like he's much more than a friend. Are the two of you engaged?" A yawning disappointment seemed to suddenly grip his interior, and it startled him that he would give a damn one way or the other.

"We're...still in the talking-about-it stage," Maggie mumbled.

Elliott's eyes darkened. "But you are talking marriage."

One lie *always* led to another...and another. Maggie's stomach clenched in protest of continuing this charade, but she forced herself to reply, if reluctantly and with very little conviction.

"I guess you could say that."

Her puny, lackluster tone of voice increased Elliott's suspicion that all was not sweetness and light with this discussion. She'd kissed back like there was no tomorrow, so Mr. Moneybags wasn't doing his duty in the physical affection department. Elliott was experienced enough to know that a man had no chance at all with a woman who was totally contented with her sexual partner. Maggie wasn't even close to being contented, and if her "fella"—whomever in hell he was—hadn't suddenly invaded her thoughts a few moments ago, she would be on the carpet this minute. They'd both be.

Shaking that image was impossible for Elliott. The ache in his groin was going to wreak its havoc for a while yet, and his staring at Maggie's mouth with hungry eyes sure wasn't going to ease his discomfort any.

Unreasonably ticked off at himself, at Maggie, and at the world in general, Elliott growled, "I've gotta go." He left abruptly, and before Maggie could do more than move into the doorway, he'd gone through the outside door.

Weakened beyond anything she'd ever experienced before, she stumbled back to her desk and fell into her chair. She'd let him kiss her. She had no one to blame for that stupidity but herself.

And then she'd lied, and, oh hell, the whole thing

was a big mess. How was she going to work with
Elliott every damned day with this between them?

The following morning Maggie sat at her desk and
shoved her purse in a drawer. Before leaving yesterday she had neatly stacked papers and file folders to
one side, thus the piece of paper positioned squarely
in the center of the blank desktop stood out like a
sore thumb. Instantly she knew what it was—another
note from Elliott.

Maggie clenched her jaw. She'd put in a bad night,
alternating between supreme regret and sublime bliss,
every damned second of her misery caused by Elliott
Sandwell, and she was in no mood for another of his
faultfinding messages. What had the first been about?
Oh, yes, something about her controlling her urge to
control. He was a hypocrite, preaching to her about
self-control when he obviously let his own urges run
wild. What she should do was crumple his note and
throw it away without reading it.

But of course she couldn't do that. Something per-
verse in her system made her pick up the paper and
focus her eyes on the handwriting. It read:

"A woman prefers a man without money to
money without a man."

Greek Proverb

Do you agree that our obvious and mutual sexual
attraction is not caused by but is in some vague
way associated with money? Your money, of

course. Or perhaps its origin. I seem to be suffering an unfamiliar (until now) malady that I cannot bring myself to openly acknowledge by giving it a name. Maybe I should leave that to you and put my trust in your kindness.

Elliott

Unlike his first note, which had contained no hidden meanings, this one was rampant with thought-provoking elements. Reading it over and over only increased Maggie's confusion about it. That "obvious and mutual sexual attraction" phrase tortured her, probably because of the awful night she'd put in debating that very...sin? Crime? Stupidity?

As far as naming his malady, that was easy. It was lust—unrequited, as it were—and could not possibly be anything else. If he considered her label unkind—although she doubted that even he would have the gall to mention the subject in person—that was just too bad. She didn't like his proverb any better than she had any of his other references to her money, and she really would like to write him a return note that would scorch his eyeballs.

She was mentally devising that scathing communiqué when her phone rang. She'd had so few calls since opening her lab that she jumped in surprise then took a moment to collect herself before answering.

"Taylor Laboratory."

"Hi. Good morning. This is Elliott. Did you see my note?"

She was nearly struck dumb by his audacity and reacted obtusely. "What note?"

"Oh. Then you haven't read it yet. I put it on your desk. Aren't you in your office?"

She heaved a long-suffering sigh and admitted with exasperation, "All right, I saw your note. What about it?"

"Do you understand it?"

"Yes, and if you think I'm looking for a man with or without money, you're so far from the truth that you wouldn't recognize it if you happened to trip over it. And another thing..."

"Whoa. Hold on a second. Forget the note. If it upset you that much I'm sorry I wrote it. I didn't call to discuss that anyhow. My primary reason for calling was to ask you to have dinner with me tonight."

"Dinner?" she echoed flatly. "What for?"

"Do we need a reason to break bread together?"

"Yes, as a matter of fact. I have a million things on my mind and none of them are remotely related to breaking bread with anyone, let alone a man who proved only yesterday and again in writing that one of the things on *his* mind is coercing me into bed. Elliott, let me put this as plainly as I can. I do not date. I haven't dated in years, and I do not intend to start cluttering my life and scrambling my thoughts with romantic nonsense at this point. You and I have an important business relationship, and I would appreciate your doing your part to keep it at that."

"Restrict our relationship to strictly business, hmm? Sorry, babe, I'm not sure I can do that." His voice became lower, deeper, with a sensual quality that caused Maggie's heart to beat faster. "Maggie, I haven't been able to get you out of my mind since yesterday, when your wet, full lips were devouring mine and my hand was between your legs. We wanted the same thing, sweetheart, and feelings that strong don't just vanish because the people involved prefer they would. Have dinner with me tonight. Who knows where a little bread-breaking might lead?"

She hesitated, then said the only thing she could say to his preposterous question. "We both know where it might lead. Goodbye, Elliott. I have work to do." She put down the phone, then sat there shaking like a leaf. He wanted to make love to her! His note said so without actually spelling it out, and so had his dinner invitation and bedroom voice.

God help her, she wanted the same thing. How did a woman forget something like that? She would remember his sinfully sexy hand for the rest of her lonely life. Elliott was making her question the dedication she'd lived with for so long, and it wasn't fair. She could not trade Hannah's life for a sexual fling with San Antonio's handsomest and one of its most sought-after bachelors, she simply couldn't! And it wasn't possible to work with Elliott during the day and share his bed—or hers—at night.

Or was it?

Chapter 5

Elliott was training his replacement at NTL. Perhaps *training* wasn't the best word, as Dr. Carlos Garcia knew his way around a medical lab almost as well as Elliott did. But Elliott had been working on four different projects in various stages of development and experimentation when he gave notice, and passing on his notes and personal observations regarding those projects to Dr. Garcia was crucial.

After seriously intense conversation with the young doctor for several hours that afternoon, Elliott's mind began wandering. There was something about his phone call to Maggie that morning that had started pestering him, although for the life of him he couldn't put his finger on it. And then without any sort of warning, the part of it that had been gnawing a hole in his gut was suddenly clear as glass. Maggie had said plainly that she didn't date now and hadn't dated for years, and that couldn't possibly be true! She had a wealthy boyfriend, didn't she? A wealthy, *generous* boyfriend?

Frowning, Elliott pondered the matter and finally reached a puzzling conclusion. Maggie had lied to him somewhere along the line, maybe this morning about not dating or maybe when she'd told him about the guy who'd given her that money. The question was why?

Something else struck him as odd, as well. If she was so involved with her big-money pal, why didn't he ever show his face at Maggie's lab? Elliott couldn't help thinking that he would have run into the guy at least once since his working arrangement with Maggie began. It was as though the man was a specter…or the figment of a fertile imagination.

But that conjecture didn't make sense. Someone had given Maggie an awful lot of money, and she'd said plainly that her benefactor was a man.

Elliott picked up a pencil and started doodling on a pad of paper. Maggie's friend was at least a millionaire, and how could an ordinary guy like himself compete with that?

Startled by his own progression of thoughts, Elliott's stomach knotted. *Was* he competing for Maggie's attention? When did that start, and why? He'd been a little bit in love numerous times, but all of those feelings had been below the belt.

Well, do you deny wanting Maggie?

Hell, no, but wanting to make love to a woman does

not necessarily mean a committed relationship! At least it never has before.

Totally unnerved, Elliott shoved back his chair, got up and walked to the window. He'd awakened this morning to gray skies, and now it was raining. In fact, from the size of the puddles in the parking lot, it had been raining for some time.

Staring outside at the spattering raindrops, Elliott realized that he felt gloomier than it looked beyond the window glass. He'd never personally known depression, for he'd been born with naturally high spirits and a positive attitude, but he wondered now if he wasn't getting his first real taste of the doldrums on this rainy day.

You want Maggie and she sure as hell kisses back as though she wants you. She put the brakes on this morning, but she hadn't really wanted to. And Maggie's been in your mind ever since. Face it, old sport, this isn't a normal case of jittery nerves over a desirable woman. You could be coming down with the one affliction you never thought would catch up with you—true love!

Elliott had succeeded in shocking the breath out of himself. He sucked in air and made an immediate decision. He would not live his life in a state of sexual and emotional limbo, and the only way out of that suffocating bind was to uncover Maggie's true feelings once and for all.

He knew of only one way to do that.

As usual, Maggie left the lab before Elliott was due to arrive. It wouldn't be long before they occupied the same workspace every darned day, so she was going to have to learn to deal with him a whole lot better than she'd been doing. For now though, she was grateful she *could* avoid him because of their differing timetables.

She drove directly to her parents' home and spent the evening with her family. By the time she drove home around nine-thirty, she didn't have the angst in her stomach that Elliott's phone call had created that morning, which made her think that just maybe she might be getting over the effects of so much emotional upheaval. She wasn't accustomed to yearning for sex, and she did not appreciate Elliott's insidious reminders that he was ready, willing and able to service any libidinous urges that might overcome her.

On the other hand, she couldn't deny his earthy magnetism and spectacular good looks. She'd noticed the same traits when they'd both been residents years ago, and unfair or not, he was even better looking now. She was positive that time hadn't been nearly as kind to her as it had been to Elliott, but then he didn't have the worries that she did, the kind of emotional stress that caused tiny wrinkles around one's eyes and mouth. She was positive that her face bore all the signs of the tension she had lived with for so long, but she'd never let anything so trivial as her own physical imperfections bother her. *And if how you look is bothering you now because of Elliott Sandwell, you're a bigger idiot than you ever thought possible!*

Sighing over the empty and hollow feeling in her

midsection, Maggie turned into the driveway of her apartment complex. After parking her car, she went inside and started getting ready for bed. She took a long hot shower and shampooed her hair, then with a towel around her head and wearing a terry robe, she decided to check her voice mail. Seated on the edge of her bed, she used the extension phone on the nightstand and heard that she had one message. After pressing the correct button, she listened to Elliott's voice.

"Maggie, I have some exciting news. I told you about my contacting Drs. Patric and Hedwig in Sweden, didn't I? To tell you the truth I can't remember for sure, but that's beside the point now. Late this afternoon I received a lengthy fax from them. Maggie, they've been working on the same theory that I've been studying and considering. What's more, so are you. I'm sure you won't mind that I checked the notes in your office, although it doesn't matter if you do, to be honest, not with this kind of headway. We're all on the same track, Maggie, and I have a gut feeling it's the right one. The fax is quite detailed, and I'm putting a copy of it on your desk so you can read it first thing in the morning."

By the end of the message Maggie's heart was pounding fast and hard. She couldn't wait until morning to read that fax, and the second she set down the phone she threw off her robe and pulled on sweatpants and an old shirt without slowing down for underwear. She put on tennis shoes without socks and then gathered her wet hair into one long twist, which she wound into a knot and pinned securely in place on the crown of her head. Grabbing her car keys and wallet from her purse, strictly the necessities for this late-evening jaunt, she ran from her apartment to her car and then pushed the speed limit all the way to her lab.

Even though she parked quite close to the building that housed her lab, she still had a short distance to walk. Rather, to run. She couldn't move slowly, not with the knowledge of that fax seeming to beat in her mind with the same fast rhythm as her heart. Was it really going to be this easy? No, *easy* wasn't the word to use so soon, for even if Elliott, the Swedish doctors and even she had all stumbled upon the right road that would lead to a successful cure for Hannah's condition, there would be myriad steps to take before any of them dared to celebrate.

Regardless, something in Maggie *was* celebrating. The joy that had lain buried within her for so long, awaiting the proper moment to escape its confines, seemed to be seeping into her system, just from the small light—ignited by Elliott—at the end of the frightening and oppressive tunnel that Maggie had been plodding through for years. She became so thankful for Elliott's brilliance that tears stung her eyes.

In a minute she saw the lighted windows of her lab up ahead and realized that Elliott must still be working. She slowed her step to battle a jab of uncertainty. She hadn't expected Elliott to be there, and however thankful she was for his involvement in her crusade, he unnerved her. She thought of how she looked and groaned under her breath.

But she was at the lab, and she certainly wasn't going to drive clear back to her apartment for some lipstick! Besides, probably the only thing on Elliott's mind tonight was that fax. And, oh, dear Lord, it *was* exciting!

Hurrying again, Maggie unlocked the lab door and went in. "Elliott?" she called.

Surprised but pleased, he appeared in the doorway connecting the anteroom and workrooms. "You got my message."

Maggie started walking toward her office. "Yes. I couldn't wait until morning to read the fax. Actually, I didn't expect you to still be here."

Elliott followed her into her office. "I know exactly how you're feeling. I've experienced this kind of exhilaration before. In research, the smallest success sends you soaring." He smiled. "Try to imagine how high we'll be flying when we hit the mother lode." Putting his hands on her desk he leaned over it and smiled directly into her eyes. "And we will hit it, Maggie, I know it now."

Her breath caught. He was a beautiful sight with his eyes shining and that glorious smile lighting his features, and if she leaned forward a mere few inches their lips would meet.

But his excitement wasn't caused by her, she thought and wished sadly that she gleamed as brightly as he did. It wasn't fair that it took hours of special attention to make herself even noticeable—such as had occurred on New Year's Eve—while Elliott glowed all the time.

Flushing to the roots of her hair, she lowered her gaze and picked up the sheaf of papers from her desk—the all-important fax.

Elliott didn't straighten up or move in any way. He was potently aroused, and if it were all because of a thrillingly successful day he would have noticed it before Maggie arrived. But the excitement he felt now was vastly different than before. Maggie looked unusually young tonight, so enchantingly beautiful in that perfectly awful shirt that he questioned his own judgment—and his eyesight.

But he knew there was nothing wrong with his eyes. Dr. Maggie Taylor had gotten under his skin as no other woman ever had—and she'd done it without flirty remarks or sexy clothes. *Hey, old sport, sex...or the promise of sex...was exactly how she got your attention New Year's Eve!*

Elliott couldn't refute that summation. Maggie *never* dressed like she had that night, nor did she ever flirt. She'd cast a line that night and he'd taken the bait exactly as she'd planned.

Maggie squared her shoulders and forced herself to look him in the eyes again. ''If you wouldn't mind, I'd like to read this now.''

Elliott straightened his back and nodded. ''Go right ahead. I'm going to get my copy and sit in here while you read it. You're going to have some questions, and since I've already discerned many of the answers, I'll be able to save you a lot of time.''

She was already starting to read, and she sat down and waved him off with a murmured, "Fine."

Elliott was badly shaken. Realizing that he could have fallen in love was a shock he'd never anticipated encountering. Especially when the lady in question wasn't the type of woman to which he was normally attracted. Glamour, a quick wit and a modern let's-get-it-on attitude were the elements that usually got his blood moving. Maggie had personified pure excitement on New Year's Eve. Since then, she'd done nothing to make him fall so hard.

Except kiss you back more than once! Yeah, that's right, she surely did do that. She's not flashy, but she's got all the right stuff. You might as well admit that it's beginning to drive you a little bit crazy.

Inhaling a long, hopefully calming breath, Elliott gathered his papers and returned to Maggie's office.

She never even looked up when he sat down.

While Maggie read with a frown of concentration creasing her forehead, Elliott's thoughts rambled. They had never eaten a meal together. They'd never sat down and just talked. He knew nothing about her favorite foods, books, movies, etc. Her rich boyfriend undoubtedly knew all those things about her, but Elliott didn't, and he sat there resenting and disliking a man he'd never met. Never even seen, for that matter. *You'd think she'd have a photograph of the guy in here, but she doesn't.* Maggie's one framed photograph was of her family. It appeared to be an enlarged snapshot, possibly one that Maggie had taken as she wasn't in the photo.

Elliott studied the people who were in the picture, Maggie's parents, obviously, and Hannah. Her sister was a pretty woman with dark hair and a sweet smile. There was a resemblance between Hannah, Maggie and their mother, although neither Hannah nor Mrs. Taylor looked to be made of steel, as Maggie did.

Bringing his gaze back to Maggie, Elliott felt a glimmer of understanding: Maggie wasn't really made of steel, she just acted as though she was. Probably because someone in the Taylor family had to be strong so they all could deal with Hannah's disease. With her being a doctor the others couldn't help looking to her for answers, and in doing so they had put a terrible burden on her slender shoulders, which she had accepted out of love. Plus, Elliot would bet, the Taylors probably had no idea of how much they depended on Maggie. Maybe even Maggie didn't realize it.

Oh, hell, he thought then, annoyed with himself over analyzing—or attempting to analyze—the inner workings of the Taylor family. There was truth in the old "walk in another person's shoes before judging them" adage. Take his burden theory, for instance. Maggie would probably rise up and brain him if he so much as hinted that Hannah was a burden to her.

Looking at her reading so intently he saw the tension in the way she held her head, in the set of her shoulders, even in her hands. He suddenly wanted to hold her, not for anything sexual but to comfort her, to add his strength to hers, to let her know that he cared and was there for her. He didn't do it, for Maggie broke the spell he seemed to have fallen under by speaking.

Without looking up she asked a question about the data she was reading. Elliott sat up straighter and gave her an answer. In a few seconds she asked another question, which he again answered, and within minutes they were discussing everything in the fax. Their conversation was technical and impersonal, and they were both so engrossed in it that neither took stock of the time.

At one point Elliott moved his chair around the desk to sit next to her, as he had numerous notes and charts that he wanted to explain. It was easier to do sitting beside each other, and for a long time they pored over papers and information with their heads practically touching. Certainly their upper arms were pressed together, and sometimes their thighs. But they were so absorbed in medical terms, theory and the professionally thrilling fax that neither noticed.

But then, abruptly, Maggie finished reading the final page. The question-and-answer session was over, and she watched uneasily as Elliott put his papers back in their proper sequence. His thigh was touching hers and exuding a warmth that seemed entirely masculine, which was really too silly to dwell upon. Body heat was the same, whether it came from a man or a woman.

Gingerly she moved her leg a fraction, just far enough to get it away from his. That was when Elliott woke up and became aware of their proximity.

"So," he said softly, "are you as convinced as I am that we're on the right track here?"

Maggie cleared her throat. He *was* referring to research, wasn't he? "Uh, yes, I'm sure we are."

"One of my never-fail signs is excitement in the pit of my stomach."

"Really. Well, since I've not yet had any real successes in research…"

Elliott turned his chair to face her. Putting his hands on the arms of *her* chair, he swiveled it to face him. "What makes you think I was talking about research?" He saw a hot light ignite in her eyes and he leaned forward to bring his mouth a mere breath away from hers. "I was, sweetheart, we both were, but that was while we were discussing the fax. All the while, though, the inner pressures were building, weren't they?"

"I…didn't feel any inner pressure," she whispered.

"You didn't acknowledge it. Neither did I, but you and I can't sit on top of each other like this for hours and feel nothing but scientific gratitude." He brushed her lips with his, and in the very next moment they were kissing and rising from their chairs at the same time. With complete grace they abandoned their seats and melted into one entity, as though they had done this a hundred times.

Maggie wasn't even surprised. Her mind was exhausted from studying the fax, then going over each speck of information with Elliott until they ran out of comments and speculation about it. It seemed, in fact,

as though her brain was far too full of medical terms
and data to absorb one more thing. The strange thing
was that her body, which had also felt exhausted only
seconds ago, now seemed restored and alive.

She kissed back hungrily and didn't care that her
eager response was completely physical. Too tired to
think, she returned kiss for kiss, and caress for caress.
Elliott's hands seemed to be everywhere, a delicious
sensation for Maggie, something that she hadn't felt
nearly enough of in her stressed-out lifetime. She
sensed his amazement when he discovered bare skin
under both her shirt and pants. She offered no explanation, not even when he unbuttoned and slipped the
shirt from her shoulders and then buried his face in
the cleavage of her breasts.

"Your skin smells like the most delicate of flowers," he said, and she heard the thickness of passion
and longing deepening his voice and turning it husky.

The flame in the pit of her stomach became a bon-
fire. Sucking in air, she slid her hands under his shirt
and then whispered, "Take it off."

He let go of her to yank the shirt over his head,
and when they embraced again the perception of her
unclothed breasts against his chest nearly undid him.
He kissed her with less tenderness, setting free his
own desire and asking silently for every ounce of
hers. He knew she was aroused, there was no way he
couldn't know. But he also knew that she was capable
of gasping out a sudden "No!" He'd never gone beyond a *no* from a woman, and he fully believed that
he never would, but if Maggie said no at this wildly

passionate moment, he wasn't sure of just how he would react. Certainly not with a smile and a casual "See you tomorrow."

No, he wanted it all. He *needed* it all, everything Maggie was and had to give. Wanting sex and wanting Maggie were two completely different things, he knew now, and he wondered vaguely within the passion-dense fog of his brain what she would say if *he* said, "I think I'm in love with you, Maggie."

But things were happening too satisfyingly fast for him to slow them down with words that just might turn her off. She had kicked off her shoes, and while kissing her incredibly sexy mouth he easily pushed down her fleecy, soft pants. She'd never been either ashamed or proud of her body, it was just part of who she was. Elliott's reaction to her nudity—"You're beautiful, Maggie, seriously beautiful"—along with the sizzling light in his eyes and the way his hands traced the contours of her figure, inspired belief and pride. For certain she had never felt her own femaleness so intently.

Without missing a beat Elliott walked them backward to the sofa. Maggie's cooperation was so exciting that he hated the moment that he had to leave her to shed his shoes and pants. Unquestionably she was sexually bedazzled, and if he did anything now to break the spell they were both under he would despise himself forever. He hurried through the task of undressing, then lay on his side on the sofa and snuggled up to her. There wasn't much room, none to spare, at any rate, and he put his arms around her and slid his right leg over hers, rather effectively surrounding her.

With his left arm under and around her neck, he kissed her lips, and his right hand went wandering. His fingertips adored her breasts, her small, tight waistline and the feminine flaring of her hips. Every part of her was perfect and womanly, her thighs, her flat belly, and her mouth that he knew he would never tire of lavishing with kisses.

His hand traveled to the juncture of her thighs, and while he ardently probed the moist, velvet depths of her mouth with his tongue, he gently but firmly moved her legs apart just enough to reach what he must.

Maggie gasped when he so skillfully began caressing her most sensitive spot. The heat and desire his touch caused overwhelmed her so quickly that she became both tearful and bold, emotionally begging him for more than he was giving.

"Elliott...please...make love to me. Do it...now."

"Yes, baby, yes," he whispered hoarsely, and moved on top of her in one fluid motion. He joined them intimately, kissing her face and lips with a groan of such pleasure that she responded with one of her own.

"Maggie...sweetheart...you're perfect."

His words sounded glorious to her. Somewhere in a nook or cranny of her mind lay the thought that she had never done anything quite as brazen or uninhibited before. Certainly she hadn't furnished her office with a sofa for this sort of usage. But having Elliott

Sandwell—gorgeous, sexy, cock-of-the-walk Elliott Sandwell—making incredible love to her and telling her that she was perfect—they *did* seem to fit together like two pieces of an erotic puzzle—turned her ordinary sofa into a magical flying carpet.

Feeling the culminating, rising tide of passion growing stronger with every movement between them, Maggie let herself go and began whimpering—not so quietly, either. She clutched Elliott to her bosom and dug her fingertips into his back. He began moving faster and said something about her being "hot…hot…hot," which made her response even wilder.

In seconds it hit her, a spiraling pleasure so intense that she began weeping. Wave after wave of the same incredible sensation washed through her, and while she was aware of Elliott's climax it was her own that held her captive.

When her rapture began subsiding, exhaustion reigned once more. This was a much different type of exhaustion than the weariness of body and brain she'd felt before Elliott kissed her. She was much too tired to talk, and she was falling asleep so quickly that she barely noticed Elliott rearranging their positions on the sofa, though she did relish the warmth when he pulled the afghan she kept folded on the back of the sofa over them.

Elliott had situated them so that he was curled around her, his front to her back. There was barely enough space on the sofa for even that tight-knit placement of two grown people, but he loved it that she couldn't—in her sleep, of course—unknowingly move away from him.

Their lovemaking had been wild and wonderful. Who would have guessed? he mused behind his closed eyelids. Who, among all the doctors and nurses that had known Maggie at Mercy, would ever have guessed that beneath her severely serious exterior had lain a woman so sensual, so *sexual,* so completely wanton once she was warmed up, that she'd nearly blown him away.

Chapter 6

Maggie was aware of being cramped and crowded long before she came fully awake. When she finally opened her eyes, saw the lights of her office and realized where she was, naked on the sofa with Elliott—also naked—wrapped around her, her heart started pounding like a jackhammer.

She remembered it all, how could she not with Elliott's manhood pressed against her derriere? *It...it was unbelievable! Do other women feel so much during sex? I never knew...I wondered, but I never really knew.*

Maggie wouldn't let herself even think that she'd missed a lot in life, but her body knew it. Every cell of her body knew it, in fact, especially the erogenous cells. *Does Elliott affect all the women he does this with in the same incredible way? He must. Now I'm*

*another notch on his bedpost. The sad thing is that
I'd like to do it again...and again. Why did my libido
have to come to life at this particular time with this
particular man?*

He was so very important to the success of her
undertaking. With that crucial information from the
Swedish doctors, Elliott had talked about how he intended to begin at once a continuation of their tests
and experiments. She knew that he was going to go
in to NTL in the morning and pick up his personal
belongings. He'd said, "Dr. Garcia is already doing
everything I did, so I'll be working here from now
on. I don't want to waste a minute in getting started."

They'd both been so high-minded, discussing the
fax and their plans, and then they'd ended up on the
sofa.

Biting her lip as the first pangs of regret struck
without mercy, Maggie tried to cautiously wiggle out
of Elliott's embrace. Because he was a deadweight
while sleeping, the arm and leg he'd laid over her
each seemed to weigh a ton.

She tried sliding over an inch and nearly fell off
the sofa. Catching herself in time, she felt Elliott stir.
Oh, no, he's waking up!

*Hey, you've got to face him sooner or later. It might
as well be sooner.*

Lifting his muscular arm *without* caution, she
shoved it away from her. She was about to do something about his leg when she heard, "What're you
doing, sweetheart?"

She swallowed dryly. "It has to be, uh, late. We should go home and get some real sleep."

"Yeah, we should. In a few minutes, okay?" Elliott moved them both so that she was on top of him!

"Elliott...we can't. Not again." Her voice was weak and not altogether steady. His arms held her in place while he nestled his burgeoning manhood precisely where he wanted it.

"Maggie, we can do anything we want," he retorted, mimicking her voice with a devilish little grin.

"This...can't become a...habit. I mean, it's just...not sensible for...two people who have to, uh, work together to be...doing this," she stammered.

"Don't be sensible, sweetheart," he whispered, and placing his hand on the back of her head, brought it down.

She watched his incredibly handsome face coming closer and knew another kiss was imminent. And another kiss would lead to more lovemaking.

"No," she said firmly just before their lips met.

"No?" He looked perplexed. "Is that a coy no or a definite no?"

"It's simply a no, Elliott. Now please let me get up."

Slowly and with a frown he released his hold on her, then watched her elude the afghan, move off of him and the sofa and immediately start to get dressed. He turned to his side and laid his head on the arm of the sofa to keep her in view.

"You're sorry we made love," he said quietly. "I wish you weren't."

"I wish a lot of things."

"You sound all torn up. We didn't do anything wrong, Maggie. *You* did nothing wrong. Please don't think you did."

Buttoning her shirt, she finally looked directly at him. "Easier said than done. For me, anyhow. I guess we all have to deal with our own conscience in our own way."

Elliott sat up. "Your conscience! Good Lord, Maggie, we didn't commit murder. Why in hell would you have to appease your conscience?"

Her eyes flashed in sudden anger. "For your information, I don't do this on a regular basis! So yes, my conscience is smarting. Yours probably isn't because you're so used to..." She stopped herself in midsentence. She had no right to judge Elliott's lifestyle, and certainly no right to do so out loud to his face.

"Sorry," she mumbled, and went to her desk for her key ring.

Elliott bounded off the sofa and took her arm. His eyes were blazing mad, and she blinked because she'd gone too far and knew it.

"The only thing you're sorry about," he said angrily, "is letting yourself feel something."

She gasped. "That...that's cruel!"

"Yes, it is. Looks like we both know how to be cruel, doesn't it?" Yanking her forward he ground his mouth on hers, kissing her as roughly as he knew how. When he needed air, he let go of her as abruptly as he'd taken hold of her, then, spinning away, he started getting dressed himself.

Shaken to her soul, Maggie hastily plucked her keys from her desk and practically ran from the office. She saw by the dash clock of her car that it was after three.

It didn't matter. She'd probably get precious little sleep now, anyway.

Battling tears, resenting Elliott one minute and her own mindless response to him the next, she drove the dark and all but deserted streets to her apartment.

Elliott drove home, as well. His eyes weren't misty with tears, as Maggie's were, however. Anger burned a hole in his gut, but it wasn't aimed at Maggie herself nearly as much as it was at her peculiar attitude. He honestly couldn't understand why a grown woman—a very passionate grown woman—would make love like there was no tomorrow and then resent her partner for taking her to the stars.

And then Elliott remembered that she had a boyfriend, a rich and possibly powerful boyfriend. "Oh, hell," he mumbled, because Maggie's personal liaison with another man only made what had taken place in her office tonight even more confusing.

He simply didn't get it, Elliott finally admitted with a heavy sigh of utter frustration. There was no figuring out Maggie Taylor, and he might as well stop trying.

As for the feelings that just kept getting stronger, no matter what did or didn't occur between them, he was going to have to learn to live with them. No, he wasn't accustomed to pining for an unattainable woman, but he'd survive.

Oh, yes, he most certainly would survive. And he'd give his all to his work. Maggie would never be able to say that tonight's events had affected his work. He would survive Maggie's undeserved rancor tonight, and he would survive working in close proximity with her all day, every day.

By the time Elliott pulled into his driveway, he was feeling a little better about the whole thing. Tomorrow, when he saw Maggie, he would act as though tonight had never happened. Since he believed wholeheartedly that she would be treating him coolly and distantly from here on in, pretending not to notice her unfriendliness was really the only thing he could do.

After all, he'd never had to beg for a woman's attention, and he sure as hell wasn't going to start with Maggie.

Maggie awoke slowly and realized before her eyes were fully open that she felt incredibly ebullient. She could not remember waking up in such a marvelous mood before—at least not since childhood—and it was a delicious feeling she wished would never end.

She lay there assessing her unusually good spirits and found herself reliving last night and the first time she had set eyes on Dr. Elliott Sandwell.

She'd been at Mercy for a week, maybe two, and she'd been walking a long corridor, heading for ICU to witness a special procedure on a heart attack patient. Maggie recalled the pressure of residency at a hospital of Mercy's renown. Every day was a learning process, every spare moment was spent in study, and the very, very few hours in between were used for sleep, of which she never quite got enough. Of course, neither did the other residents.

But lack of sleep definitely affected some more than others. She did blame a portion of her stress on Hannah's illness, which was as yet undiagnosed. Named or not, though, Hannah had contracted something frightening, and she was never far from Maggie's conscious thoughts.

At any rate, she'd been walking, undoubtedly with a frown of concentrated worry, as was her habit, when she saw two young male doctors coming toward her. Everything—good and bad—fled her mind as she stared at the taller man. Never had she seen anyone so stunningly beautiful, man or woman. And his smile! He and the other resident were obviously enjoying a carefree conversation, because they kept smiling and even laughing.

Maggie had panicked. What if they said hello, or worse, stopped to talk to her? They would recognize her as a resident, just as she recognized their status, and they honestly looked to be the kind of devil-may-care guys who talked to any- and everyone.

But all they did was flip her a casual, "Hi, how're you doing?" when they passed by, which caused her such intense anguish that she decided on the spot that she despised Dr. Elliott Sandwell. Oh, yes, she'd seen the name tag on his jacket, and she had also recalled hearing his name more than once in the short time she'd been there. He was the main topic whenever the female residents and nurses discussed men.

Now, many years later and lying in the comfort of her bed, a startling fact came to light. She hadn't despised Elliott at all! She'd fallen for him at first sight and hadn't let herself admit it because he very definitely had not been hit by the same bolt of lightning.

So, what about now? He'd acted struck by something last night. His lovemaking had been intense enough to stand *her* on her head. Not literally, of course, but emotionally she'd given him everything.

And then she'd taken it all back—or tried to—by being mean and hard with him.

"I have to apologize," she whispered.

Still, there was something she must do before going to the lab and facing Elliott, and it had to be done exactly right. She would worry about Elliott's reaction to an apology later on.

Even if she had finally faced her feelings—and she knew now that she loved Elliott with all her heart—she could not dwell solely on romance.

In her case, there was life—and possibly death—outside her own sphere of existence. She could not ignore it.

When Maggie pulled her car into her parents' driveway, it was immediately apparent that neither was at home. Hannah was still in her pajamas and bathrobe, but she opened the front door when Maggie rang the bell.

"Maggie, how nice!" Hannah stepped back from the doorway.

Maggie went in and gave her sister a hug. "Hi, sweetie." Hannah shut the door, and Maggie asked, "Where are Mom and Dad?" having noticed that her mother's car and father's pickup truck were gone.

"Dad's been using his truck to haul some junk to the dump for a neighbor, and Mom decided to do her grocery shopping early today. Neither of them should be gone very long."

"It doesn't matter. I came to see you." Quickly she did a visual check of Hannah's eyes and skin color. "You look quite well today."

"I feel quite well today. Maggie, you worry too much about me," Hannah said gently.

"That's just not possible, Hannah." Smiling, Maggie took her sister's arm. "Let's sit in the den. There's something I'd like to tell you."

"Sure, okay. Would you like some coffee or tea? Have you had breakfast?"

"No, no and yes. But thanks." Maggie settled her sister on the sofa, then took a nearby chair. "Hannah, something wonderful occurred during the Christmas season and I didn't tell anyone about it for what I still think was a very good reason."

Hannah's eyes lit up. "You met someone! Oh, Maggie, I'm so happy for you."

"Honey, that's not it. Well, in a way I suppose it is, but it didn't start that way." Maggie rolled her eyes, then laughed. "I'm probably confusing the stuffing out of you, right?"

"Sort of...I guess."

"Okay, let me start at the beginning. Some time back I was one of the physicians who cared for a man named Ryan Fortune. Have you heard of the Fortune family?"

Hannah frowned slightly. "I think I might have. Hasn't the Fortune name been in the newspapers quite a lot?"

"Over the years, yes, but then there are quite a lot of Fortunes and from what I've read, heard and seen with my own eyes, the Fortune family is not what one would label subdued or inactive. First of all, they are immensely wealthy and have been for generations. Hannah, you and I have lived such an ordinary life that it's almost impossible for us to visualize the way the Fortunes live. Mom and Dad scrimped and saved and went without themselves to provide us with an education, and they did it out of love."

"We've always been loved," Hannah agreed. "That's one thing I've never doubted."

"Same here. But getting back to my story, I saved Ryan Fortune's life while he was in the hospital, and..."

"You actually saved his life! Oh, Maggie, how wonderful it must be to be a doctor."

"Yes," Maggie said softly, not expanding her one-word reply because her profession had so many facets. It was wonderful, yes, but it also had a dark and difficult side. It wasn't always easy, that was the one thing she could have added to her brief response to

Hannah. Leaving that subject entirely, she told Hannah about Ryan's Christmas gift.

When she had finished, Hannah's jaw dropped and she gaped at her sister. "You're not serious."

"The reason I didn't tell everyone right away was because I didn't want to give you false hope. You see, Hannah, I opened my own lab with that money and hired the very best researcher in all of Texas to find a cure for your condition."

"The man you mentioned before."

"Yes, Dr. Elliott Sandwell. Hannah, we think... both he and I do...that we're going to succeed. Not today or tomorrow, but possibly yet this year. In conjunction with some other doctors, we're all working in the same vein, and everyone is quite optimistic." Maggie looked at her sister with a loving expression. "I only learned all of this last night, and this morning I knew that it was time to give you the same hope that fills my heart and soul. Dearest sister, tell me I've done the right thing."

"Oh, Maggie." Hannah covered her eyes with her hand and wept quietly.

Chapter 7

Maggie drove away thirty minutes later with so much love in her system that she felt like crying herself. But she didn't want to walk into her lab with red eyes. If Elliott had done as he'd said last night, then he would be there, and she would really like to look her best.

A glance in the rearview mirror at herself made her feel dissatisfied. She wanted to be beautiful—or as attractive as possible—today, and she wasn't. Her hair was down and she'd curled it some, but she no longer liked so much hair hanging around her face. She was thirty-two and believed that she looked every day of it—sometimes more. What she needed was a good cut from a good stylist. It wouldn't make her look twenty again, but nothing could do that.

Besides, she wasn't at all unhappy with her age,

just with the fact that most of the time any good looks she did have were camouflaged by out-and-out dowdiness. Heaven help her, she would never twist her hair into that tight bun again, or as Elliott had called it, "that *frigid* bun." He knew now that she *wasn't* frigid, far from it. And if he accepted her apology there was no telling where their personal relationship might go.

Where do you want it to go, Mag?

She was afraid to form a definitive reply to that question, and to avoid doing so turned her thoughts back to her appearance and getting a new hairstyle.

Not all shops welcomed walk-ins, but there was one in the same part of the city as her lab that catered to the harried schedules of medical personnel. That was not the shop Maggie had used for her glamour-girl persona on New Year's Eve, and thinking of that memorable evening Maggie suddenly knew the reason why she had chosen that showy out-of-character method of meeting Elliott again. He'd looked at her the way she had dreamed he would years ago. He'd even kissed her at midnight, and if she hadn't been so out of touch with her own feelings then, their entire relationship since that night might have been completely different.

Sighing heavily, Maggie turned into the parking lot of the mall and found a space near the beauty shop. She turned off the ignition and then just sat there. Her own thoughts had brought down her good mood considerably. What, really, did she hope to accomplish by apologizing to Elliott? Surely she wasn't expecting extreme gratitude from him, and then a declaration of undying love? After all, last night had been remarkable and unique for her, but it had probably been just another sexual interlude for him. Another conquest.

Groaning, Maggie put her head down on the steering wheel. Her emotions were out of control; she couldn't both love and hate Elliott, could she?

Elliott had been at Maggie's lab for several hours. He'd done exactly as he had said last night, gone in to NTL, spoke to the managing director about leaving today as his replacement was fully cognizant of his work and completely capable of taking over, then stowed his few personal belongings in a cardboard box and left for good.

When he first got to Maggie's lab he'd felt some surprise that she wasn't there, but once he started concentrating and theorizing on the best way to reach the final step in that cure for Hannah's rare blood disease, he forgot about everything else, including Maggie. In truth, he didn't think of her again until he heard her unlock the front door and come in.

He started toward the doorway to say hi, but then changed his mind. Maggie's intense regret last night still smarted, and he really wasn't sure of what their relationship was now. If it were all up to him, it would be something that he'd never known before, the kind of loving committed relationship that led to marriage, kids and growing old together. Acknowledging feelings that serious for a woman was so foreign to his nature that his internal organs felt as though they were tied in knots, something else that was pretty darned foreign to him.

In her office, Maggie sat at her desk. She knew Elliott was there because the security system had been disarmed. Nervously she took a small mirror from her purse and studied her hair again. What if he hates it!

Whatever Elliott or anyone else thought of her new style, it was done. Actually, the more she looked at it, the more she liked it. It almost touched her shoulders, so it wasn't as though she'd had it cropped, for heaven's sake. And it curved around her face in a most beguiling manner. The streaking was minimal, appearing more as natural golden highlights than anything manmade. She came to a final decision on her new look: She really did like it, and she had far too much on her plate to worry about other people's opinions. Even how Elliott would feel about it, she added to herself. If he didn't like her new style and said so, she was not going to lose any sleep over it.

Putting away both the mirror and her purse, she began sorting and stacking the papers that she'd left strewn across her desk last night. She read bits and pieces from the papers as she organized them, and a good twenty minutes went by before she wondered why Elliott hadn't at least stuck his head in and said hello.

Her stomach was suddenly churning. He's angry...he's hurt...oh, damn.

She knew that her moment of truth had arrived. If she was going to apologize, it was time she got to it. Rising slowly from her chair, she sucked in a long, hopefully calming breath and quietly walked from her office.

Peering through the open doorway of Elliott's favored workroom, she saw him standing at one of the long granite-topped tables with various beakers, bottles and experimental tools laid out in front of him. Just looking at his back caused Maggie's heart to skip a beat. She loved him, adored him and wished with all her might that he would turn, see her and confess immediately that he felt exactly the same way.

But she knew in her heart of hearts that was not going to happen. A nearly silent sigh whispered through her.

"Elliott?" she said softly.

He held a test tube containing a pink-hued liquid up to the light, studied it and said, "Yes?"

"I got here a short while ago. You probably didn't hear me come in. What are you working on?"

"One more idea," he said without inflection, and then added, "I heard you."

"Oh." Wasn't he going to look at her at all? Would it be funny or horrible if he never noticed her hair when he finally did look at her? "I went to see Hannah. I thought she should know about our progress."

"I agree. How about your boyfriend? Did you tell him of our progress, as well?"

Was that lie going to haunt her into the hereafter? "Elliott," she said, fully intending to set him straight on that subject.

"Of course, there's progress and then there's progress,'' Elliott said coolly. ''Some kinds are a lot more fun than others, wouldn't you agree?''

He was referring to their lovemaking! How could he talk so callously about it?

''You're not a very nice person, are you?'' she said frostily. ''Be that as it may, I came in here to apologize for my behavior last night after our little stint on the sofa. *I* wasn't very nice about that, and I'd just as soon not be in your rude, egotistical and overbearing league any longer than I have to be.'' Turning quickly, Maggie returned to her office, this time slamming the door shut behind her.

Elliott was thunderstruck and apparently glued to the floor. But when he got past the shock of Maggie's apology, he rushed after her. Her office door was closed and its message was clear: Leave me alone!

''To hell with that,'' Elliott muttered, and reached for the door handle. He pushed the door wide open and saw Maggie standing at the window with her back to the room.

''Good Lord, what've you done to your hair?'' he asked in a horrified tone of voice.

Maggie spun around. ''You...you arrogant jerk! My hair is none of your business, nor is anything else about me.''

''Oh-oh, I sure said the wrong thing. Your hair looks great. It just surprised me.''

''Oh, go fill a beaker...or something!''

He stood there staring at her. ''You apologized. May I do the same?''

She tossed her head disdainfully. ''You, apologize?

The great Elliott Sandwell, apologize? Lord have mercy, I just might faint dead away.''

"Maggie, did you or did you not apologize for regretting, as you put it, our little stint on the sofa?''

"I apologized for something," she muttered. "And you were so gracious about it, weren't you?''

"No, I was a jerk about it, and I'm sorry. I'm sorry about that boyfriend crack, too.''

Maggie heaved a sigh. "Let's set that record straight, all right? There is no boyfriend and there never was.''

Elliott frowned. "But the money...you said...''

"I said it was a gift, and you asked if it was a gift from a man. I said yes and you assumed the rest.''

"Why didn't you deny it?''

"Because I didn't want you chasing me around the office!''

"Well, you sure as hell didn't run very fast last night!''

Maggie threw up her hands. "You could drive anyone stark raving mad!''

"So could you!" Elliott advanced on her. "Who gave you the money?''

"Ryan Fortune.''

"*The* Ryan Fortune?''

"Yes.''

"For God's sake, why?''

"So I would find love and happiness and...and discover how important having my own family is," Maggie shrieked.

"Can't we talk without yelling?''

Embarrassed over her lack of control, Maggie took a breath. "I'll try. Along with his check, Mr. Fortune gave me a letter during the Christmas season. In it he wrote that I should feel free to use the money any way I saw fit, but that I should find someone who...who makes my heart sing."

Elliott took another step toward her, bringing the gap between them down to mere inches. "Did I make your heart sing last night?" he asked softly.

She was taken aback and couldn't speak for a moment. What was happening here? Dared she think that her dreams might be coming true at this very moment?

"Are...you hoping that...you did?" she stammered awkwardly.

He reached out and cupped the back of her neck with his hand. "I'm hoping for that and a lot more, my love."

"What did you say?" Her eyes were big as saucers.

"My love. Maggie, it's how I've been thinking of you lately. Is that all right with you?"

Her heart *was* singing! Oh, Lordy, she thought, it really can happen. "Yes," she whispered. "It's more than all right with me."

Elliott lowered his head just enough to mate their lips. It was a gentle, tender kiss, and it turned Maggie's knees to mush.

"We have a lot to talk about," Elliott said while looking deeply into her eyes. "You have to meet my family, and I yours." Maggie gave her head a shake, and Elliott laughed. "What was that for?"

"I'm wondering if this is real or if I'm still asleep and dreaming."

He put his arms around her and held her close. "We're both awake, sweetheart, and this is as real as anything ever gets. Listen, there's one thing we have to talk about right away. I told you about my financial advisor doing such a good job for me, but I didn't say how good. Maggie, I'm not quite as well off as you are, but I have enough money to buy into the lab. Would you ever consider a partnership?"

She was snuggling in his arms, absorbing his warmth, basking in the first true love of her life. "A partnership in everything?" she murmured.

Elliott leaned back enough to see her face. "I couldn't have said it better, but I should have. Yes, my love, a partnership in everything."

"Of course you may buy in, if you want to."

"We're a terrific team, Maggie, and you and I together could make this lab a real success." Elliott paused briefly, then quietly added, "I love you, Maggie."

She thought she would perish from overwhelming happiness. Her eyes filled, but he was beautiful even through a mist of tears.

"I love you, Elliott."

"When did you know?"

"The first time I saw you."

His mouth opened but nothing came out of it for

several seconds. "I...had no idea," he finally said, sounding anguished.

"I'm not sure that I did myself. Not at the time. But I know now that it was love at first sight for me."

He took her hand and brought it to his lips. "I'm so sorry," he said huskily.

"Don't be, please. You had your life, I had mine. Fate planned for us to get together this year, not that one."

A devilish twinkle appeared in Elliott's eyes. "Fate and a red dress."

Maggie blushed. "That was so childish of me, drawing your attention with a dress like that."

"Childish? Oh, no, there's nothing childish about that dress, my love. When am I going to get to see you in it again?"

Maggie moistened her lips with the tip of her tongue. "Would this evening be soon enough? At my apartment?"

Elliott took a satisfied breath and smiled. "I'll order dinner brought in."

"Wonderful," she murmured.

It seemed that everything was settled and perfect, and they sealed their love with a kiss that went on...and on...and on.

* * * * *

*Be sure to watch for the exciting
conclusion of*

THE FORTUNES OF TEXAS:
THE LOST HEIRS
*in Silhouette Desire as
the villain who poisoned Ryan Fortune
is caught and
Gunnery Sergeant Sam Pearce faces his
toughest assignment yet in*

*DID YOU SAY TWINS?!
And now for a sneak preview of this
scintillating title,
please turn the page.*

One

"Okay," Gunnery Sergeant Sam Pearce told himself as his gaze raked across what looked like miles of shopping aisles. "Let the battle begin."

A man could live on hot dogs and frozen burritos. But his life was about to change, he reminded himself as he snatched a cart free, and it wasn't as if he had a choice now, was it?

"Strained carrots, strained spinach. They really expect kids to eat this stuff?" he asked aloud of no one.

"It's hard to gnaw on a good steak when you don't have teeth," Michelle Guillaire quipped and then braced herself, waiting for his reaction. It was ten years since the last time he'd touched her and yet, her skin was humming. When she'd first seen him in the grocery store she'd told herself that they were grown-ups. Adults. They could be friends. But the sudden rush of heat pouring through her now, put the lie to that idea.

Sam went completely still for a long moment, then turned around slowly to face her. The minute those deep green eyes of his locked with hers, Michelle felt her knees liquify. Oh for heaven's sake. It was just like old times.

"Michelle."

No warm welcome in *that* voice, she thought, but at least he hadn't snarled at her. She swallowed hard, forced a smile and said, "Hi, Sam. I heard you were back in town." In fact, the minute he'd moved back to San Antonio, it seemed everyone she knew had made sure she heard about it.

His hands closed tightly on the two jars of baby food he held, and she noticed his knuckles whitening. "Yeah. Been back several months now."

Oh, this was going well. "So what are you up to?"

"My neck," he said darkly, "and sinking fast."

"What?"

"Look at this," he said, holding up the jars of baby food and waving his right hand at the shelf in front of him. "How're you supposed to know what to get? And if it's formula, what kind? Liquid? Powder? Ready to drink? Mixable?"

Her lips twitched. "I thought you liked beer."

His gaze snapped to hers. "I do. And right now, I could use one."

Michelle thought she detected a glimmer of panic in his eyes, but that had to be a mistake. Nothing and no one scared Sam "Storm" Pearce. "What's going on, Sam?'' she asked and told herself it was simply curiosity that had prompted the question.

"Oh, nothing," he muttered, setting the jars of food back onto the shelf, as if half expecting them all to come tumbling down. "Just the end of the world as I know it."

"Thought that happened last year."

"What?"

She shrugged. "I saw the article in the newspaper. You know…about you being one of the Fortunes?" She could only imagine how weird that had been for him.

Sam shifted position and his scowl darkened. "That's got nothing to do with this. That's…" He shook his head. "Hell, I'm not sure what that means yet."

Okay, she thought, his problem had nothing to do with him suddenly inheriting not only wealth but also an extended family. What else could it be? "Sounds serious."

He folded his arms across his chest, planted his feet wide apart in an "I dare you" posture and blurted "I just became a father."

"I…" she said, searching for the right thing to say. She hadn't heard anything about Sam having a wife. By the look on his face, she was guessing "congratulations" weren't in order. "Boy or girl?" she forced herself to ask.

"Twin girls."

Twins. Imagining two babies with his brilliant

green eyes, she strangled a little sigh of pure envy. "So, when did this happen?"

"A couple hours ago."

"Are you serious? Shouldn't you be at the hospital with your wife?"

"Huh?" Sam gave her a look, then shook his head. "I'm not married. You don't understand. The twins aren't newborns. These babies are nine months old. These babies are my goddaughters. Their folks died in a scuba diving accident a few days ago and, in a few hours, I'm flying to Hawaii to pick them up. Just call me Mr. Mom."

"Is your apartment ready for them?"

"I bought beds for them a while ago if that's what you mean. They'll be delivered when I get back."

"That's part of it. There's lots more things you'll need," she told him and started to launch into a list when another thought occurred to her. "Look, Sam, why don't I just go back to your place with you and help you get set up?"

His features tightened and, for a moment, Michelle thought he might refuse her. And maybe that would be for the best. Being alone with Sam in his apartment probably wasn't such a good idea. It had been ten years, but judging by the trip-hammer rhythm of her heartbeat, ten years wasn't long enough to curb the kind of desire they'd had for each other.

But she wasn't the same girl he'd known. She could deal with this. Since he still hadn't spoken, Michelle said, "Look, you said yourself you don't have much time. If I help, you'll get done in half the time."

He finally nodded abruptly. "Okay," he said. "I appreciate the offer."

Michelle plastered a smile on her face and asked, "What are friends for?"

"Is that what we are?" Sam wondered aloud. *"Friends?"*

"We could be," she said softly. "And it's better than enemies."

"I was never your enemy, Michelle," he told her and his voice was soft and rough. "It'd probably be easier if we didn't talk about the past. Why don't we just start over?"

But as they headed to the checkout aisle, Michelle told herself that just because they weren't going to *talk* about their past didn't mean that they both weren't *thinking* about it.

FORTUNES OF TEXAS: THE LOST HEIRS
Fortune Family Tree

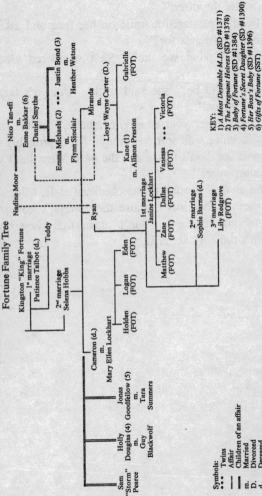

KEY:
1) *A Most Desirable M.D.* (SD #1371)
2) *The Pregnant Heiress* (SD #1378)
3) *Baby of Fortune* (SD #1384)
4) *Fortune's Secret Daughter* (SD #1390)
5) *Her Boss's Baby* (SD #1396)
6) *Gifts of Fortune* (SST)

Symbols:
••• Twins
——— Affair
———— Children of an affair
m. Married
D. Divorced
d. Deceased

FOT Romance takes place in original Fortunes of Texas 12-book continuity

July 2001
COWBOY FANTASY
#1375 by Ann Major

August 2001
HARD TO FORGET
#1381 by Annette Broadrick

September 2001
THE MILLIONAIRE COMES HOME
#1387 by Mary Lynn Baxter

October 2001
THE TAMING OF JACKSON CADE
#1393 by BJ James
Men of Belle Terre

November 2001
ROCKY AND THE SENATOR'S DAUGHTER
#1399 by Dixie Browning

December 2001
A COWBOY'S PROMISE
#1405 by Anne McAllister
Code of the West

MAN OF THE MONTH

For over ten years Silhouette Desire has been where love comes alive, with our passionate, provocative and powerful heroes. These ultimately, sexy irresistible men will tempt you to turn every page in the upcoming **MAN OF THE MONTH** love stories, written by your favorite authors.

Available at your favorite retail outlet.

Where love comes alive™

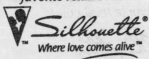

V *Silhouette*

INTIMATE MOMENTS™

is proud to present

Romancing the Crown

*With the help of their powerful allies,
the royal family of Montebello is determined
to find their missing heir. But the search for the
beloved prince is not without danger—or passion!*

This exciting twelve-book series begins in January and continues throughout the year with these fabulous titles:

Available at your favorite retail outlet.

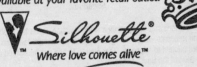

V *Silhouette®*
™ *Where love comes alive™*

Visit Silhouette at www.eHarlequin.com   SIMRC